# Gotta Love A Cowboy

## Want Ads 1

## Sandy Sullivan

**EROTIC ROMANCE**

**Secret Cravings Publishing**

www.secretcravingspublishing.com

**A Secret Cravings Publishing Book**
Erotic Romance

Gotta Love A Cowboy
Want Ads 1
Copyright © 2011 by Sandy Sullivan
Print ISBN: 978-1-936653-77-5

First E-book Publication: March 2011
First Print Publication: September 2011

Cover design by Beth Walker
Edited by Ariana Gaynor
Proof read by Mahalia Levey
All cover art and logo copyright © 2011 by Secret Cravings Publishing

**PUBLISHER**

Secret Cravings Publishing

www.secretcravingspublishing.com

# Dedication

This book is dedicated to my friend Tess MacKall.

You saw me through the beginnings of this story and I'm sorry

we weren't together to see if come to publication. I still have you

to thank for this.

—

# GOTTA LOVE

# A COWBOY
## Want Ads 1

### Sandy Sullivan

## Chapter One

**Wanted**
*Experienced horse trainer for difficult animal*
*and other horses on the property.*
*Needs to be the best of the best.*
*Excellent pay for six months work.*
Room and board provided.
Call…

Heat rose off the dry desert floor in rippling waves. The temperature had already hit the high nineties, and it wasn't even noon yet.

Ann Marie Skolack stepped out on the long porch surrounding the stark, white ranch house and sighed. Late afternoon sunlight filtered through the trees over the house, casting shadows on the ground. A small breeze rustled the leaves overhead and made the wind chimes at the corner of the porch tinkle with a soothing, musical sound. But the obvious neglect screamed at her from every turn. One corner of the porch sagged with the weight of the roof. Flakes of white paint littered the ground near the windows. Graying boards ran the length of the porch and needed painting. Fences needed mending, the cattle needed bringing round, fields required bush hogging and the men hadn't had a break in months. Things she'd have to take care of herself, since her husband was no longer here. John had been her savior and friend, and his death some seven months ago left her feeling alone. Two white rockers stood in silent reverence to their time together. Many a night they'd spent sitting out here, watching the sun go down and the stars appear in the nighttime sky. She ran her palm lovingly over the white wood, remembering the day John had presented her with them.

"It's a surprise, Ann Marie. Now stop trying to get me to tell you what it is," John told her during dinner on Christmas Eve nine years ago.

"Just a hint?"

"No. You'll find out soon enough."

The next morning, he'd awakened her early with a kiss. "Come on. Your present awaits."

The cold morning air bit at her cheeks when he took her outside to see the two gleaming, white rockers on the porch.

"We'll sit here and rock until the sun goes down, or when the grandkids come over to visit."

A tear slipped down her face. John had been so proud of those two chairs. She shook off the sadness, not willing to spend time dwelling on the past with so much to do.

A loud snort from near the fence brought her thoughts back to the present. She smiled at the sight of the streak of black running back and forth along the paddock fence. Black Jack, her pride and joy, stopped on his rear haunches and peered over the railing. Her dusty boots sounded hollow on the three steps of the porch when she went down and around the edge of the house to reach him.

"Do you want a treat, big boy?"

The horse nickered and tossed his regal head, sending his glossy mane whipping through the air. Hard, black hooves stomped at the dry ground, sending dust flying in several directions.

With her hand outstretched, she rubbed the horse's nose while he sucked up the sugar cube in her flattened palm.

"That's it, sweetheart. You are such a big baby, aren't you?"

After a quick nudge against her shoulder, Black Jack spun around and took off like a shot across the pasture, hooves flying, pounding the dirt and grass like thunder.

On the horizon, a cloud of red dust bloomed from the direction of the main highway. If he wasn't coming to the Double S, a person had no reason to be on this road. It had to be the trainer she was expecting.

Several moments later, a black dually stopped in front of the house, kicking up gravel and flinging it in several directions.

Shielding her eyes from the glare of sunlight, she watched while the driver's door popped open and black, pointed-toe boots hit the dirt as the man stepped out. Long legs encased in a pair of Wrangler jeans gave way to trim hips and a narrow waist made even more noticeable by the large, silver buckle. A western-style shirt with the sleeves cut off stretched across an impressive expanse of chest, and a cocky smile graced his face. His eyes were shaded with a pair of mirrored, aviator sunglasses, and soft-looking, dark curls peeked out beneath his straw cowboy hat.

*Lordy. Any sex-starved woman in their right mind would be interested in that. Wait! That's me! The sex-starved part, anyway.* Fingers touched her bottom lip, just to make sure she wasn't drooling. What woman would be crazy enough to let him out of her sight? He was one hell of a man in one hell of a sexy package.

The man slammed the truck door and swaggered toward her with a roll of his hips and the walk of a man confident in his sex appeal. "Mrs. Skolack?"

*Breathe, Ann Marie, breathe.*

"Yes?"

"I'm Travis Brooks."

"Welcome to the Double S."

"Is your husband home?"

"My husband died over seven months ago, Mr. Brooks."

Whipping the hat off his head, he clenched it in his fist as a frown marred his features. "I'm sorry, ma'am."

"He left this earth doing what he loved."

He dropped his gaze to the ground at his feet, giving her a clear view of thick, wavy black hair with no sign of gray anywhere. "Yes, ma'am."

*Manners. I like that.*

"Would you care to come inside? It's warm out here and I just made some lemonade."

"Much obliged. It's gonna be a scorcher today."

"Afraid so."

When his tanned hand held the screen door, she noticed the clean, short fingernails, calluses on his palms, probably from holding reins, and no wedding ring. His better than six-foot frame towered over her five-foot-five, but she could still feel his warmth of his breath on her neck.

"You aren't from around here, are you, Mr. Brooks."

"No, ma'am."

Her steps took her toward the kitchen, and she had to chuckle at his formality. "Call me Ann Marie. Ma'am makes me feel old, and I can't be much older than you, if at all. Besides, if you're going to be working for me, we should try to be friends."

Sensing he no longer followed, she turned to find him still standing next to the screen door, hat in hand and sunglasses dangling from his fingertips. Blue eyes the color of the sky stared back.

"Is there a problem, Mr. Brooks?"

"I won't work for a woman."

"Excuse me?"

"I'm sorry, but if there ain't a man around here, I can't take the position."

She cocked her head to the side and planted her hands on her hips. "Let me get this straight. Because I don't have a husband, you refuse to do the job."

Pulling his shoulders back, he straightened to his full, impressive height. "That's right."

"Well, if that's not the most arrogant, self-righteous, stubborn, pig-headed, chauvinistic thing I've ever heard." Her eyes narrowed. "Are you a man of your word, Mr. Brooks?"

"Of course."

"Well then, you have no choice but to work for me. You agreed to the job, and the ad said what the job entailed. To break and train my horses for a period of six months."

"But I didn't know you were a woman out here alone."

"Why is that a problem?"

"Women need a man to take care of them. They shouldn't be running a ranch."

"Even though it's none of your business, let me explain something to you. My husband and I ran this place together. Never once was it his job to take care of the ranch and mine to cook, clean, and bear children. We shared in the responsibilities of our home, and I'm very capable of handling it on my own." Her steps took her back in front of him so they stood toe-to-toe. "I have lived my entire life around horses and cattle. I can ride and rope better than most men. If it weren't almost a hundred degrees outside, I'd show you. We can go to court if you so choose, Mr. Brooks, in order for the verbal contract we have to be enforced, but I don't think you want to do that. Am I correct?" Her foot tapped with an aggravated tempo, and her breaths came out in angry bursts.

His eyes narrowed into irritated slits and a nervous tick appeared in his jaw. "No."

"Good. Then we have an agreement." She turned back toward the kitchen, expecting him to follow. "A room in the barn has been set aside for your use, or you may stay in the bunkhouse with the other hands. Makes no never mind to me. Meals are provided each morning and evening. You will have the weekends to yourself. I don't tolerate the men coming home drunk, and they know this. If you plan on drinking until you can't walk — stay in town."

"Yes, ma'am."

The cabinet door to the left of the large farm sink revealed several rows of cups. Grabbing two, her next stop was the freezer for ice.

"The men call me Ann Marie. Most have been here from before John and I married. They are loyal and protective." Once she handed him one of the glasses of lemonade, she moved toward the dining room table. "Take a chair, Mr. Brooks."

"Since you've managed to wrangle me into staying against my better judgment — call me Travis."

"All right, Travis. Where do you call home these days? I've done my homework and know where you grew up, but do you have a permanent house somewhere?"

He tipped his drink to his lips and swallowed several big gulps. The movement of his throat mesmerized her as she watched each time the liquid go down. Dark whiskers shadowed his jaw, and the insane urge to feel them scrape against her skin made her nipples pucker. She took several sips of her own in a vain attempt to squelch the heat racing through her. The sweet, cold liquid slid down her throat, quenching her thirst, but not the hunger in her blood.

"Amarillo."

"Do you go from place to place, training horses?"

"It's my job."

"And you're good, from what I've heard."

"The best."

"No modesty there," she replied, studying his rugged features.

"I'm sure you've done some checking, Ann Marie. Otherwise, I wouldn't be here."

"You answered my ad, I checked you out, and here you are. I was very selective with where I placed my classified, so only the best would see it."

"What do you want from me?"

Her gaze skimmed over him again, and she tried to think of how to explain her plan. "I'm sure you saw the black stallion out in the paddock."

"Yes," he replied, narrowing his gaze.

"I want him broke to ride and race. He's fast."

A honk sounded outside and he turned toward the sound as the pounding of boots hit the porch.

"Mom?"

"In the kitchen, Ty."

At eight years old, her son Tyler already stood tall for his age. He took after his father with his big brown eyes and blond hair, but in temperament, he was just like her.

*Bang!* The screened door slammed against its frame, and she heard him scramble through the house, racing toward the kitchen.

She glanced at Travis, knowing she would have to explain who the stranger sitting across from her was and just why he was there. Ty would be upset at having another man around the horses.

Sliding to a stop near her, Ty blurted out, "Can I spend the night with Jimmy?"

"Not tonight, son."

"But, Mom!"

"Mind your manners."

"Yes, ma'am." Ty cocked his head to the side and looked at Travis. "Who are you?"

"Tyler Alan," she growled.

"It's okay. Name's Travis Brooks," Travis said, holding out his hand.

Tyler ignored the offered handshake and gave her a sidelong look.

"Mr. Brooks is here to train the horses."

"But...that's Daddy's job," he said, pain evident in his voice.

"I know, Ty, but your dad isn't here anymore and I can't do it alone. I need someone to work with the stallion."

"Dad was 'posed to do that."

"Tyler, we'll talk about this later."

"You brought another guy here?" Anger and hurt made his tone rise. "How could you do that, Mom? It's not right." Tears shimmered in his eyes, and his Adam's apple bobbed up and down as he forced a swallow.

"Tyler..."

"You don't love Daddy anymore!"

"Your dad meant everything to me, but I need someone to break Black Jack and help with the other horses. Mr. Brooks is one of the best."

"I don't care. He's not Dad!"

"Ty, is it?" Travis asked, coming to his feet.

Tyler nodded, and pulled his shoulders back trying be older than his eight years, but his bottom lip quivered with the emotions he felt.

"Listen, Ty. I'm not here to take your dad's place. It's my job to break horses, and your mom needs help with that. I'll be moving on once the job is finished."

Tyler glared at Travis, and Ann Marie sighed.

Maybe I should let him go to Jimmy's. It would be a good thing to get him away from the house for a night. Let him come to terms with Travis being here. Plus, it would put an end to his questions—for now.

"Okay, Ty. You can spend the night at Jimmy's, but I want you home first thing tomorrow. Understood?"

"Yes, Momma." Tyler gave Travis one last look and disappeared down the hall.

"I bet he's a handful."

"Yeah. You could say that. More so since his father died."

"Didn't mean to pry," Travis murmured.

"It's fine. I need to talk to him. That's all. Explain things, you know."

When she stood, their eyes met and held. The look on his face gave her pause as the heat of his stare scorched her skin with its intensity. His gaze dropped to her lips, and he frowned.

"Do I have a wart on my nose or what?"

"Huh? Uh, no. Why do you ask?"

"You're frowning while you're looking at me. A woman doesn't like to be frowned at by a man. It makes her feel lacking."

"Sorry."

Several seconds of uncomfortable silence stretched between them, and she continued to observe his unconscious signals. How his hand clench at his side like he wanted to touch her, but wouldn't, the narrowing of his eyes and the small movement of his gaze down to her breasts. Heat zipped from her nipples to her pussy.

After a rough clearing of her throat, she said, "Follow me, and I'll show you the barn and your room." Without another word, she walked through the living room and out the front door.

They stepped out onto the porch and started across the front toward the large structure in the distance, but she was very much aware of his trailing behind her and the feel of his gaze on her ass. She let a small smile play on her mouth when he came up beside her.

"How long have you lived here?"

"Ten years."

"Child bride?"

"I don't consider twenty-two a child bride, but you might."

"You're thirty-two?"

"Yes. I told you I couldn't but much older than you. Why? How old are you?"

"Thirty-five."

"Kind of old to be breaking horses still, aren't you?"

His steps came to a sharp halt

She laughed and turned to face him. "I'm kidding. Lighten up, will you? Are you always this serious?"

A smile lit up his face, and her heart tripped over itself.

The man was downright drool-worthy handsome, but when he smiled, she couldn't breathe—couldn't think. "No."

"No, what?" she asked, as they reached the barn and she pulled open the door.

"No. I'm not usually this serious."

"Good. I can't handle a man who can't take a joke." She moved toward the office at the end of the long, dirt walkway, keeping the conversation going so she wouldn't have to think about what she'd like to do with him. "So. Any family left behind?"

"No wife, if that's what you mean."

"Well, I would hope not. I'd be rather pissed off if my husband took off all the time, running all over the country."

A warm chuckle left his lips, and the sound sent shivers down her arms. Rubbing them to calm the goose bumps, she approached the door and opened it for his inspection.

"This will be your room. Or would you rather stay in the bunkhouse?"

"No. I'm kind of a loner. This will do just fine."

"All right," she said, flipping on the light to illuminate the space. "There's a double bed against the wall, a private bath with shower through there. A small office is down the walkway a little farther, with a computer and files. I need you to keep good records on your training schedule and how far along you are with the horses, but your priority should be the stallion. I'll review your notes on a regular basis."

"How far did your husband get with the horse?"

Capturing her lip between her teeth, she debated on how much to tell him.

"If I don't know, it'll take that much longer, because I'll have to start from scratch." His eyes narrowed. "What's wrong? Didn't your husband work with him at all?"

Pain and grief rode her hard, and probably showed in her features. To this day, she fought with the urge to put the stallion down or believe in him—believe in the dream she shared with John.

Moving toward the window, she stared out over the pasture, watching the black beast as he pawed at the dirt under his hooves.

*"That animal is such a free spirit. I almost hate to tame him, but he's a winner. I know he is."* Her husband's words haunted her. Black Jack had been his obsession from sun up 'til sun down each day. An obsession that had cost him his life. Would Travis walk away if he knew the truth?

"John worked with him some." The calm inflection of her voice gave away nothing of the nervousness she felt.

"How much is some?"

"He had a saddle on him." Terror gripped her heart.

*I can't explain. What if Travis won't train him?*

"You need to be more specific. I can't do my job if I don't know how he reacted to certain things. A saddle, a bridle, a bit…"

"You'll have to check John's records. I'm not sure."

"What aren't you telling me?"

"Nothing. Black Jack is just high-spirited. That's all."

"There's more. I can tell by your voice. What is it?" he demanded.

With a gasp, she spun around. The suspicion in his eyes sent trepidation down her back. "There's nothing else to tell you."

"Nothing, huh?" Both arms crossed over his broad chest. "Do your damndest, Mrs. Skolack. If you want to sue me, then so be it. But I refuse to work with you if you don't trust me to do what needs to be done for that animal."

Travis stepped out of the room and started back down the hall. Anne Marie quickly fell in step behind him.

"Travis, please. I need you. No one else will touch him."

He whirled and faced her. "Why?"

Tears rolled down her cheeks. She dropped her gaze to the barn's dirt floor.

He stepped closer. "Tell me," he said, his voice dropping an octave to what she assumed to be his coaxing voice.

"Because Black Jack was responsible for my husband's death."

* * * *

Travis couldn't believe what he'd heard. "Responsible? How?"

Ann Marie lifted her face and met his gaze. Gut-punched. That's the effect her tears had on him. He didn't need this. What the hell had he gotten himself into?

"Yes. John and I had high hopes for Black Jack to run in the quarter horse races, but John was having a difficult time with the training."

"How difficult?"

A heavy rush of air left her lips, and with a weary sigh, she sat on the bench next to the wall. Not sure if she would tell him the truth, he waited, anxious to know just what happened.

"John had gotten gear on him. A saddle and bit, but Black Jack didn't like it." One shoulder lifted in a shrug. "He's a real pussycat … with me, at least. John wouldn't let me near him, though. The…" She swallowed hard. "The day John died, he'd taken Black Jack out for his first ride."

Tears glistened on her lashes, and he felt like a vice squeezed his heart. The moment he'd seen her standing on her porch, she'd taken his breath away. When she'd lit into him about backing out of the contract, her blue eyes had spit fire, and the no nonsense woman captured his attention. She barely came to his shoulder, but he could already imagine what the taste of her lips would be like. Her long, brown hair lay in a ponytail down her back, but he could tell by the width of the tieback holding it in place, it had to be thick. Breasts big enough to fill a man's hand pressed against the front of her blouse with each ragged breath she took. Worn jeans hugged her hips and emphasized her long legs. His cock strained against the front of his pants, and he cleared his throat while he shifted his stance to relieve some of the pressure.

"John left the house around noon that day. When the sun started to set and he hadn't come home, I sent some of the men out looking for him." Her lips pressed into a thin line. "They came back with his body draped over another horse."

"Do you know what happened?"

"Not for sure. We all assumed Black Jack threw him. There was so much blood." She shivered and he wanted to bring her into his arms." The coroner listed severe trauma to the head, as the cause of death."

Travis frowned. There'd never been a horse he couldn't break to ride. Ever. Not since he started training at the age of fifteen.

*Do I want to take on this horse, knowing it cost a man his life?*

Not realizing she'd gotten up and moved closer to him, he was startled to feel the warmth of her hand on his arm. His belly clenched at the touch of her skin, and his cock twitched in his jeans.

"Please, Travis. Don't walk away from me. I need you."

*Ah hell!*

His guts tied into a knot at the sadness and hope her eyes. He knew what it felt like to lose someone you loved way too early and to watch all your hopes and dreams die with them. "All right. I'll stay."

"Thank you," she whispered, brushing her lips against his cheek. His hands automatically went to her waist and held her within his embrace for a moment. The brush of her breasts against his chest had his dick ready to explode. When she leaned back, her eyes seemed brighter and her pupils were dilated, almost encompassing the blue. Her breathing came out a little faster and a flush of color had splashed over her cheeks. He could smell her arousal. The perfume of her need filled the space around them, but he resisted the urge of his body to take this beyond business.

After a moment, she stepped back. "I'll leave you to get settled in your room. You can start tomorrow, if you'd like."

The sexual tension eased when she moved away.

"That'd be fine."

"Breakfast is at six sharp. Cook hates it when the men are late."

"Will you be there?"

*Why the hell did I ask that? What do I care if she's there?* It surprised him to know that he wanted her to be. The idea of sitting across from her at breakfast appealed to him somehow. To see her beautiful blue eyes. The sprinkling of freckles across her nose. That stubborn chin. He hadn't had a woman in a while, and it would explain his reaction to Anne Marie more than anything else, except she was different. Smart, tough, yet soft. All woman. Maybe more woman than he had a right to want, too. After all, Catherine did a damned good job of making him feel worthless.

She smiled and brushed the remaining tears from her cheeks. "Yes. I usually eat with the men. Besides, that way I can introduce you to the group. They'll accept you a little better if I tell them you're here at my request and not another wanderer passing through."

"Do you get a lot of those?"

"A couple. Seems word has gotten out that I'm running this ranch alone. The world is made of all kinds of men," she said, her cheeks blushing. "And I guess some think they could take advantage of a widow, especially with a spread this big."

Drifters came with the territory of owning a ranch, but the thought of one of them taking advantage of her hospitality and working his way into her bed on the off chance of getting his hands on her place, didn't sit well with him. Ann Marie didn't seem like the type to fall for a man's pretty words and compliments. She was strong. She had to be to keep the respect of the men who worked for her. Protectiveness came naturally to him. Growing up with lots of sisters would do it to a man, but the unusual, intense feelings he had for Ann Marie worried him. He shifted from one booted foot to the other, not comfortable with where his line of thought was traveling. "How many acres do you have?"

Her eyes narrowed. He'd raised suspicion with his question. No doubt about it, she was a smart one. But she had nothing to worry about from him. Six months and he was gone.

"Just askin'. Curious is all," he said, hands spread, palms up.

"Five thousand, plus or minus a few."

"Really?" He cocked an eyebrow as he whistled through his teeth. "That's impressive."

"Thanks. I'll die keeping it." Her gaze darted around the barn for a moment. "Well, I should get back to the house. I've got some bookwork I need to finish."

"You do the books, too?"

"Yeah. I managed to get my accounting degree after John and I got married so I could keep the books for this place. One less expense."

Admiration for Ann Marie grew in leaps and bounds. The acreage she had didn't impress him. Hell, he'd been to a few spreads in his days that would make this place look paltry in comparison. "I guess I'll see you in the morning, then."

"Guess so. If you need anything, let me know."

"Thanks. I will."

Her eyes sparkled with the smile that lit up her face..

*Damn, she's pretty. And totally off limits. The last thing I need to get saddled with is a widow, her kid and a ranch that would tie me to one place. Nothing but heartbreak in all that. Never again.*

"I'll talk to you in the morning. Sleep well, Travis."

"You, too."

With a quick glance, she made her way back down the dirt aisle and disappeared from his sight.

A quick rush of air left his lips as he tipped his head back on his shoulders and set his hands on his hips.

*Maybe a shower will do me good. A cold one at that.*

He unbuttoned his shirt and shrugged it off his shoulders. Tossing it across the foot of the bed, he unbuckled his belt, letting it hang from the loops. He strode toward the shower, but pulled up short at the sound of two quick raps to the door. Turning around, he took three steps toward the door and pulled it open, surprised to see Ann Marie again.

*That wasn't just a hiss between her teeth, was it?*

Her gaze slid down his chest and stopped at his waist. A swell of urgent need rushed through him at the look in her eyes. When her gaze returned to his face, she slipped her tongue over her lips. Travis fought the urge to sweep her up in his arms and kiss her until they were both breathless.

"I…uh…sorry. I thought I'd offer you something to eat since I wasn't sure if you'd eaten. It's a bit of a drive from Amarillo."

*Oh, I'd like to eat something all right.*

"No thanks. I stopped at a little restaurant in town before I drove out to the house."

"Okay. Good. I'm glad you aren't hungry."

*I didn't say I wasn't hungry. I'm starved—just not for food.* "I'll be fine until tomorrow."

Shifting from foot to foot, she appeared anxious. The blazing look of desire in her eyes told him exactly what had her wound up tighter than a weathervane spinning in a tornado. He leaned his shoulder against the doorframe, his cock tight against the front of his jeans. Maybe he'd just push the issue a little and see where it led. He damn sure wasn't looking for a relationship, but a little fun between the sheets? Maybe it was wrong to even think about it. After all, she was a lonely widow, and he assumed others had tried to take advantage of the lack of a man around, but there were things he just couldn't deny. One of them was how much he'd like to get between her gorgeous thighs. And judging from the expression on her face and the heat in her gaze, she might like a few months of uncommitted sex. "Something else I can do for you?"

His question seemed to bring her to her senses, and she stiffened. "No. I didn't mean to disturb you."

Right. She didn't need him any more than he needed her. Too complicated—on both their ends.

"You didn't. A shower sounded good. That's all."

"I guess I'll see you tomorrow, then."

"I'll be here."

"Night."

Travis watched her walk toward the big entrance. The sway of her hips in those snug-fitting jeans had him almost coming in his pants.

*Damn, she's got a nice ass.*

She glanced over her shoulder, smiled, and walked outside.

*Definitely a cold shower.*

# Chapter Two

*A nice warm bath will relax me so I can sleep.* Her shoulders felt tight and her back hurt from getting tossed by one of the mares that morning, but she feared the tenseness and jumpiness had nothing to do with the goings on at the ranch. Travis Brooks had her on edge — a sexual edge she wasn't sure she liked.

When she reached her bathroom, she turned on the hot water and splashed in a few honeysuckle-scented bath beads. Her hand skimmed down her lower back, trying to ease the ache settling there. Her butt would be sore come morning.

Stripping off her clothes, she eased into the soapy water with a heavy sigh.

"God, I love a hot bubble bath."

Closing her eyes, she tried to relax. But flashes of blue eyes and a handsome face appeared behind her eyelids. Travis could be a problem if her attraction to him meant anything at all. Seeing him open the door to his room with no shirt on had made her feel hot, flush and wet, all at the same time. She'd recognized the appreciation in his gaze, the hunger in his eyes. What would it feel like to kiss him? To smooth her hands over his chest and simply give in to all of the heated sensations he aroused in her.

*That's crazy. The last thing I want is a man around here, other than to work, and that doesn't mean work on me.*

Her relationship with John had been one of convenience. They hadn't really loved each other at the time of their wedding. He needed a wife to help him run the ranch, and she wanted out of her parents' house. John hadn't been a handsome man by any means, with his hawk-like nose, small black eyes and crooked grin, but she'd cared for him in her own way. There hadn't been a mean bone is his body. He'd been ten years older than she, but he'd turned out to be the perfect husband. Tender, easygoing and patient. Lord, he'd been so patient with her. The last thing she'd wanted was for a man to touch her. John knew his way around a woman's body, though, and for the most part, with his gentle teaching, she'd learned to accept his touch.

But enjoy it? That was a whole different thing.

The whinny of the stallion in the pasture next to the house brought her thoughts back to the intriguing stranger in her barn.

*I have a feeling Travis' touch would be so different.*

But there was no reason to contemplate such a thing, was there? A man like Travis surely had women throwing themselves at his feet on a regular basis. One trip to The Watering Hole and he'd have half a dozen females ready to lick his boots or something else."

She sank farther into the tub, the hot water relaxing the tight muscles of her back.

Blue eyes surrounded by long, soft-looking lashes swam in front of her. Lips with a crooked grin and a flash of white teeth forced her to smile. Firm muscles with a smattering of dark chest hair pushed a moan from her lips. She wanted to run her hands over those plains and valleys, and slip her fingers through the crisp curls to find out how they felt.

She shook her head, thinking she must be crazy. *Good grief, I just met the man a few hours ago.* But Lordy, did that little trail of hair from his belly button that disappeared into his boxer briefs ever make her think of seeing just what he had under those tight Wranglers!

Happy Trail? Wasn't that what they called it? *Mmm...I wonder how far it goes.*

Teeth captured her lip and she chewed, fighting the moan bubbling in her chest. The bundle of nerves between her legs throbbed with a need she hadn't felt before. Her fingers slipped between her parted thighs to brush against her clit. Her breath quickened into little pants.

John had known a lot about sex, and she really didn't have any complaints about how he'd treated her in the bedroom, but she'd often wondered if there could be more to it. There had been too many nights when she'd taken matters into her own hands after John finished and rolled over to go to sleep. Since his death, she had even ventured into buying a toy to help keep her body's needs under control,

Travis made her think about those needs and how to satisfy them with something other than cold plastic, like warm, male flesh.

One finger slipped over the sensitive bud and found a satisfying rhythm that would bring her to the peak of release while she imagined Travis running his tongue over her breast. The image of his eyes, dark with desire as he sucked one nipple into his mouth and rolled the other between his fingers swirled through her mind and left her breathless.

She dipped two fingers inside her pussy while another finger worked her clit faster, harder. The thought of him touching her, sucking her nipple, brought her to the end she sought. Lifting her hips, she climaxed, moaning and groaning his name.

A forced exhale and she struggled to her feet to grab a towel. Standing on one foot then the other, she dried off, slipped on her nightgown, and then walked into her bedroom.

"Great, Ann Marie. Masturbate to thoughts of the new guy at the ranch, even if he is gorgeous, rugged and smells like horses and man. Desperation doesn't play at all in this scenario. Oh no." The curtain moved away from the window with the brush of her hand and she could see the light in the window of his room. "I'm lonely. Nothing more. John's been gone a long time and I'm a healthy, thirty-two year old woman with needs. Acting on those needs with Travis would be a huge mistake, so if fantasizing about him helps me take care of them without making that mistake, then I don't see a problem with it."

A soft knock, brought her attention to the doorway as Tyler pushed it open.

"Mom, I'm going to Jimmy's now. His mom is picking me up." A horn sounded outside. "That's her. I'll see you in the morning."

"All right. Have fun and behave yourself."

"Aw, Mom."

The door clicked shut, and he disappeared. Her little man seemed to be growing up before her eyes and it made her a little sad to think she might never have another child to hold.

The covers were pulled aside with a whoosh. Cool sheets slipped along her skin as she settled beneath the comforter. She sighed and closed her eyes, waiting on sleep that never came. Too many thoughts crowded her mind. The ranch, Ty growing up, her hopes for racing Black Jack…

And Travis.

Thunder rumbled in the distance, and her gaze darted around the room. Lightning slashed across the sky in a bright flash and Ann Marie sat bolt upright when her room lit up like the Fourth of July.

Wind rustled the trees, and rain pelted the house's tin roof. She winced at the ping of hickory nuts hitting the side of the house. Goose bumps rose on her skin, and she shivered in the cooling air.

*God, I hate thunderstorms.*

* * * *

Travis raked his fingers through his hair and looked up at the starless sky. After his shower, he'd wandered outside, wanting to curb the lingering desire in his blood.

One large raindrop plopped against his face. The icy bead cut a path down his neck, disappearing beneath the collar of his T-shirt.

The sky opened up and water came down in sheets, soaking the material within moments, molding the cotton to his chest like a second skin. Hell, he needed cooling off.

*I should have high-tailed it as soon she said she didn't have a husband.*

Unfortunately, the challenge of breaking a difficult horse had called to him the moment he caught a glimpse of the magnificent animal behind the fence. The stallion's jet-black coat had glistened like onyx in the bright afternoon sun, contrasted only by one handful of white hair near his head. When the horse flipped his mane from side to side and stomped his hooves in the dirt, Travis had been spellbound. He'd never seen such a beautiful specimen of horseflesh.

Shit. Who was he kidding? Yeah, he wanted to train the horse. The opportunity to prepare one who might win at the American Quarter Horse Races could be the crowning glory to his career. No doubt about it. Every man needed to test himself and his abilities. But the woman he'd met today aroused thoughts in him he'd tried hard to forget—feelings he hadn't felt in a very long time. A man would be a fool not to want her and fight to protect her. Her kind of woman came with a price and it usually meant the ball and chain of marriage. The kind a man wanted by his side, working with him, living with him and growing old with him, not a quick roll between the sheets—one to lie down with him each night and hold close. To bury his cock deep inside her with one swift thrust, and hear her scream his name as she climaxed around him.

Damn it. The real reason he'd stayed was Ann Marie, but he had to stop thinking this way. Six months to gentle the horse? But hell, in six months he'd be the one tamed if he didn't get a handle on the way she affected him.

A high-pitched whinny rose above the crashing sounds of the storm and traveled across the yard.

He squinted, trying to see through the sheets of rain, and got a big surprise. The big, black stallion reared and pawed at the air.

Travis smiled. "Well, well. What do we have here?" He strode toward the paddock railing. "Shall we see how ornery you really are, big boy?"

Black Jack tossed his head and whinnied louder.

Travis approached the wooden barrier separating them, his hand outstretched. Black Jack settled down and sniffed Travis' palm. Without warning, the horse tried to bite, but Travis was ready for that flare of temper and pulled his hand back.

"Ah. So, that's how it's going to be, huh?" He propped his elbow on the fence rail and stared. "You and me are gonna get real close. I don't break animals like you—I tame 'em. Breaking something so magnificent would be a shame."

Hooves slashing the air, the horse reared again as if informing Travis that he wouldn't go down without a fight. A quick spin on his hind legs and Black Jack disappeared through the curtain of rain and into the inky night.

Travis smiled and retreated to the dry barn and his room, stripping off his soaked shirt as he walked. The sticky jeans came next, over his hips and landing on the floor in a wet pile.

He walked inside the florescent-lighted bathroom and turned the shower knob. Steam fogged up the mirror within seconds. Stepping into the stream, he tipped his head back, the hot liquid pricking his skin like tiny needles. Water ran down his chest in rivulets as he closed his eyes.

Flashes of memories beat against the back of his eyelids, and he fought the urge to drown in the images. It wouldn't do a damned bit of good to relive those days, but sometimes he couldn't help it. Seeing Ann Marie's little boy had been the trigger.

*"Daddy, follow me."* Adam laughed, running on pudgy little legs toward the water's edge.

*"Stay close, buddy."*

*"Water,"* his boy said, pointing at the lapping waves, and then facing him.

*"I know. Come here, son."* He grabbed the giggling boy up in his arms and hung him upside down. *"You can go into the water in a minute. We need to get you changed first."*

*"Travis, don't do that. He'll throw up. We ate thirty minutes ago,"* warned his wife.

*"Oh quit worrying, Catherine. He'll be fine. He loves it."*

*Adam giggled again as Travis tickled his stomach and then set him on his feet.*

*"Let's get your swim trunks on. Then you can go in the water with Daddy," Travis said.*

*"Water." Adam pointed at the bright blue not fifty feet from their blanket.*

*"Yep," Travis replied, shooting an exasperated glance at his wife.*

Slapping his hand against the shower wall, he forced his eyes open, not wanting to remember anything else. Catherine had seemingly been the perfect woman. She had everything—long blonde hair, big green eyes, legs that could stop traffic. But on the inside, she was a cold-hearted bitch. "Catherine," he whispered. Why had he ever married her?

They'd been on vacation in Orlando when it happened. Anger churned inside of him—anger at Catherine—but a rage against himself that ran so deep he had no hope of ever cutting it loose. He squeezed his eyes shut again, the hot spray of water stinging his skin, his son's voice calling to him, pulling him back.

*"Water!" Adam squealed. Travis laughed, picked up his boy, and walked toward the waves. Once they reached the edge, he set Adam down and kept an eye on him while he splashed through the surf, giggling at the way the foam tickling his feet.*

*Every few minutes, he'd look back at his wife. On the last glance, he saw another man sitting next to her on the blanket. The tinkle of her flirty laughter reached him at the water's edge. Travis ground his teeth together in frustration.*

*When he and Adam walked toward her, the other man took off in a hurry, leaving him questioning her, but as usual, she denied everything and had packed up their things to go back to the room. An argument started, but instead of fighting with her, he went to the bar, leaving her and Adam alone in the room. When he'd returned an hour later, they argued more, and he told her he wanted to get a separate room. That's when he noticed his son  wasn't lying on the bed napping like he'd thought, and Catherine informed him she'd put him in the bathtub.*

He leaned against the cool travertine tile of the shower. A choking sob broke from his mouth, and he let the tears flow.

*Ten fucking years!*

He'd lost his son ten years ago, and he still blamed himself. If he hadn't been arguing with Catherine… If he hadn't left him alone with that bitch, his son would still be alive.

His wife had walked out on him after Adam's death. No surprise there. She'd blamed Travis, but not as much as he blamed himself. The tears finally stopped, but the ache for his son would never go away. He turned off the tap and stepped from the shower, grabbed a towel and dried off. Returning to the bedroom, he reached for his duffle to get some clean clothes and noticed there were no sheets on the bed. Shit. Now he'd need to either make a trip to the house or out to the truck for his sleeping bag.

With a tug of his fingers, he slipped on a pair of worn jeans and tugged a T-shirt over his head. He snatched up a pair of socks and hurriedly put them on, followed by his boots. .

*I sure didn't figure in gettin' all the way dressed again.*

The loud sizzle of lightning and a crack of thunder heavy enough to rattle the windows moved through, hitting the transformer near the barn with a loud pop, sending the whole area into darkness.

"Great. I'm gonna get soaked, and it's dark as hell out here," he grumbled, sprinting for the door.

The air felt sticky and hot. Beads of sweat formed along his upper lip. Rain plastered his hair to his head and water trickled down his back.

The ranch house sat about a hundred yards from the barn, but with the unrelenting lightning, he could clearly see the outline and made a beeline for the front porch. A sidestep here and a jump there had him dodging the growing puddles in the yard. Mud still managed to cake his boots and leave footprints on the porch when he got to the top step. Four quick stomps of his feet dislodged the majority of the dirt, but left globs of muck behind.

He rapped his knuckles against the door and waited.

*Maybe I should get the sleeping bag.*

About the time he turned to go to his truck, the door opened behind him, and when he turned, he sucked in a ragged breath at the sight of Ann Marie.

She stood in the doorway, holding a hurricane lamp. With her hair tousled and falling around her shoulders, she looked like an angel come to carry him away. The light flickering from the lamp outlined the terror in her eyes. Breaths came from her lips in little rasping pants. Every rush of air pressed her breasts against the gaping front of her nightgown and made him fully aware of her hard, knotted nipples.

"You okay?" he asked.

"N-no." Clutching the gown's filmy material in her fist, she balled the fabric into a knot and twisted it. "I h-hate storms."

"Oh. This is a bad one all right. Sorry to disturb you, but there aren't any sheets on the bed ."

"S-sorry about that. Come in and I'll get you some."

Inside, silence engulfed him. Shadows shifted, slithering along the walls, sending a nervous shiver over his arms and the hair rising on the back of his neck. ." You'd think I believed in ghosts or something," he murmured and chuckled to himself.

"Why?"

"Nothing. The shadows from the lamp—and the lightning is eerie."

"Yeah. It is kind of weird, huh?"

A warm chuckle left his lips as he jabbed his fingers through his wet hair. He squinted into the darkness, trying to follow Ann Marie. Working his way behind her, he whacked his shin on the coffee table. "Son-of-a-bitch! Damn it, that hurt."

"Are you okay?" she asked, a tremble in her voice.

"Yeah, just hit my shin on the table."

"I should have warned you."

One hand rubbed the wounded leg as he hobbled toward the hallway. A second later, the lights came back on with a crack.

"The generator," she said, as light flooded the room. A big, leather couch graced one wall, with several throw pillows lying across one end and what looked like a handmade quilt across the back. Large end tables sat on both sides with a multitude of magazines scattered over the rugged top. A fireplace took up almost one whole wall of the room, and he moved to get a closer look at the pictures lined up along the mantle.

Travis smiled and picked up a photo of Tyler running through a sprinkler.

*Kids.* For a moment, the image of his son wavered in his mind, but he pushed it away, refusing to give in.

The next photo he picked up appeared to be a wedding picture of Ann Marie and a guy he assumed was John. They seemed happy, and Travis didn't quite like the tightening of his gut at the smile on her face. He returned the frame to its spot. Several more showed images of her over the years, one painting the inside of the house, another arranging a baby's room—tears on her cheeks as she cradled Tyler in her arms the day of his birth. It was like looking through a window at the scenes going on inside, but not being a part of it—kind of like his own life after Adam died.

"This is nuts," he grumbled, placing the last photo back on the mantle. He followed in the direction Ann Marie had disappeared.

"Here you go," she said, meeting him in the doorway, sheets stacked in her arms.

Another loud boom of thunder shook the house. Ann Marie jumped like a scared rabbit. He'd never seen anyone so terrified of a storm. She trembled like a leaf, and all he wanted to do was put his arms around her and take away the fear.

Instead, he said, "Thanks."

"You're welcome."

They walked into the center of the living room, and he motioned to the pictures on the mantel. "Nice photos. It's like seeing a movie."

"I love taking pictures."

"It shows. You're very photogenic yourself."

"Yeah, right. I'm usually the one behind the camera, not in front of it."

Her gaze dropped to the wood floor, and he noticed her bare toes peeking out from under the hem of her nightgown.

*Pink nail polish? I never would have pegged her to be the frilly, nail polish type woman.* But the thought was a pleasant one.

"Anyway, these storms tend to move off quickly, so you can get some rest soon," he said, hoping to reassure her somehow.

"I sure hope so. It makes it real hard to sleep. I jump every time it flashes or crashes." Her palms slid down her arms and back up. "I guess I'll have to hide under my bed until it's over."

"That bad, huh?"

"Yes." Another round of thunder rolled through, and her eyes widened in terror and shifted from side to side.

Damn it. She really was spooked. "Want me to stay for a bit?"

"Would you?" she asked, her voice small and weary.

"Sure. Got some coffee?"

"I can make some."

"Sounds good."

A little smile formed on her lips, and he had to swallow the lump that threatened to choke off his air. His dick jumped to attention behind the fly of his jeans. Her hand cupped his face for a moment, and the softness of her palm felt wonderful against the roughness of his whiskers. What he wouldn't give to feel her lips under his—even for a second, although he knew seconds or even hours, would never be enough.

"Thank you for staying," she whispered. Her lips parted, inviting a kiss he wanted so badly to give her, but he knew it would be a huge mistake.

"You're welcome."

Her hand slipped away, but the warmth of her skin remained. The sway of her hips beneath the filmy nightgown, and the faint swish of the material when she turned toward the kitchen, made his hands itch to touch what lay concealed from his gaze.

He followed like a puppy, sniffing at her, absorbing the scent of honeysuckle wafting behind her.

In the kitchen, she stood at the counter preparing the coffeemaker. First the coffee in the filter, then the water from the sink. For some reason, the whole thing became erotic.

*Making coffee shouldn't be this damned nerve-wracking or make me this fucking horny.*

A rough clearing of his throat brought her attention to him, and she gave him a curious look over her shoulder as he took a seat at the breakfast table.

"It should be ready in a few minutes. This machine doesn't take long."

"Great."

More lightning flashed, followed by several loud claps of thunder and he saw her white-knuckled grip on the countertop and her gaze fixed out the window over the sink.

Without thought, he stepped behind her and laid his hands on her shoulders.

Another loud crack, and she was in his embrace, with her face buried against his chest.

His arms automatically went around her back to pull her closer. The scent in her hair, the feel of her skin, the press of her breasts, sent his control right out the window.

Skin quivered and breathing hitched, but he wasn't sure if it had to do with her fear or the unbridled lust zinging between them at every touch.

The nightgown she wore did nothing to hide how her nipples puckered into tight little buds. There would be no mistaking the rigid shaft pressing into her belly. Hot breath flittered over his neck. Soft lips felt like butterfly wings on his skin.

"Darlin'," he growled, low in his throat.

She tipped her head back and met his gaze with wide, seeking eyes and said, "Kiss me, Travis."

Mouths fused, tongues sought and hands roamed as he lost himself in the heat of the moment and the feel of her. The nightgown crawled up her body with a tug of his fingers, exposing every last inch of exquisite skin. One sharp tug and it fell into a pile on the floor beside them. Both hands cupped her ass and lifted her in his arms to sit her on the countertop. Her head fell back against the cabinet behind her, baring her neck for his mouth. The silky panties between her thighs did nothing to hide the dampness there from his gaze. Her breasts took his breath away. They fit perfectly in his palms as he molded them to his touch and rasped his callused palms over the tight nipples. He nipped the skin of her jaw, licked a path to her ear and nibbled her earlobe with his teeth, encouraged at the soft moans and intimate whimpers coming from deep inside her. The stroke of her hands seemed hesitant at first, but the more he slid his tongue from ear to shoulder, the more she explored the expanse of his chest. Harsh, rasping breaths filled the air. The rapid fluttering of her heart at the base of her throat told him she felt the pull, too. Her eyes sparkled in the dimly lit room, and her lips begged for the return of his kiss. Her fingers plucked at the edge of his tee shirt and pulled it from the waistband of his jeans. Seconds later, it joined her nightgown on the floor.

"You are so beautiful," he whispered, burying one hand in her hair. The weight of her tresses in his palm and the silkiness of her hair did funny things to his insides.

"I need you."

"I'll take care of you." His stomach quivered as she skimmed her fingertips down his abdomen to the edge of his jeans. The timid touch of her hand made him wonder, but when her lips slid across his shoulder, all thought disappeared.

Her panties skimmed down her legs with a sharp tug of his fingers, leaving her open and eager. Pussy lips glistened with her juices, and saliva flooded his mouth at the desire to taste her.

One finger slid over her clit and between the lips, bringing a deep moan and a high-pitched whimper to her mouth. She planted her heels on the edge of the counter and shifted her butt closer to the edge.

"Oh yeah," he murmured, dropping to his knees and nuzzling the crisp hair at the juncture of her thighs. He blew softly over her clit and felt her thighs quiver. The scent of her need drove him past the point of control.

With the touch of his tongue, she moaned, "Ah, God."

Two of his fingers slipped into her tight passage as he pulled her clit into his mouth. He could already feel the muscles of her vagina vibrate with the need to come. It wouldn't take much to send her over the edge. Her fingers tangled in his hair and held his head in place.

"Mmm," she hummed, the pitch of her cries getting louder and higher. "Oh yes. Oh yes. Please."

Cream flooded his mouth and ran over his fingers when she climaxed on a loud cry.

"Easy," he whispered, continuing to lick and sooth her trembles.

Grabbing his wallet, he retrieved a condom and then dropped his pants around his ankles as he stood. He glanced at her face to make sure she hadn't changed her mind. The way she licked her lips and fastened her gaze on his cock, he didn't think she had. With his dick safely encased, he stepped between her thighs and eased the head into her pussy.

"You feel amazing."

"Now, Travis. Please. I want you inside me."

"Need to go slow. It's been too damned long. Otherwise, this will be over way too fast." His teeth hurt from grinding them together to forestall the inevitable explosion of cum.

She wrapped her legs around his waist and planted her heels against his butt. Her movements shoved his dick all the way in, and he fought the urge to come right then.

"I need this. I need you."

"Fuck, darlin'. Hang on, honey." Both hands grasped her hips and he pulled back so only the head remained and then shoved his cock back inside her, over and over. The rush of ecstasy left him panting as if he'd run a marathon. Heat curled up his legs, rushed through his pelvis and he knew he couldn't stop it. His thumb found her clit and brushed against it quickly to bring her along for the ride. "Come for me, darlin'."

"Oh God. Oh God," she panted.

Her pussy felt like a vice when she came apart and climaxed with his name on her lips.

# Chapter Three

Morning brought to light Travis' greenhorn status when he stepped into the bunk house dining area for breakfast as the inquisitive looks passed over him. He shot a glance at the men surrounding the long table.

"Who the hell are you?" The voice belonged to a man sitting at the far side of the table. Given the man's dark complexion and eyes, Travis guessed he had some Mexican ancestors somewhere in his lineage.

Travis stuck out his hand to the speaker and said, "Travis Brooks. Mrs. Skolack hired me to train the horses. Got in yesterday."

"Manuel," he said, taking Travis' hand, then motioned to an empty chair next to him. "Haven't seen Ann Marie this morning. She's always here before the rest of us."

"I'm sure she'll be along in a minute or two. Had a late night with the storm and all."

Manuel's eyebrows shot up. "And you would know this how?"

Travis knew when to keep his mouth shut, and talking about what happened between him and Ann Marie the previous night, would be like cutting his own throat. He murmured "thanks" to the cook who set a plate in front of him.

"None of your business, Manuel," Ann Marie declared as she stepped through the doorway.

"Sorry, Ann Marie. Just askin'." Manuel picked up his napkin and wiped his mouth.

Ann Marie introduced the rest of the men sitting at the table, and despite the misgivings she'd mentioned about him being accepted, everyone seemed to be cordial enough.

The heat in her eyes when they came to rest on him would have singed his hair, if he'd been closer. A quick glance from the top of her thick, brown tresses to the tips of her cowboy boots, and all the feelings and desires rushed through him.

*Making love to her was a huge mistake. One I can't repeat while I'm here.*

But being inside her sweet heat bordered on ecstasy—something he'd never felt in his life, and he knew she'd felt it, too. The looks coming his way across the table could have set the place ablaze if there'd have been dry grass around. A quick tumble between the sheets, or in their case, on the kitchen countertop, seemed like a great idea at the time. In the light of day, not so much. God, she'd tasted like heaven. All woman and made for a man's touch.

"So, where you hail from, Travis?" Manuel asked.

"Amarillo."

"Been trainin' long?"

"About twenty years, give or take. Never met a horse I couldn't tame. I ain't aimin' to start now."

Manuel looked at Ann Marie. "He gonna break the stallion?"

She nodded, and Travis said, "That's the plan."

A chorus of groans and shifting chairs echoed in the room.

"Good luck with that one." Manuel shoveled a forkful of food into his mouth. "That ornery bastard killed John."

Travis eyed Manuel. "Maybe he did, maybe he didn't." Riding a wild stallion was questionable. And without knowing exactly what had happened, Travis was hard-pressed to blame the animal.

Manuel stared at Travis for several seconds, but didn't reply.

Conversation turned to other ranch business, while thoughts whirled through Travis' mind. After several sly glances, Manuel asked, "When are you gonna start with Black?"

"Soon. The sooner the better."

"Can I give you a bit of advice?"

"Sure."

"Don't get between him and Ann Marie. The horse is taken with her. Just don't work with him whenever she's around."

Travis thought about what Manuel was trying to say for a few seconds, then asked, "Why? What do you think he'd do?"

"Kill you."

\* \* \* \*

Travis decided to spend the first day oiling the equipment and getting familiar with the setup of the ranch. Bringing several pieces of tack into the office, he laid each one out on the desk and flipped on the computer.

The arena he would have to work with could only be described as impressive. Its dirt floor and circular shape would keep the animal moving if he wanted to do lunge work. But finding out where each animal stood with its training would be first on his list.

Ann Marie had given him a shy glance over her shoulder and then disappeared after breakfast, leaving him to wonder at the look.

Shaking his head to clear his thoughts, he focused on the computer screen and clicked on the files he needed.

Black Jack.

Ann Marie's Dream.

Tyler's Pony.

Spirit Runner.

Lucky Lady.

Obviously, John and Ann Marie had numerous top of the line horses on the ranch. He recognized quite a few of the names on the computer screen as either some he knew personally or those whose sires had bloodlines longer than his arm.

Travis whistled through his teeth. "Damn. The list goes on and on," he said, looking over each name until he clicked on Black Jack's file.

For the next few hours, Travis read every note John had made on the stallion and his progress, which turned out not to be much. John had also written about the dream he and Ann Marie had for the beautiful animal and how they hoped he would become their prized possession.

One particular note read:

*February 10, 2009*

*Had Black in the arena today. He did well with the halter and lead, but balked*
*with the bridle and pads. I need to work more with him, but I don't have the time.*
*Imperative that I get the cattle rounded up and ready to ship. Taxes due and*
*credit has already been extended by the bank to the max.*

Travis didn't want to read any further. The entry appeared personal, and he felt as if he were prying. Besides, he really didn't want to know.

The tack on the desk needed cleaning. Someone wasn't doing their job if the equipments condition said anything. *I'll have to ask Ann Marie. This stuff is filthy.*

Lifting one of the bridles, he unhooked the bit and scrubbed it with the rough brush he'd brought in with him to get the loose dirt off before he cleaned them with saddle soap.

The scent of leather filled his nostrils, giving him a sense of home and putting him at ease. He closed his eyes, thinking about the way Ann Marie had smelled last night. She'd been fresh from a bath. Her skin had been so soft, so...

His eyes flew open. "Get those thoughts right out of your mind. The woman is off limits no matter what happened last night."

Picking up the various bridles, he shoved his way out of the office and down the walkway toward the washroom in the back. A quick flick of the wrist and warm water poured into the sink. Dribbling some saddle soap into the water, he turned the tap off and grabbed the soft brush he found on the shelf above the sink. Dirty horse tack, he couldn't handle.

Just a mild scrubbing and it would be clean and ready for use. Upkeep and repair on the equipment would be a priority as long as he worked on the ranch.

*Maybe I can pay Tyler to do this.*

"Hello there," Ann Marie said from the washroom doorway. "How are things going? I hope breakfast wasn't too big of an ordeal."

He glanced at her for a moment and went back to the task at hand. Too many thoughts ran through his mind. Her body open for him on the kitchen countertop—the way she tasted, and the scent of honeysuckle on her hair. Soft lips and passion-filled eyes distracted him from her presence for a moment.

"Something wrong?"

"Huh?" His gaze went to her face while he continued to scrub. "Sorry. No."

"I asked how everything was."

"Fine. I'm cleanin' up some tack. Filthy stuff you've got here."

"Doesn't surprise me. John handled that, and I believe he'd farmed the chore out to one of the hands. A few left right after his accident."

"Why?"

"Same reason you stated. They wouldn't work for a woman."

Heat crawled up his neck, and he dropped his gaze back to the task at hand. "Sorry. I guess it's a man thing."

"I suppose so."

"I went over a few of your husband's notes on the horses. You own some impressive stock."

"Some of the best."

"Have you bred any of the mares this season?"

"No. With John's death, and dealing with Ty and everything after…"

"I understand. Are there any you want bred? I can get that done for you, but we need to get moving. It's getting later in the season, and you don't want late foals, necessarily."

"I believe there are two John mentioned breeding."

"I'll look over his notes and see which ones. Do you want them bred to the stallion?"

"Preferably, yes. Any foals from Black Jack will be awesome."

"If we breed now, they'll be mid-year foals. Take into consideration; I won't be here for the births."

*Why does the thought of leaving make me feel like shit? I can't stay here. I won't. It's too much like settlin' down.*

Ann Marie refused to meet his gaze.

"Listen, about last night," he said, setting the bridle on the side of the sink and drying his hands.

"Um, yeah." Her eyes seemed brighter—almost like she'd thought about it too much since they'd parted. "We shouldn't have. I mean, it was a really bad idea, and one we can't repeat."

"No problem."

Frown lines appeared between her eyebrows. "We should pretend it never happened. You know, forget about it and move on."

"Sure."

She rocked back on her heels and stuffed her hands in her pockets. "It was a weakness on my part. It's been a long time since I've been with a man and you're very handsome. But any kind of relationship between us wouldn't be a right."

"Who said anything about relationship?"

"Well I…I mean I kind of assumed, since we'd slept together—"

"We didn't sleep, Ann Marie, we fucked. Big difference. I won't get involved with a woman beyond sex." He traced one finger down her cheek. "Don't get me wrong; I enjoyed it immensely, but I'm not going to be here beyond six months."

"Okay. Fine. It won't happen again, and we won't mention it after this. Agreed?"

"As you wish," he replied, and turned back toward the sink.

"We have a wonderful vet. A guy named Charlie Miller. One of the best."

"Charlie Miller? That name sounds familiar. I went to school with a Charlie Miller."

"He's supposed to be out here tomorrow to check on one of the mares. A piece of barbed wire caught her in the leg, and it got infected."

"Which mare?"

"Ann Marie's Dream."

A smile twitched at his lips at the name. Figures John would name a horse after her.

His gaze roamed over her frame from the top of her straw hat to the tips of her black boots. Flashes of memory of their night together haunted him. The firmness of her thighs when she'd gripped his waist and forced his cock deep into her sweet pussy with her heels against his butt. How her breasts had molded perfectly to his palms. Pink areolas tightened into hard nubs, begging for his mouth. His cock pressed insistently against the fly of his jeans, and he stepped closer to the sink so she wouldn't see. "Nice name."

"I didn't name her. John did."

"Is she your personal mount?"

"One of them, yes."

"I'll check her myself later and see how it's healing."

"Vet skills, too?"

"A little. You know how it is when you're a trainer. You have to be able to spot troubles with the animal you're working with, whether it's physical or mental."

"True enough."

He continued to work the soap through each piece of tack until all the dirt and grease were gone.

"Something else I can do for you?" he asked, aware she continued to stand at the door watching him. Just her presence set him on edge. He felt every breath, every movement and every sigh, she made. Did she realize having her close like this made him want to set her on one of the saddles against the wall and see if last night was only a fluke?

"Um…I thought maybe you might be up for a ride?"

"Ride?" Alone out in the middle of nowhere, the two of them. What the hell? Is she trying to drive me insane? Surely she knows she's playing with fire here.

"I want to go down by the river, and I hate riding alone. I thought maybe you'd like to see some more of the ranch."

"I guess I can. These pieces need to dry a little. I can't oil them until later anyway."

A radiant smile flittered across her lips, lighting up her face and making her eyes sparkle like diamonds in the sun, even though uncertainty rolled across her face like a cloud.

*Breathe. In and out. In and out. Remember, she's totally off limits.*

"I'll saddle a couple of horses," he replied, not sure if he would be able to keep his hands off her. A groan rumbled in his chest with the intoxicating scent of roses that met his nose.

God, this would be a long ride.

* * * *

Thirty minutes later, they mounted and rode toward the tree line in the distance.

Riding normally gave Ann Marie much-needed alone time, time to forget, to think. Today would be different. Travis was at her side, and she had a sneaking suspicion his presence would be a major distraction.

But that's what she'd wanted, wasn't it? Last night shouldn't have happened. Bad idea. Getting involved with one of her employees didn't bode well for a continued, uncomplicated business arrangement, and that's what they had, a business arrangement.

The far off screech of vultures as they circled overhead told her they'd better check out whatever lay dead or dying over the hill.

"Let's ride over there," he said, almost reading her mind. "It might be one of the cows or horses."

At a full gallop, they raced across the dry desert floor, avoiding scrub trees, rocks and tumbleweeds. The closer they came to the area below the scavengers, the more Ann Marie's stomach rolled, with the stench of rotting flesh from a dead animal carcass.

"I can't get any closer," she said, stopping her mare several feet away, even though he gave her a curious look. "I have a really weak stomach when it comes to dead things."

A soft chuckle and a cocked eyebrow told her he didn't believe she could have that weak of a stomach and be a rancher, but he didn't say a word.

After he'd taken a look, he trotted his horse back toward her while she admired the cut of his shirt, the fit of his jeans and the line of his jaw. His thighs gripped the horse and his hips rolled with each movement. Powerful and fit. Memories of last night flooded back. The same hips powering forward, driving his cock into her pussy and making her almost beg for release.

She shook her head to clear her thoughts and bring them back to the curious fact of his sleeves cut off on all the shirts she'd seen. Not too many cowboys she knew preferred their shifts like that.

"Are all the sleeves cut off your shirts?" she asked, to take her mind off the dead animal and the memories of his lovemaking. She kind of liked being able to see the muscles in his arms bunch and roll with his movement.

The cocky grin sliding across his mouth, made her heart skip a beat.

"Not all. It's easier to work with the horses without having something around my forearms. It keeps my arms free in case the horse tries to bite or kick. Why do you ask?"

"Curious, I guess." Tearing her gaze away from his sexy form, she asked, "So what was it?"

"Calf. Been dead for awhile. Several days at least."

Bile rose in her throat and she fought the urge to hurl.

*Don't throw up. Don't throw up.*

"You okay? You look a little green."

*Throw up.*

Almost pitching herself from the saddle, she ran toward a stand of trees and puked up her breakfast.

Warm hands pulled her hair back from her face and held the mass until she finished. A damp handkerchief found its way into her hand.

"Thanks."

"You're welcome."

"Sorry."

"For what?"

Her watery eyes met his and she caught the glint of silver as he handed her the canteen. A quick rinse of her mouth helped.

"Losing my breakfast in front of you. Not a good impression of the boss lady."

"Not like I haven't seen people puke."

She shrugged her shoulders and stepped back. Being this close to him, smelling his aftershave, his hands in her hair, did things to her insides she would rather not deal with right at this moment.

"I guess we should get back to the house. I need to brush my teeth and have a bite to settle my stomach."

"No problem. I've got work to do anyway." A smile lifted the corners of his mouth and crinkled the skin near his eyes. Her stomach fluttered like a million butterflies beat on the inside to get loose. "Boss lady is pretty demanding, you know."

"Is she now? I need to talk to her, then, and make her understand you need time to yourself on occasion, too."

A warm chuckle left his mouth." You do that."

His laughter sent shivers down her arms.

When they'd remounted, they pulled their horses around to head back to the house.

"Is Ty around today?" he asked.

"No. He hasn't come back from his friend's house yet. Why?"

"I figured he could help me clean up the barn. Like every other kid I know, he'd probably like to earn a little extra cash."

"You don't need to pay him, Travis. He gets an allowance for doing chores."

"Yeah, but a little extra helps when they want something special from the store."

"All right. If you want to, but don't make it a habit. I don't want him bugging you all the time for money."

"He'll have to work for it. I'm a pretty hard taskmaster."

Silence stretched between them for a few moments and, she wondered how much of herself to expose to this man. "I've tried to get him to take on more responsibility since his dad died, but he's so angry all the time."

"I'm sure he misses his father a lot."

"I guess so."

"Speaking of your husband…"

"Yes?"

"I get the impression it wasn't a love match."

"No." She didn't elaborate. It wasn't any of his business, but she wanted to talk—needed to talk to someone.

They rode up to the front of the house and dismounted.

"Tie the horses up and come in, please, so we can talk."

Travis hesitated behind her.

"Travis?"

"Yeah, I'm coming."

With a shake of her head, she walked into the kitchen and made coffee. She had to hope telling Travis some of the problems of her past wouldn't make him feel sorry for her. Pity wasn't an emotion she could handle from this man.

The strong brew dripped into the pot with a gurgle, and she moved back toward the living room to find Travis sitting comfortably on the couch, his booted feet crossed at the ankles.

For a brief moment, she wondered what it would feel like to lay her head on the muscles of his chest and let him take all the heartache and pain away. *I need to get those thoughts out of my brain this minute. The last thing I need is another man, especially one who makes me think of long walks in the moonlight and hot, sweaty sex between the sheets.*

"Coffee should be ready in about ten minutes or so." She sat down next to him, and the clean smell of his hair met her nose. Some type of musky scent emanating from his skin wrapped itself around her senses and made her hands tremble and itch to touch.

The crash of glass upstairs startled her, and she jumped and ran for the stairs.

"You want me to come?"

"No, it's fine," she called to him from over her shoulder. "It's probably Tyler or the cat. I'll be right back."

At the top of the stairs, she paused and inhaled a deep breath. She edged along the narrow hall, cautious, stopping short at Tyler's room where she found nothing out of place. The next room was hers—the one she'd shared with John. Peeking around the corner of the door, she noticed one of her glass figurines lying shattered on the wood floor.

*Meow.*

The large black and white cat whined from the window seat.

"Damn cat," she grumbled. "You know you aren't supposed to be in here." Ann Marie swatted at her, and the cat meowed again, but scooted out the door.

She picked up all the larger sized pieces of glass and tossed them into the trash, making a mental note to bring up a broom and dust pan later to get up the tiny slivers that remained. With the crisis over, she decided to get out of her jeans and into a pair of shorts before going back downstairs. She changed quickly, her thoughts centered on Travis and the discussion they were about to have—and that sexy body of his. Was she ever going to get used to having all that male muscle around her?

Heat zipped across her chest and down her abdomen to settle low in her belly at the thought of their tryst last night. Months of no man around except the ranch workers, left her needy. It never occurred to her to cross the line of boss and employee with any of the other men, but with Travis, it became almost natural to take him into her body and savor the time together.

"Enough, Ann Marie. Yes, the man is gorgeous, and yes, you wanted him, but you need to put a stop to this insane instant attraction for him. No good can come of it anyway."

The steps creaked and groaned as she stepped on them, and she realized she needed someone to look at them. One more thing she had to take care of.

She rounded the corner to find Travis sitting on the couch with his boots crossed at the ankles.

"Let's go into the kitchen and have some coffee. We can talk more."

Once he settled into one of the dining room chairs, she poured him a cup of the steaming brew and set it down in front of him.

"Do you take anything in it?"

"No. Black's fine."

"Typical cowboy."

With a quick flash of white teeth, he grinned, showing off that elusive dimple she'd seen a couple of times.

"So you told me you grew up near Amarillo."

"Yep. I'm the eldest boy in a bunch of girls. I have a baby brother, but he's a lot younger than me. Four sister's between us, and I spent all my time chasing boyfriends away from the house until they all grew up."

A bubble of laughter left her lips, and he smiled again.

"How come some lucky woman hasn't snapped you up before now?"

That brought a frown to his sexy mouth.

"I'm sorry. Never mind."

"No, it's fine. I haven't really found anyone I wanted to get serious with during the last ten years, I guess. Besides, I ain't the marryin' kind anymore. Don't need a wife or kids. I'm fine on my own. I travel. I come and go as I please. No woman tellin' me what to do, where to be…"

One set of strong fingers wrapped around the coffee mug and lifted it to his lips. Long, dark eyelashes covered his impressive baby blues, blocking her from seeing anything in his expression other than avoidance.

She cocked one eyebrow and tilted her head. "Loner. Got it."

"Don't stay in one place long enough to get close to anybody."

His gaze stopped on her for a moment, and she forgot to breathe.

"Do you ever go home? I mean back to Amarillo?"

"Yeah, about once or twice a year, dependin' on the jobs I have. My mom wouldn't have it any other way. I have to be there for Christmas, or she'd tan my hide."

Her gaze dropped to the milky substance in her cup.

"What about you? Does your family visit? I don't think you told me where you're from."

She jumped to her feet and walked to the sink, placing her cup inside. Talking about her mother and father left a bitter taste in her mouth, and she would rather avoid the subject altogether.

"Did I say something wrong?"

"No. I don't talk about my family."

"Bad blood?"

"Not with my sister, Kelly. In fact, she'll be coming to live with me soon. I don't talk to our parents anymore, and Kelly is finally old enough to leave that hellhole."

"Whoa. Sorry I asked."

A heavy sigh escaped her lips. "Its fine, Travis. I haven't seen my parents since I married John ten years ago. My father is a senator and my mother is a stay at home mom. He's an abuser, both physically and mentally. I left when I could. My mother refused to leave him and she wouldn't allow Kelly to leave and come here with me until she turned eighteen."

"Did you ever report it?"

"Of course I did! No one would believe me. He's got every judge, cop, and lawyer in his fucking pocket."

"What's your maiden name?" His question brought her gaze to his. Why would he care? He was only there temporarily.

She shook her head, refusing to answer.

*It wouldn't do anyone any good if he knew.*

He stood and moved to stand in front of her, trapping her against the sink with one hand on each side, next to her hips.

"Tell me, Ann Marie," he whispered, dropping his voice an octave.

"No," she murmured, hating the way he sent her heart skipping a beat as his breath caressed her lips.

"Let me help you."

"It's not your fight, Travis."

"I'm making it my fight. I can't handle men who abuse women. He should be in jail, not in our government."

"Leave it be. It doesn't matter. He can't hurt me anymore."

"He's still hurting you emotionally, darlin'." She didn't think his mouth could get any closer, but it did, hovering bare centimeters from hers. "You married John to get away from him, away from them."

"I married John because I loved him."

"You didn't, not at first. I can see it in your eyes. He made you comfortable." Travis ran a finger down her arm, sending the hair rising on her flesh in its wake. His gaze dropped to her lips, and she ran her tongue over the parched surface. "I make you nervous."

"Yes."

"Why?"

"I don't like how you make me feel."

*What a frickin' lie! I love how he makes me feel, how he makes me want things I never had.*

"How do you feel when I do this?" He nibbled the corner of her mouth. "Does it make you want more?"

Her lips parted, but no words came out.

Lips brushed softly against hers, and she closed her eyes. They continued across her cheek to her ear.

"Does my kiss light a fire in your belly you want to quench? John never made you feel all warm from only a look, did he."

"No," she whispered, while her hands grasped at his forearms, desperately trying to right her tilting world.

He sucked her earlobe between his lips and nipped at the skin with his teeth. Her nipples puckered into tight little nubs.

"Tell me your maiden name, darlin'."

"Boyd," she sighed. "It's Boyd."

"Leo Boyd is your father?" he asked, as he continued to tease the skin.

"Yes," she whispered, loving the feel of his lips on her neck and ears. John never did those things. He wasn't one for foreplay. Oh, he took his time, but it was to help him get wound up enough to have sex with her, not to help her get ready for him. Their sex life could be classified vanilla to a fault.

The feel of Travis pressed against her breasts, his lips brushing over her skin, the smell of his musky scent mixed with horses, sent heat straight between her thighs. She loved the smell of horses on a man.

A tortured moan slipped from her mouth, and she tipped her head to the side, leaving her throat open for his continued play.

"Like it?" he asked against her neck.

"Oh, God, yes. I…" Her voice trailed off on a moan.

One hand palmed her breast, rasping lightly against the nipple through her bra and shirt.

* * * *

Passion clouded her blue eyes. She wanted him, wanted him like a woman wants a man to satisfy the deep, gnawing ache she felt, to fill the void left in her belly when she hasn't been with anyone in a long time.

With a weary sigh, he stepped back, but she held on and wouldn't let him go far. The throbbing between his legs almost drove him past the point of reason.

*I can't make love to her again. It wouldn't be fair, but right now, all I want is to bury my cock deep inside her hot little pussy.*

"I'm sorry," he murmured, pressing his forehead against hers.

"For what?"

"Taking advantage of you."

"You haven't…yet."

A dry chuckle left his lips. "Yet."

"Travis—"

He stopped her words with one finger to her lips. "Don't." Teeth nipped at the pad of the digit, and he fought the groan in his chest, struggling to escape. "I don't want to hurt you."

"You can't."

"Yes, I can."

Without another word, he turned and walked away, letting the screen door slam shut behind him while he hurried for the barn.

*Cold shower. Definitely need a cold shower.*

His dick screamed with want—the undeniable need to fuck Ann Marie. How long had it been since he'd made love to a woman?

*Made love? Where the hell did that thought come from?*

"Oh, Travis, old boy. You are in way over your head, and you haven't even been here a goddamn week."

He reached his room, stripped off his clothes and went into the bathroom. The shower came on with a twist of his hand on the cold spigot.

A deep breath rattled his chest, and he fought the high-pitched squeal as he stepped into the icy water.

"Fuck, that's cold!"

His cock eased its achy awareness seconds later, but as visions of Ann Marie with her passion-filled eyes swam in front of his closed eyelids, it sprang back to life.

"Son of a bitch! Okay. Only way to take care of this problem, other than running back to the house and throwing her down on the bed, is to get myself off."

Wrapping his palm around his stiff erection, he let images of her sweet face, luscious lips and sexy smile dance inside his head.

In his fantasy, she'd kneel in front of him in the shower, her pretty pink lips lifting in a smile as her hand cradled his balls. The head of his cock disappeared between her pouty lips.

*Aw, hell!*

Both hands wrapped in her long hair, twisting it around his fist, letting his fingers massage her scalp while she sucked him deep—so deep he could feel the back of her throat. The muscles of her mouth and neck worked over him, sucking and swallowing, bringing him to brink before she eased up and let him slide almost completely out. The hand cupping his balls rolled them and squeezed lightly, while she took him back into her warmth. Her finger trailed back to his ass, fingering the hole, but never delving into the forbidden area. She grasped both of his butt cheeks in her hands and held him to her, not letting him out of her mouth until he shot cum clear to the back of her throat and she swallowed every drop.

A tortured growl spewed from his lips as he stroked his cock until his load shot into his hand. On shaky legs, he slumped against the edge of the shower and inhaled sharp, raspy breaths between his lips until he felt strong enough to walk.

\* \* \* \*

Determined to put his obviously uncontrollable issues with Ann Marie out of his mind, Travis got dressed. He didn't feel he had the mindset to work with the stallion today, but there were plenty more horses that needed his attention.

A pretty, painted mare stuck her nose over the fence and whinnied.

"Well, hello there, beautiful. I wonder what your name is."

"Misty," a small voice said behind him, and he turned to find Tyler standing several feet down the walkway.

"Is she yours?"

"Yeah," Tyler said, dropping his gaze to the dirt floor, kicking at a protruding rock.

"Do you ride a lot?"

The negative response from Tyler made Travis wonder why.

"How come? She looks to be a real sweetheart."

Tyler shrugged, but his gaze remained fixed on the rock.

"How long have you had her?"

"Since before I can remember."

"Did you ride with your dad?"

Another negative response, and Travis wondered why. It seemed odd with his mother and father so into horses and ranch life that Tyler wasn't.

"Would you like to ride with me?"

The boy raised his face, and immediately, Travis could see what the problem was. Tyler had a fear of horses.

*I wonder if Ann Marie knows this.*

"Come here, Ty."

He took a step back and vigorously shook his head.

"It's okay. I won't let her hurt you. "

Travis knew Tyler wanted to by the look on his face, but for some reason, terror gripped the child.

"Did something happen to make you afraid?"

"I'm not afraid," Tyler grumbled. "I don't like 'em. That's all."

Travis moved to a bench across from the stall and sat down. "Can I confess something, Ty?"

"I s'pose."

"I was scared to death of horses once too."

The boy's eyes widened in disbelief. "You were?"

"Yep."

Tyler sat down next to him. "Really? You aren't just telling me a story, are you?"

"No. A horse bit me once. Right here." Travis pointed to his thigh. "I wouldn't go near another one for nigh on five years. My daddy wasn't happy. You see, my mom and dad have a big cattle ranch near Amarillo. It wouldn't do for their eldest son to be scared of horses."

"How'd you get over it? I mean you ain't a scared of 'em now."

"No, I'm not. I found me a pretty little mare like your Misty there and worked with her for a long time—months. I rode her every day, no matter how scared I was. Pretty soon, she and I got to be real close. I knew she'd never hurt me. Not to say there aren't horses out there that are downright mean, but I learned to avoid situations that would get me hurt."

"Did mom tell you my dad got killed by the stallion when he was out ridin'?"

"Yeah."

Tyler dropped his gaze to the floor again for several moments. "Will you help me?"

"Help you?"

"Yeah. Learn not to be afraid anymore?"

Travis swallowed hard. He knew how much it took for Tyler to ask him for help while he faced the fact that his father wasn't here anymore.

His heart clenched, and he closed his eyes for a moment. Adam would have been about Ty's age if he would have lived. His little boy. His son. They would have worked the horses together. He would have taught Adam from early on, how to train and carry on his legacy, but now nothing remained but the pain.

Despite his own pain, his need to block the immense weight of guilt and sorrow wrenching his guts, he found himself saying, "You bet."

Tyler stood and glanced at him. "Thanks, Mr. Brooks."

"Call me Travis, okay?"

"Sure."

The boy moved back down the dirt hallway without another look in his direction.

He and the boy might be able to come to some sort of compromise during his time on the ranch. Tyler needed a father figure, badly, but Travis knew he couldn't do it for him—didn't want to. The only child he wanted to be a father to was no longer alive.

*I'm here for only six months. I can't get too involved. The last thing I want or need is a wife and a kid.*

\* \* \* \*

The next morning, Tyler came into the barn as the sun began to climb in the sky. Travis had been up since daybreak, grooming the horses, cleaning out stalls and finishing up the tack.

"Hey, buddy," Travis said.

"Hi."

"You're up mighty early. I figured you'd be sleepin' in since it's the weekend."

"Nah. I always get up by six."

"Would you like to help me?"

The kid's eyes widened. "Do what?"

"I need to brush Misty down and clean her hooves."

After one harsh exhale, Tyler moved closer. "I s'pose."

"Here." Travis handed him the curry comb. "You comb her down, and I'll go behind you with the grooming brush. Then we'll do her feet together."

"F-feet?" Tyler asked, with a nervous twitter in his voice.

Travis had to smile. He knew it took a lot of courage for the boy to get this close. "It's okay, Ty. I won't let her hurt you."

Tyler's fingers shook when he took the comb from Travis' hand.

With a small nod, Tyler moved to the mare's side and ran the comb down her coat.

"Put a little more pressure behind it. The curry comb is to get all the deep stuff off. The dirt, sweat and grime under the surface. The one I have will do the top coat."

The horse shifted, and Tyler squealed and jumped back.

Travis coaxed the boy close again and said, "The main thing you need to be careful of is walking behind her. Put your hand on her butt so she knows you're back there, and stay close to her tail. It's much harder for her to kick you like that."

Once one side was brushed, Tyler hesitated a moment, then laid his hand on her and walked behind her to reach the other side.

"See. She won't hurt you."

The kid tugged at Travis' heart strings, but getting involved with Ty would hurt them both. Pain and heartache were nothing new to Travis. Losing his son cost him a lot. The several months following Adam's death, he had drunk himself into oblivion on more than one occasion. After a while, he realized drowning himself in a bottle of whiskey wouldn't bring his son back, no matter how much he tried.

Travis pushed the painful thoughts down and focused again on Tyler. "How's school going?"

"Fine. I wish summer would get here, though," Tyler replied, not realizing the ease with which he continued to brush the mare. Almost like he was born to it.

The more time he spent with Tyler, the more Travis saw the gentleness of Ann Marie's spirit in him. Ann Marie was tough on the outside, but her hard shell could be cracked to show the heart of the woman beneath if one lucky guy managed to penetrate her outer defenses. Making love to her didn't count. It was a moment of weakness on her part, he figured, but the thought bothered him.

*I don't need to be that man. She needs husband material, not a drifting horse trainer.*

"How long do you think it will take you to break the stallion, Travis?"

"Not sure. I work with them until I get where I want to be. Black Jack's stubborn and ornery, but we'll get there."

When they finished brushing the mare, Travis grabbed the hoof pick and motioned for Tyler to stand beside him.

"Ever done this?"

Tyler shook his head and stepped back, his eyes bright with fear again.

"Okay. I'll show you. You can do her other side." Shifting his shoulder against the mare's side, he tugged at her foot to encourage her to bring it up for him. "Get her foot in your hand good and steady, and use the sharp end to scrape all the shi...uh, stuff out of her hoof."

After he'd cleaned the first one, he  shifted to the horse's hindquarters. "Your turn."

*Poor kid.*

Travis helped Tyler get the mare into position and instructed him on what to do. Luckily, the little mare was well trained. The hoof came up in Tyler's hand without much pressure.

"You're a pro already, buddy."

"Really?"

"Yep."

Tyler puffed his chest out and squared his shoulders as a wide grin spread across his face. Travis' thoughts turned to Adam again, and it broke his heart to think of how much he could have taught his son about horses and how he would have loved to seen the same look in his son's eyes.

"How about we saddle her."

"S-saddle her?"

"Sure. You don't have to ride, if you don't want to. You can just walk her around, but you need to know how to saddle and bridle her."

"O-okay."

"Follow me." They walked down the aisle to the tack room, pulled out the bridle, saddle and blanket. Travis figured the best way to deal with the boy's fear had to be facing it head on and pushing him when he wasn't sure.

Once they stood near the horse again, Travis said, "We'll do the bridle first. Hold the bit between your fingers like this and slide it between her teeth."

"I-I can't, Travis."

"Yes you can. Here. I'll stand behind you and help. Take the bit and put it against her teeth. She'll open her mouth without you having to do anything else."

The bit slipped inside without a problem, and Tyler grinned

"Now, loop the headstall over her ears and buckle the chin strap under her jaw."

After the bridle was secured, Tyler exclaimed, "I did it!"

"You sure did." Travis ruffled the boy's hair and grinned. "Let's get her saddled. You already did the hardest part."

Within moments, they had the mare saddled and ready to ride.

"Can I get on her?"

"You want to, buddy? You don't have to, you know. You've done great already."

"I want to. She doesn't seem so bad anymore. Kind of like a big baby."

Travis chuckled. "We'll take her into the arena then, so it's a controlled area." The two of them walked out into the center with the mare trailing behind Tyler. "Do you know how to mount?"

"Yes," Tyler replied, sliding his left foot into the stirrup and swinging his leg over the back of the saddle.

"Do you want me to lead you around?"

"I think I can do it. I've watched Mom and Dad."

"Go for it, then, but I'll be right there by the side of the arena in case there's a problem. Okay?"

Tyler nodded and kicked the mare in her sides. A huge grin spread across his face when the mare took several steps forward and walked around the arena.

"I'm doin' it! I'm ridin'!"

"Great job, buddy."

Sadness pulled at his heart while he watched Tyler riding around the arena. *It should be Adam I'm teaching to ride. My son should be here, not buried in the ground in Amarillo.* His fingers cut a path through his hair as a frustrated sigh left his lips.

With his back to the doorway, Travis didn't see the car pull up outside in the front of the house until he heard the door slam.

He turned around, and his heart dropped into his stomach. Anger flushed through him so fast, he fought the urge to put his fist through the planking surrounding the arena.

The leggy blonde faced him and smiled. "Travis."

"Catherine."

# Chapter Four

"What in the hell are you doing here?" Travis asked, a snarl pulling at his mouth.

"I came to see you, sugar. I thought we needed to talk."

"I have nothing to say to you, Catherine. Get back into your car and crawl back into whatever hole you slithered out of."

One painted fingernail trailed down his chest.

"Oh, Travis, honey."

"Can I help you?" Ann Marie said coming up to stand beside them. Her eyes narrowed into agitated slits. "I'm Ann Marie Skolack. Welcome to the Double S."

"I came to see my husband."

"Husband?" Ann Marie asked, her gaze shooting to him.

"Ex-husband," Travis growled, pulling her hand away and dropping it. "How in the hell did you find out where I was?"

"Private investigators do a wonderful job."

"What do you want, Catherine?"

Catherine glanced at Ann Marie, and then back to him. "Do you really want to talk in front of her?"

*Shit.*

"No. Follow me." He spun around and walked toward the barn, expecting her to follow. She wanted something, and he aimed to find out what.

When they reached the office, he pushed her inside and slammed the door behind them. "Now. What the hell do you want, and don't give me any runaround, Catherine. I'm not in the mood."

Tears well up in her black-rimmed eyes, but he knew they weren't real. The woman didn't have a heart.

"I wanted to apologize, Travis. I realize now how much I love you,, and how sorry I am things ended the way they did. Adam meant everything to me and when he died, I…"

"Don't ever mention my son's name. You have no right."

"I have every right. He was my son, too."

"You didn't give a shit about him. He died because you weren't watching him in the tub that night. You were too fucking busy talking to your latest conquest or whoever on the phone."

The anger simmering under the surface almost brought him to his knees. The guilt tore at his heart, but there was no way he would let her back in. He loved her once, but now he could see her for what she was. A gold-digger. Wind of his good fortune with training must have reached her, and now she thought she could weasel her way back into his good graces and get her hands on some of it.

"But I love you…"

"Don't," he growled, pointing one finger in her face. "You never loved me, and you don't now."

The real Catherine reared her ugly head. A snarl left her lips. "Are you fucking that little bitch who owns this place? Trying to get your hands on her property, Travis?"

"What happens between me and Ann Marie is none of your business, and if you must know, I have enough in the bank to buy this place two or three times over. I don't need to fuck her to get it, if I wanted to." The door swept open with a twist of his hand. "If you'll excuse me, I have work to do. I'm sure you can find your way out."

He left her standing in the middle of the office with her mouth opening and closing like a guppy.

* * * *

Noonday sun burned bright in the clear blue sky above, and sweat rolled down between his shoulders to soak his shirt.

*Damn, it's hot today.*

"Travis?"

Her sweet voice drifted to him on the stale air. He'd avoided being alone with her for the last week. Hell, he'd avoided her, the best he could for the last several weeks, but she'd caught him in the large arena on the side of the barn, working with the stallion today. After the tryst in the kitchen, he'd been walking around with a perpetual hard-on, with no relief in sight.

"Yeah?"

"Why don't to take a break for a bit? It's got to be a hundred degrees out here."

"Ain't got time."

"Yes you do."

"You want this animal broke or not, Ann Marie?"

"You know I do, but not at the cost of you dropping from heatstroke." Her arms were hooked over the railing of the enclosure, and her breasts pushed against the wood.

*Ah, hell. So much for avoidance.*

"Come sit on the porch for a bit and drink some water or lemonade. I don't want to have to be takin' you to the hospital."

"I'm born and raised Texan, ma'am."

"That doesn't mean shit, and you know it. Come, sit, before I get me a whip and tan your hide."

One eyebrow cocked and he smiled, thinking about how cute she looked, ordering him around and standing there with her hands on her hips. Her little bit frame, at no more than five feet five to his six foot, didn't stand a chance if he wanted to squash her. Not that he would hurt her in any way, shape or form. Smacking a woman around made a man about the size of a June bug, in his way of thinking. "All right, fine, woman. If that will make you happy, so you can quit buggin' me."

A grin lit up her face, and he swallowed the lump threatening to choke him. She had no idea of her sex appeal, and the way every glance, every smile, twisted his gut into knots.

Making love to her had whetted his appetite beyond normal thinkin' *Maybe I need to make a trip to the local honky-tonk.* A quick glance at Ann Marie changed his mind. *Who the hell am I kiddin'? The woman I want is right here.*

He looped the lead rope around the fence to keep the stallion close and walked toward the porch.

So far, he'd managed to get a halter and lead rope on the horse, but damn, the animal was about as stubborn and bullheaded as his mistress. The horse had brains, too. The first day Travis had wanted to work with him, it took him all day to even get close to the ornery shit. Late that afternoon, the damned horse walked right up to Ann Marie, like he was the tamest thing anyone would ever want to touch, and took the sugar cube she held, right from her hand. She had petted the damned animal like a dog and then watched as he spun on his heels and took off across the pasture in a cloud of dust.

The porch of the house sat close to the pasture he'd be working in. It took twenty steps or so to reach her side. One slim hand held out a tall glass of lemonade, and before he knew it, he'd swallowed the entire contents in half a dozen swallows.

"I must have been thirstier than I thought."

"See."

"Smart-ass." The rocker next to her looked mighty inviting. A groan almost rumbled from his lips when he sat down. "Where's Ty?"

"Doing his homework over at Jimmy's." Her eyes met his and he felt like he was about to drown in the blue depths. "Thanks for taking him under your wing."

"No big deal." One shoulder lifted in a shrug. "I didn't get a chance to ask you about it in the last few days, but do you know why he's afraid of horses?" Her eyes widened and he felt like an ass for revealing what the boy had kept a secret from his mother, too. "Never mind."

"No." She laid her hand on his arm, and he felt the warmth clear to his balls. "Is that what he told you?"

"Sort of. In the barn a couple of weeks ago."

Her eyes closed and she exhaled a sharp breath as she tipped her head back on her shoulders, baring her neck to his gaze.

*All I want to do is suck the rapid fluttering of her heart at the base of her luscious throat between my lips and…*

"Travis?"

The sound of his name on her lips brought his thoughts back from the erotic zone they seem to permanently inhabit these days.

"Sorry. I was thinking. What did you say?"

"I asked what he said."

"Not a lot. I guessed from his reaction to the mare he said belonged to him."

"Misty?"

"Yeah."

"I never knew," she whispered, looking off into the distance.

"Don't beat yourself up over it, Ann Marie. He's a boy. Boys don't like to confess their fears, especially to their moms."

"I bet you have never been afraid of anything."

One hand pushed a strand of hair behind her ear, and his fingers itched to do the simple task, for her.

*Yes, I have. I'm scared to death of you.*

"I have. I had a fear of horses, too, for a while. One bit me when I was a kid. I wouldn't touch one for long time."

The hand found his arm and he wanted nothing more than to pull her onto his lap and kiss the daylights out of her.

"You didn't. Really?"

"Yep. Had to get over it, otherwise my dad would have killed me."

"I wish his father was here."

With those six little words, she crushed his nuts into dust and stuffed them in his mouth.

*She doesn't want you, you idiot. She wants her husband back.*

Her gaze fastened on him for a split second, and then she looked back out over the pasture again.

"John and Ty had a close relationship. But I'm not sure if he ever knew Ty feared horses. Don't get me wrong—I miss John, and I know Ty does too, but we never had a traditional marriage in the sense most folks have." A small laugh bubbled from her lips, and her cheeks flushed in embarrassment. "You don't want to hear about my farce of a marriage."

"If you want to talk, go ahead. I'll listen."

The glass in her hand came up to her mouth, and he couldn't breathe while she sipped and swallowed.

"I've told you a while ago, I married John to get out of my parents house and get away from the abuse, which is true. I met my husband at the feed store one day when I went with the foreman on my parents' place. My father never did anything that resembled labor. He had employees to do the rough work like break the horses, round up the cattle — you know. Normal ranch stuff."

He nodded in understanding, but didn't say anything, hoping to encourage her to continue to talk.

"John was a lot older than me." A dry chuckle left her lips. "At twenty-two, I thought I knew everything, of course. John wasn't handsome in the regular sense of the word, but I loved him in my own way. He needed a wife to help him run this place, take care of the house and all. I needed someone to love me, but they had to be patient, too. I wouldn't even let John kiss me for months."

"Your father didn't…"

"You mean did he sexually abuse me? No. But I sure never wanted a man to touch me. John couldn't even get close to me for a long time. And sex? Forget it. We were married quite a while before I ever let him make love to me." Pink flushed her cheeks, and she pressed her hands against them. "I can't believe I'm telling you this."

His heart broke for her and the shit she'd gone through for so long. If the plans he'd put into motion when she'd given him her maiden name so many weeks ago came to fruition, her father would pay for what he had done.

Grasping one of her hands, he folded it between his two palms. He wanted to help her heal. Her husband had started the job, but she still harbored a pain deep in her soul, one no one had been able to touch yet. It shone bright in her eyes.

*Whoa there, cowboy. Take a step back and think.*

A rush of air slipped from between her lips, and she tugged her hand from his grasp.

"I'm sorry. I shouldn't have burdened you with my issues."

"It's fine, darlin'. You needed to talk. I have a good ear." He tugged on his left earlobe and she laughed. "Havin' been raised with a bunch of sisters, I had to learn to listen."

"It must have been miserable being the eldest boy."

"Nah. Not really. I learned to understand women very well by the time I turned eighteen."

"So why hasn't somebody wrangled you to the altar again? You'd be one hell of a catch, Travis Brooks."

"I won't ever get married again, or have kids."

"Been burned besides your ex?"

He stood and walked to the railing of the porch. "I've had my share of women."

The next moment, she wrapped her arms around him from behind and laid her cheek against his back.

"What happened?" she asked.

Tears closed his throat for several minutes. Thoughts of his son had brought too many tears in the last few weeks. Maybe it was being around Tyler. He didn't know, but he sure felt like breaking down right now in front of Ann Marie.

"You met my ex-wife."

"Yes."

"The bitch from hell."

"How long were you married to her?"

"Five years. We went on a vacation to Florida for a week. I wanted to work on the marriage, but she didn't. I had a feeling she'd been cheating on me, but I didn't have any proof." A sharp inhalation of breath and he continued. "I had a son."

"Had?"

"He died when he was three. He drowned in the hotel bathtub because I wasn't paying enough attention to him. I'd been arguing with Catherine over her wanting a divorce. She told me she'd never wanted our son because he'd ruined her figure. I went down to the bar, had a couple beers. I went back upstairs two hours later, and she'd left him in the bathtub. By the time I found him, he was…"

One tear slid down his cheek and he brushed it away angrily.

"God, Travis, I'm so sorry," she whispered.

"Nothin' to be sorry for." He turned to face her. There were tears on her cheeks. "Why are you crying?" He brushed them away with his thumb. "Don't cry, darlin'."

"I can't help it. I don't want to even imagine the pain that caused you." Her lips brushed his palm.

"Ann Marie, don't."

"Don't what? Want you? I can't help that either." Fingers gripped his shirt front and she tugged him closer. "You make me feel things I never knew existed. You make my belly quiver and flutter like a million butterflies are loose in there. After you left me in the kitchen several weeks ago, I wanted nothing more than to follow you into the barn."

"You need a husband—I can't be that."

"Right now, I don't need a husband—I need a man. I need someone to take care of this gnawing ache I have to be held, caressed and filled until I come so hard, I can't breathe. John never did that for me. Can you? Can you be the man I need right now? I'm not asking for promises, Travis."

"Aw, fuck," he growled, his dick so hard behind the fly of his jeans, he thought he'd explode from need.

With one quick swoop, he scooped her up in his arms and moved toward the front screen door. It opened with a sharp tug.

The stairs loomed in front of him, and he took them two at a time.

"Where?" he asked with a tortured groan.

"Last door on the right." Her lips pressed against his neck.

*God, she has me on fire.*

In seconds, he laid her gently across the large bed and followed her down.

"Do you have any idea what you're doing to me?" he asked.

"If it's anything like what I'm feeling right now, yeah, I have an idea." Fingertips trailed up his back and then tangled in the hair at his nape. "Did you lock the door?"

"Shit. No." He rolled off and stumbled toward the door as she giggled softly behind him.

"We don't want Ty walking in."

"Isn't he gone?" He stopped at the side of the bed, his hands coming to an abrupt halt at his waist instead of finishing stripping off his shirt. At this moment, he wanted to do nothing more than feel her skin, strip her of every piece of clothing she had on and bury his cock inside her.

"Yeah, but you never know with him if he'll come back in the middle of the day." She kneeled on the bed and reached for his belt loop. "Come here." Her fingers made quick work of the rest of his shirt. He almost came apart as her lips touched his chest. Her tongue grazed his nipple, bringing it to an aching point, and he growled low in his throat. Soft hands slid up and then back down his spine.

He wound his hands in her hair, twisting the strands around his fingers.

"Darlin'. What you do to me. You're driving me crazy."

Her eyes met his and he could see the heat raging through her, by the fire in her gaze. "Good. Now you know how I've felt since you drove up to the house, all male in your cowboy boots and Wranglers."

Forcing her back, he followed her onto the bed, kissing his way from her fingertips, up her arm to her shoulder, along her neck, nipping at her earlobe, and then stopping a mere hairsbreadth from her mouth.

"You're about the sexiest woman I've been around in a long time. God, I want you so bad, I hurt."

"I'm glad I'm not alone."

The lips that softened under his were kissable and tasted like heaven. A low moan escaped from her mouth. His tongue delved into the silky depths. Tongues stroked, licked and explored. He tore his mouth from hers and skimmed across her cheek to her ear." You've got too many clothes on, darlin'."

"Mmm…'pears to be a mutual problem there, cowboy."

He nipped at the soft skin below her ear while one hand tugged at the bottom of her cotton shirt. Women with curves, all soft and warm, tied him up in knots. He didn't care much for the stick thin kind of a girl. Plump breasts, nice ass, curvy hips, she had everything he needed and then some.

Callused fingers danced up her stomach, and she moaned.

"Sorry about the roughness," he murmured.

She grasped his face between her palms and looked into his eyes. "Don't you be sorry about having working hands. I love a man who works hard for a living, and calluses are your brand. They feel fantastic on my skin." With her pupils dilated like they were, he could almost believe she had the same desire for him he had for her.

She sat up, whipped the shirt over her head and unsnapped her bra. In nothing flat, she flipped them off the bed, reclined against the pillows and tempted him with a smile.

*Damn, she's got pretty titties.* Dusky areolas, nipples puckered, and waiting for his tongue, begging for his mouth, quivered slightly when she took a deep breath. He palmed the right one and smiled when she sucked in a ragged breath. "Lordy, you're beautiful."

"I want your mouth, Travis."

"My pleasure, darlin'." Lips replaced his hand, sucking the hardened bud into his mouth. One palm rasped over the other breast and then rolled the nipple between his fingers.

Two hands grasped the back of his head and held him in place while he tongued first one breast then the other.

The button on her jeans gave to his insistent fingers. Parting the edges, he slipped under the elastic of her underwear to slide through the nest of curls guarding the spot he wanted.

An almost inhuman sound came from her mouth as one finger touched her clit. Her hips lifted in time to the movement of his fingers

*Did her husband never give her pleasure? Didn't he care whether she enjoyed sex or not?*

"Please, Travis," she begged, her head tossing from side to side on the pillow.

The low whimper of need coming from her pleased him. He left her side for a second to remove her pants and toss them across the room. His shirt and jeans followed hers.

The silkiness of her flesh on his hair-roughened skin almost sent him over the top, but the look on her face, the dazed, heavy eyes, had him harder than he'd ever been in his life. The scent of arousal in the air, her need, drove him past the point of reason.

Lips cut a path up the inside of her thigh. Slick cream glistened on her pussy when she spread her legs. The need to taste her sweet essence pulled his balls up tight against his groin.

*I don't think I've ever been this damned horny.*

One quick swipe of his tongue on her clit, and he thought he'd go mad from wanting her. Pussy lips quivered under his mouth. He moaned and speared her slit with his tongue. He slid two fingers into her pussy while he held her hips to the bed with his other hand. The walls of her vagina gripped him tight. In and out, he dipped, trying to bring her to the brink of insanity with him. This was for her. His need could wait.

Passion spiraled out of control in her as she shuddered and quivered under his hands and mouth. He could feel her need to climax with every breath. Every muscle in her body pulled tight with desire until he sucked at her clit, and finger fucked her until she flew apart with a tortured groan.

Once the trembling calmed, he kissed his way up her stomach, to her breast for a swift lick to her nipples, before he hovered over her lips and waited.

"Oh, my God, Travis. I … that was amazing."

"We're just getting started, darlin'." He nibbled her lips. "Didn't John ever do that for you?" Her gaze shifted away until he brought her focus back to him with a tug on her chin. "Ann Marie?"

"No," she whispered.

"I'm sorry, honey."

"Why?"

"Because a man should make it good for you, too, not just for him. If he doesn't, he's not much of a man at all."

"Show me."

"Oh, I intend to," he said, running his tongue across her bottom lip. He coaxed her to open for him her mouth and let their tongues duel. The strokes of his tongue had her wiggling beneath him in seconds.

Over her cheeks he moved with his lips, nibbling her earlobe with his teeth, down the soft skin of her neck. He took her nipple in his mouth and sucked. One finger dipped into her pussy and spread the lingering wetness over her clit. He worked her body, stroking, licking, and caressing until she moaned his name. He bumped against her waiting warmth with his cock.

With one word, his desire almost shriveled into nothing. "Condom?"

"Ah, hell!"

"It doesn't matter."

"Yes, it does. I'm not going to take the chance. I can't." He stood quickly, pulled on his jeans, shirt and boots and left her lying naked on the bed with a quick glance and an "'I'm sorry," he walked out.

* * * *

"Oh, my God! He didn't walk out on me, did he?" She scrambled off the bed and peeked out the window of her room to see him walking briskly across the yard toward the barn. "Holy hell!" The curtain dropped back into place, and she paced across the carpeted floor. "Okay, think Ann Marie." Capturing her lip between her teeth, she chewed it, trying to understand what happened. "I mentioned the condom, and that's when all hell broke loose." She snapped her fingers. "That has to be it. He said he wouldn't have any children, ever. He must be afraid I'll get pregnant. But he has no idea I've been on birth control. We never had that conversation. A condom is important, but I … maybe we should have talked about it." Picking up her T-shirt off the floor, she slipped it back over her head and grabbed her jeans. "Shit. It's not like I'm an old hand at this kind of thing."

"Mom?" Tyler yelled from the bottom of the stairs.

*Well, it's a good thing we didn't get into something, from the way the interruptions going on.*

"I'm in my room."

Tyler peeked through the doorway a moment later. "I'm going to go riding with Travis."

"Can I talk to you for a minute, buddy?" she asked, taking a seat on the chair by the window.

He took several steps into the room. "Sure."

"Sit down, Ty." She shifted in the chair and sighed. This wasn't going to be easy. She didn't want Tyler to think Travis had broken his trust by telling her about his fear of horses. "I don't want you to ever think you have to keep things from me, okay? I know boys don't always want to talk to their mom. I get that, but you're my son. I'm here for you in whatever way you need me to be. The last several months have been rough without your dad here, and I want you to know I appreciate how good you've been and how you've taken on some of the responsibilities around the ranch."

"But Travis is here to help now, too."

"Yes, he is. He's a good man, Ty."

Tyler dropped his gaze to the floor and asked, "Do you like him, Mom?"

"Sure. He's nice and all that. Good with the horses. Works hard…"

"That's not what I mean. Do you *like* him?"

Not quite sure how to answer him, she hesitated.

"I don't think Dad would like Travis being here."

"I'm sure you're probably right, but Dad isn't here anymore, and I have to do what I think is best for our home."

One of his slim shoulders lifted in a shrug. "I think Travis is a good guy. I want him to stay." Tyler walked to the window and looked out for a minute before he turned back toward her. "Can I go ride now? Travis is going to help me with Misty."

"Of course. Have fun."

She watched him disappear out the door and sighed.

*What the hell am I going to do about Travis?*

Hearing sounds coming from outside, she turned toward the window in time to catch Travis ride out of the barn, with Tyler on Misty bringing up the rear. The devastatingly handsome man glanced up at the window, and she could almost feel the desire radiating from his look.

*This has got to stop. Either he's going to have to make love to me again, or he's going to have to leave. But do I want him to leave?*

The home phone rang and she turned to answer it.

"Hello?"

"Hey, sis."

"Kelly? Where are you?"

"At the bus station. Can you come and get me?"

"Sure, honey. I'll be there is about fifteen minutes." She hung up the phone, grabbed her shoes and walked downstairs. Tyler would be occupied with Travis for a while. Good thing. Maybe she could get her mind off her handsome horse trainer for a few moments. With Kel at the house, their alone time should be cut to almost nil.

Ann Marie pulled the truck into the station a short time later. Within moments, she was swallowed up in a hug from a petite, dark hair girl.

"You're sure a sight for sore eyes, sister."

"I'm so glad you're here, Kel." She squeezed her sister's shoulders. "Thank God you finally got away from all the craziness."

Kelly winced as she touched her arm, and Ann Marie's eyebrow rose in question. "He left me with something to remember him by."

"That son-of-a-bitch," she whispered, and crimped her eyes closed. "I should have blown his nuts off when I had the chance."

"Then you'd be in jail, Ann Marie."

"Yeah, but he wouldn't have been able to hurt you or Mom anymore." She grabbed her sister's bag and walked toward the double doors leading outside. The truck wasn't far." How's Mom, by the way?"

"The same. She'll never leave him, you know."

"I'm sure. If she wouldn't do it to save her children from the abuse, why would she now that we are both gone?"

Kelly shrugged, and Ann Marie shot her a quick glance over the bed of the truck.

"How is my nephew doing?"

"Good. Tyler was out riding with Travis when I left."

"Travis? Some new guy I don't know about?"

"There's nothin' goin' on between me and Travis, Kel. I hired him to break the stallion and work with the other horses John hadn't gotten to."

"Uh-huh. That's why you're blushing."

She put her hands on her cheeks. "No, I'm not."

"Yes you are. I think it's cute. I hope things work out for you. You need another man around."

"I do not," she replied as they both got settled in the cab of the truck.

"You do fine on your own running the place, but John wasn't the right man for you."

"But—"

"No, Ann Marie. He wasn't. He loved you in his own way, and I'm sure you loved him too, but he didn't have your heart pounding, didn't make your legs weak when he looked at you and he didn't make you cream your panties with a kiss."

"Kelly Leanne Boyd!"

"Well, it's true. If you settle for less with another man, you're crazy."

They pulled up at the house several minutes later, and she could see Travis and Tyler in the pasture.

*Damn, the man has a nice ass in jeans, and the way he rides...* She shifted uncomfortable on the seat.

"Is that him?" Kelly asked and then glanced across the truck.

"Yeah."

"Hot damn, sis! You did good. Now wrangle that man into your bed and you'll be all set."

"I can't believe you said that," she replied, popping open the door.

They stepped out and walked toward the fence as Travis and Tyler rode in their direction.

"Travis Brooks, this is my sister Kelly. Kel, this is Travis."

"Howdy." He tipped his hat and smiled, and Ann Marie's stomach flipped.

"Well, ain't you one fine hunk of a man."

"Kelly," Ann Marie growled. "Knock it off."

"I'm only admiring the view."

Travis blushed under his tan, and she had to fight the laughter bubbling in her throat.

"Uh ... hey, Ty? Let's put these two up for now. We've worked 'em pretty hard." He pulled his horse around and rode for the barn with Tyler right behind him.

"I'm so embarrassed," Ann Marie said, even though she never took her eyes off his back.

"Why?"

Ann Marie grabbed her sister's hand and walked toward the house. "You are way bolder than I am. I would never say those things to him."

"But you're thinking them."

"Well yes, but that's different."

"I don't see why. He's a nice looking man, muscled in all the right places, even though he's too old for me. I'm thinkin' he's right up your alley, sis. Besides, I bet he makes you all wet and tingly, doesn't he."

She rubbed her arms to calm the goose bumps as she remember their tryst this morning upstairs, and how he made her come so hard with his mouth. John never even suggested doing those things to her, much less actually did them.

"Has he kissed you yet?"

*Oh yeah, he's done more than kiss. His tongue did wonderful things to me—things I'd only ever imagined.*

"Listen, Kelly. What goes on between Travis and I is none of your business, and I can't believe we're having this conversation."

"If he hasn't, do you want him to?"

The back screen door banged against the doorframe and Ann Marie turned around to meet the intense blue eyes of the man in question.

# Chapter Five

"Ty wants you to come see him on Misty."

"Sure," she said, following him back out the door even though her sister's gaze followed them.

He slowed his steps to match her shorter ones.

"When did your sister get here?"

"She called not long after … um…you left."

"About that."

"Yes?"

"I'm sorry."

"Why? Nothing happened."

He scowled at her words, not liking her rendition of the events in her room.

"Well, something happened, but not all the way."

"I should have been prepared. I wasn't."

The warmth of her hand on his forearm penetrated his shirt, and sent heat straight to his groin. The last thing he'd wanted was to walk away from her earlier, but not having a condom and taking the chance she'd get pregnant wasn't in the cards.

"There's something I need to tell you." She stepped closer and the scent of honeysuckle drifted to his nose. "I'm on the pill."

"You are?"

"Yes."

"Why didn't you say so before? I mean we would still need protection for other things, but knowing that would have taken part of the weight off my shoulders." The hat whipped off his head, and he ran his fingers through his hair. "Damn it, Ann Marie. You should've told me you were on the pill!"

All sounds around them stopped, and several sets of eyes focused on them while they stood in the middle of the yard.

"Can we have this discussion somewhere else? I don't want the hands knowing who is in my bed and who isn't," she hissed under her breath.

"Sorry."

They fell into step and continued toward the large structure.

"Hey, Mom!" Tyler yelled from the middle of the enclosed arena.

"Hey, baby. You look great!"

Ty trotted the mare around the enclosure.

"Kick her into a canter, Ty," Travis instructed.

The boy nodded and nudged the mare into a slow gallop.

"Thanks for everything you've done for him. I never even imagined he had a fear of the horses."

"He's a good kid."

"Yeah, he is. I'm proud of him."

"You should be."

"Lord, it's been a long time since I've shown a horse. I used to do a little rodeo stuff, too."

"You used to show?" he said, propping one boot onto the railing.

"Yes, and I miss it. I need to get back to it soon."

"There are a lot of competitions around, especially in the summer months. How about we check a couple out, take Ty and hit one."

With a saucy tilt of her head and twinkle in her eyes, she said, "Are you asking me on a date, Mr. Brooks?"

"No. I—..."

"I'm kidding, Travis."

*Quit reading shit into everything. She might be interested in a quick romp, but that's it and so am I. A long term relationship isn't in the cards.*

"How about this weekend? I think there's one in Houston. That is, if you aren't busy with the ranch stuff."

"It's a date," she replied with a grin lifting the corners of her mouth. At the sight of her smile, he felt like kicking his own ass. Ty rode up to the fence, and she reached over to stroke the mare's nose.

"Are you ready to put her away, Ty?"

"Yeah. Are we having dinner at the house tonight, since Aunt Kelly is here?"

"Yep. I'm even cooking."

"Oh boy," the boy grumbled and Travis laughed.

"Wait a minute there mister. I happen to be a fair cook."

"Sure, Mom." Tyler dismounted and grabbed the mare's reins. "Can't Aunt Kelly cook instead of you?"

"Tyler!"

"Sorry, but you burn everythin', Mom."

"I do not." With all five foot five inches of her frame, she got indignant and he almost grabbed her and kissed her silly.

"How about if I cook?" he suggested. "I'll even run into town and get some ribs. How long has it been since your barbeque has been used?"

"Since Dad died," Ty answered with a frown.

"Well, then, I guess we should fire it up. What do you say?"

"All right. How about I go to the store with you? I can make salad or something," she shot Tyler a mock glare. "Something I can't burn."

"Sure. I'd love the company."

"Let me check with Kelly and see if she can watch Ty. I'll be back in a few minutes."

"I'll help Ty put Misty away."

"Okay. I'll meet you at the house in fifteen minutes?"

"Perfect."

He couldn't help but watch her pretty little butt sashay across the yard, especially when all he wanted to do was bury his rock hard cock between those tempting thighs.

"Do you like my mom, Travis?" Tyler asked, diverting Travis' attention.

"Of course, Ty. If I didn't, I wouldn't still be here."

"What I mean is, do you *like* her."

Travis hesitated. This conversation could go nowhere fast.

"Do you want to kiss her?"

"Why don't we put that mare away?"

"You're avoiding my question. Do you want to kiss her?"

*I want to do a hell of a lot more than kiss her.*

"She's a mighty pretty woman, Ty. I don't know many men who wouldn't want to kiss her, including me."

"That's what I thought." Tyler opened the gate and started down the dirt walkway, never once looking back at Travis.

"I wonder what that was all about." He shook his head and followed to make sure the boy got the gear off.

*Since when did I get so caught up in her life? This is bad news. At the rate I'm goin', I'll be tied up in everything here in nothin' flat.*

An hour later, they bumped along in his truck toward town. Thoughts of her and Tyler becoming part of his life didn't sit well, and Tyler's questions brought his attraction for Ann Marie to the forefront of his mind. It felt way too domesticated for him.

"Why the frown?"

"Huh? Oh, nothin'."

"Bullshit, Travis."

His head snapped around so fast, she laughed.

"I'm thinkin'. That's all."

"About?"

"Nothin'."

"Typical man," she grumbled and looked back out the windshield.

After several minutes, he said, "I was thinking about somethin' Ty asked me after you left the barn."

"And?"

"He asked me if I liked you."

A snort left her lips.

"What?"

"He asked me the same thing earlier, and somehow I think he wanted to know more than whether I thought you were a hard worker and good with the horses."

"Yeah, I got the same impression. He emphasized the like part and asked me if I wanted to kiss you."

"So, what did you tell him?"

"Not much. I kind of avoided answerin' him directly."

Moments later, they pulled into the parking lot of the local grocery. Several women stood outside chatting, and he walked around the front to open her door, every set of eyes found them and stared.

"Damn."

"What's wrong?"

"I didn't think about how this would look to your neighbors."

She shrugged. "So? I don't care what a bunch of busybodies think."

"What about your reputation?"

"I never had much of one anyway, Travis. Most of these old biddies knew John and I got married without knowing each other very long. They don't like me much, and I don't care for them either. I have more friends in the men of this town than the women."

His palm found the small of her back.

"Hey, Clark," she said, waving to the portly man behind the checkout stand.

"Hi, Ann Marie. Who's the fella?"

"Travis Brooks. He's breaking the horses for me."

"Nice to meet'cha," Clark said, and the two of them shook hands.

"You too," he replied.

"Doin' some shoppin'?"

"Yeah. Ty doesn't want me to cook."

Clark's belly rolled when he laughed, and Ann Marie blushed. "That youngin'." Clark's mood soured a bit, and he asked, "How's he doin'?"

"Good. Getting some pretty good grades in school, even with everything going on."

"I'm glad. He took his daddy's death pretty hard."

"He sure did." By the shift of her eyes, he got the impression she wanted to move on.

"Nice to meet you, Clark, but we should get moving. We've got some hungry kids back there to feed."

"Sure. Nice talkin' to ya. Hope to see ya around a bit, Travis."

The two of them walked down the meat aisle with Ann Marie shifting glances to the other women.

*Even if she says she doesn't care, the looks are making her nervous.*

"These look good," she said, grabbing the first package beneath her fingers. "Let's go."

Within moments, they'd returned to his truck with only the basic necessities for dinner. "I want to make one more stop."

"Oh?"

"Yeah." He didn't say anything more as they drove down the street, and he pulled into the parking lot of one of the local drug stores. Running inside, he grabbed the box he wanted, paid the cashier and returned to find her chewing her lips.

The plain brown bag dropped in the space between them on the bench seat.

"What's this?"

"Open it."

A soft smile lifted the corners of her mouth and she pulled the edges of the bag apart. Rolling laughter bubbled from her lips. "Condoms?"

"I didn't want to be caught with my pants down again and nothing to show for it. I had the one in my wallet, but I don't make a habit of keepin' them stocked. I wasn't sure if we would get into the same situation again."

"I want you, Travis. I'm not ashamed to say it. I have needs, and if you are okay with a short term relationship, so am I."

"It's fine with me, darlin'."

She pulled the box from the bag and asked, "Ribbed?"

He shrugged as he felt heat crawl up his neck.

"You're blushing. I'm sorry. I didn't mean to embarrass you. I didn't expect this, but I'm glad you thought of me, and I guess this means what happened earlier will happen again?"

"I'm sure hopin', darlin'. I've had a hard-on since I walked out of your room. Do you have any idea how hard it is to ride like that?"

"I can imagine."

Once he pulled out onto the street headed back for the ranch, he said, "Listen. I'm sorry how things went."

"I understand, Travis."

"No, you don't. If you're okay with a physical relationship, then we're good. I don't want you to get any ideas of anything permanent."

"I know. You told me from the beginning, you aren't the settlin' kind. I respect that about you. You know your mind, and no one is going to change it for you."

*Wait just a damned minute here. Ain't I the one supposed to be shuttin' things down before they get too serious?* His gut clenched at the thought of walking away from her when his six months ended. *Damn it!* His grip on the steering wheel tightened. *Let it go. She wants a good time, then that's what I'll give her.*

They rolled into the yard to find Kelly sitting in one of the rockers, with Tyler in the other.

"So, when do we eat? I'm starving," Tyler said, and Travis had to chuckle at the boy's appetite. Now he knew what his mom meant about growing boys and how they eat all the time.

"Soon, buddy. Fire up the grill. We got ribs."

"You're cooking, right, Travis?"

"Yes, he's cooking, Tyler," Ann Marie grumbled.

Travis laughed as he walked around the back to where he'd seen the grill. Tyler kept the conversation lively while he cooked, talking about his dad and mom and gave away a few secrets Travis thought Ann Marie might not want him to know. Like how she liked to read "those girlie books" in the bathtub. He assumed what Ty meant was romance novels. Tyler also told him about a man. One who came over quite often for a while, and one he'd seen Ann Marie kiss on the porch one night.

"His name's Jared McElroy. His dad owns one of the places up the road."

Jealousy burned in his gut with Tyler's words and he wasn't sure he liked the feeling. "When did you see him last?"

"Um… right before you came, I think. I ain't seen him in a while." Tyler looked straight at him. "Why?"

"Curious. That's all."

"I ain't seen Mom look at anybody like she looks at you."

Travis didn't think he wanted to get into the kind of conversation this one was working into, so he changed the subject.

Once dinner finished cooking, they sat at the picnic table, laughing and teasing each other while they ate.

"This tastes great, Travis," Tyler said. "You need to let him cook all the time, Mom."

"Save it, mister. No kissin' up to me now," she grumbled good-naturedly.

" Don't pick on your mom like that. She made awesome…salad." He wrapped an arm around her shoulder, pulled her to his side and gave her a wet, barbeque-faced kiss on the cheek.

"Ewww!" Tyler grimaced and laughed. Travis grinned and bit into the rib in his hand.

"Thanks. I'm going to have a take a shower after dinner now to get all the barbeque sauce off."

He wiped his face with his napkin and whispered near her ear. "Can I help?"

* * * *

Heat went straight to her belly at the feel of his lips against her cheek. *Good Lord, the man can make me hot from a simple kiss.*

The words he whispered sent all kinds of intriguing images spinning through her mind starting with what it felt like to have those lips on her pussy in the shower or out. She didn't care. The need for him drove her past caring even if he wouldn't be there past Thanksgiving.

"What's the matter, darlin'? Cat got your tongue?"

"You are impossible." Grabbing her plate, she stood and walked toward the back door of the house. The screen banged against the doorjamb when she walked inside and stuck her plate under some running water to rinse it. Lost in thought, she never heard him come in behind her until he laid his plate in the sink, too.

"Hey. You okay?" Tugging on her hand, he turned her to face him.

*God, I want him to kiss me so bad.* Lips tingled for the pressure of his mouth. "I'm fine."

"Then what's the problem?" Fingers trailed up her arm, leaving goose bumps in their wake.

"Nothing. I—"

"I didn't mean to embarrass you out there."

"You didn't. I'm not sure I want Kelly or Ty thinking there is something going on between us."

"There is, isn't there? I mean we do plan on more hot and heavy sex at some point, right?"

"Well, yes, but—"

"But what?"

"Not here—not in the house. It would be too easy for them to hear or interrupt."

"How about later, after Ty's gone to bed and Kelly's not paying attention, you come out to my room. No one will know what's going on that way, even though I know your bed upstairs is more comfortable than mine." One slow lick along her neck and she pushed the moan in her throat back down. "I even have a shower," he whispered.

The back screen door banged against the frame again as Ty and Kelly followed them inside and Travis stepped away, leaving her shivering for the warmth of his body.

*Damn it! This is nuts!*

"I'm going to go upstairs and get my stuff settled," Kelly said with a wink and a smile. "I'll see you in the morning, sis."

"Okay."

"Come on, Ty."

"I'm not ready to go upstairs, Aunt Kel…"

Kelly clamped a hand over his mouth and pulled him out of the room, leaving her and Travis standing in the kitchen staring at each other.

"She wasn't very slick, huh."

"No, she wasn't, but it did the trick," he answered with a grin.

Nipples puckered hard against her shirt, almost begging for his touch. The lump in her throat threatened to close off her air. His lips brushed hers, and she whimpered. His thumb slid across the nub, forcing a sharp exhale from her mouth.

"Come out to my room," he murmured, running his tongue along her lips.

"I can't."

One hand snaked up under her T-shirt, and the abrasiveness of his calluses almost had her coming in her pants.

"I want you."

"Travis, please."

"Please what, darlin'?"

"I need… I want…"

"I'll go out first. Follow me in about fifteen minutes," he whispered against her lips. "I'll wait for you."

Without so much as a backward glance, he disappeared out the screen door, letting it slam behind him.

* * * *

*She's not coming. I've been stood up. I'll be damned!*

Travis paced back and forth across the floor in his room. He'd left Ann Marie in the kitchen over an hour ago, expecting her to follow shortly, but she hadn't knocked on his door, and now he stood there looking like an idiot.

*This is fucking crazy. Why am I so worried about her coming to me? It's not like I can't go into town and get laid if I wanted to.* With a snap of his fingers, a slow smile spread across his mouth.

Throwing on a clean shirt and jeans, he brushed his boots and stuck his straw cowboy hat on his head. A few swipes of cologne, and he grabbed his keys, stuffed a condom in his wallet and pulled open the door.

Quick steps took him to the driver's side door of his truck. With a swift glance up at her window, he slid inside and turned the key.

Fifteen minutes later, he drove into the parking lot of the local honky-tonk.

*I'll be damned if she's gonna make me horny, then leave me high and dry. I'm sure there are at least one or two women in here I can hook up, with and I don't have to worry about getting involved. Hell, maybe I'll find two willing females to have a threesome with.*

The smoke filled bar looked like the typical cowboy bar he'd seen a thousand times. The women outnumbered the men, two to one. Neon lights flashed different brands of beer from every corner, and a band twanged on the stage, trying desperately to sound like something out of Nashville. He wasn't here for the music or the alcohol — he came for the women.

"Hey, gorgeous." A leggy brunette slid up to his side and wrapped her arms around his neck.

"Well lookey here. What's your name, honey?"

"Brandy. How 'bout you handsome?"

"Travis."

One fingernail raked down the buttons on his shirt, and she glanced through her lashes. "Well, Travis. What do you say we do a little dancin'?"

"Sure," he replied, taking her hand in his and leading her out to the dance floor.

When they reached the wooden area set aside for two-steppin', he pulled her back into his arms and swayed to the beat of the latest Dirks Bentley song.

"You must be new 'round here. I would remember you anywhere."

"Yeah, I'm new. Well, sort of. Came into town to do a little work on one of the ranches."

"A real cowboy, huh?"

"Can't get much more real than me."

"Mmm… you ride?"

He chuckled low in his throat. The women loved it. "You could say that."

"How 'bout you ride me?"

"Now you're talking, sweetheart." His palm cupped her ass cheek and pulled her closer. "You got somewhere we can go?"

An hour later, he slipped out of the cheap motel room and cussed all the way to his truck.

"Goddamn it!" Pulling the door shut, he slammed his hand against the steering wheel. "Fuck! I've never had a problem lovin' a woman before. What the hell?"

*Never mind that I couldn't do anything to Brandy without seeing Ann Marie's face.*

"Great! Just fucking, great!"

Tire spun and gravel flew as he ripped out of the parking lot and onto the highway, headed back for her place.

* * * *

Lights reflected off the front window. Ann Marie stopped and peeked out to see Travis' truck pull up near the barn.

Capturing her bottom lip between her teeth, she chewed the inside.

*I need to talk to him and find out where he went. He wanted me to come out to the barn, and then disappeared.*

"All right. One foot in front of the other." Blowing a frustrated breath, she pulled open the door on the front of the house and walked down the stairs.

The big door of the barn opened with ease, and moments later she stood in front of the door to his room. A ray of light shone underneath. She fortified herself with a steadying breath and raised her hand to knock until she heard cuss words coming from the other side of the door. The thing bothering her was her name was attached to several.

With a frown, she knocked twice.

"What?" Travis yelled, opening the door.

"Sorry. I…"

*Ah hell!*

Bare muscled chest, flat, six-pack abs and the happy trail she remembered, met her eyes.

"Where'd you go? I came out here a little while ago and you were gone."

"I went into town. What can I do for you?"

Confused, she tilted her head to the side and said, "You told me to meet you out here."

"Two hours ago, Ann Marie," he grumbled and stepped back, allowing her to enter behind him.

The sweet fragrance of a definite feminine perfume met her nose.

*Son of a bitch!*

"I don't believe you! I didn't show up on your schedule, so you took off, and hooked up with some bimbo?"

"What the hell difference does it make? There's nothing between us. It was supposed to be a quick fuck. You didn't show. I found a substitute."

Her eyes burned with tears she refused to let fall.

"Fine. I understand now, and I'm sorry I disappointed you. But let me tell you one thing, Travis Brooks. I dance to no one's tune, but my own. I don't need you except to train the horses. Do your job and do it well, and stay out of my way."

She spun on her heel and slammed the door behind her. Tears fell in earnest down her cheeks as she returned to the house and her lonely bed

# Chapter Six

*Two damned months. It's been the longest two months of my life.*

Travis rolled out of the double bed in his room and stumbled to the shower.

*Too fucking many cold showers–I know that much.*

The spigot turned on and the cold water sprayed out in a wide stream.

"Son of a bitch, that's cold." Shivers rolled down his back as the water hit his shoulders like tiny needles. "I'm gettin' real tired of jackin' myself off too. We need to get this shit settled between us. Otherwise, I'm gonna lose my mind."

One hand palmed his cock and he tried desperately to bring himself some relief, to no avail.

"All right. I've had enough of this shit. I'm takin' that woman to bed tonight if it's the last thing I do. I'm not walkin' around with this permanent hard-on anymore."

He shut the water off, dried his body with one of the towels and then slipped it around his neck.

Tonight was Friday, and by God, he planned to make the best of it. His work with the stallion had progressed well for the last several weeks. Now, if the distraction of Ann Marie would leave him alone, he would have been a hell of a lot happier. Oh, she was polite when they ran into each other, but she avoided being alone with him at any point. If she caught him somewhere by himself, she would excuse herself and disappear.

Tyler on the other hand, sought him out at every turn. The boy had become a constant shadow. Not that he minded, but he hoped the boy didn't get too attached. Breaking the heart of the kid didn't sit well with him, but he couldn't bring himself to get too close to the boy.

A soft whistle came from his mouth while he dressed. The thought of finally getting between her thighs again put him in a pretty good mood. He adjusted his belt buckle and then slipped on his socks and boots.

"Mornin'," he said when he stepped out into the sunshine and came face-to-face with Manuel while he and several others hands walked toward the kitchen for breakfast.

"Mornin'. You're pretty chipper today," Manuel replied, falling into step beside him.

"Workin' on it. I've got some plans to get the stallion to run some this afternoon."

"Oh yeah?"

"Yep. He's ready."

Manuel whistled through his teeth. "Pretty brave of you, compadre. Make sure someone knows where you'll be so we can pick up the carcass when you don't come back."

Travis laughed good-naturedly. "I'll do that, Manuel, but I don't think it's necessary. Me and the stallion have an agreement, you see."

"Ah. Well then." A hearty chuckle left his mouth, and he slapped Travis on the back. "That makes all the difference in the world, mi amigo."

Finding a seat, he sat with the rest of the men, and the cook dished up breakfast.

The moment she came into the room, he could feel her and smell her. Dick at attention, heart hammering against his ribs and mouth watering to taste, his gaze captured hers, and he knew she wanted him, too.

Pupils dilated and nipples puckered into tight little nubs that poked at the front of her shirt. Lips parted, and she released an audible sigh. It was like no one else existed in the room but the two of them.

"Hey, Ann Marie," Cook said, drawing her attention away as he waved and motioned her to a seat next to Manuel, setting set a plate down in front of her.

"Good morning, gentlemen. How is everyone this morning?"

Several hands grumbled a greeting, but her eyes focused on him.

"Travis."

"Ann Marie."

"I want to go over your files on the horses this morning. I have a meeting in town later with a potential breeder, and I need to be able to give him information."

"Certainly. Anytime. The office is open."

"What are you working on today?"

"I'll be taking the stallion out for a run later, after I do some work in the arena with a couple of the others."

She nodded and refocused on the plate in front of her.

The need to get her alone drove him to distraction, but he knew if he tried now, she'd run.

*Patience. I need to be patient. Taming her will be no different than taming a skittish filly. She doesn't trust me, and I can't blame her. I let her go on thinking I bedded that chick over a month ago. In fact, I couldn't because of her. If I'd told her what happened, we could have had wild sex right then, and all this waiting would have been over with.*

"Travis?" she asked, bringing his attention back from getting her between the sheets.

"Sorry. I was thinking. What did you say?"

"Would you like to go with me to meet the breeder? I've been thinking, and it would be good if you could talk to him, too. You could explain your training program and how well Black is doing, and how he's taken to the bit and saddle."

"Maybe. What time are you leaving?"

"One o'clock."

"All right. I'll meet you at the house at one and go with you."

Lips turned up in the first smile he'd seen from her in weeks, and he felt like someone punched him in the gut.

*The ride into town with her is gonna be hell.*

Blowing out a frustrated breath, he finished his breakfast while he attempted to keep his focus on his food and not on the gorgeous female sitting two seats up and on the other side of the table.

"I've got work to do," he grumbled coming to his feet and putting his plate on the cart.

Her gaze followed him. He could feel the heat of her eyes on his back, and he was seriously tempted to take another cold shower or drag her into a warm one with him.

The tack room door loomed in front of him. With a cuss under his breath, he pushed open the door to retrieve the bridle, saddle and blanket he needed. The light flipped on with the flick of his fingers on the switch and he shuffled his way to the back corner.

\* \* \* \*

Travis didn't know it, but Ann Marie watched him work the mare in the arena all morning. The same thing she'd been doing for the last several weeks. Ever since he'd come home from the bar that night smelling like another woman. The man had turned into a serious distraction.

*What do I care if he's sleeping with someone else? I mean, it was my intention to have raunchy sex with him too. What hurt the most? He didn't even let me explain why I didn't come right out there. Is it my damned fault, my mother called for the first time in ten fucking years?*

Every bunch of the muscles of his back, every angle of his chest and plane of his six pack abs, sent heat straight to her middle. There was no denying her need for the man. A little wiggle of her butt on the window seat of her room did nothing to relieve the pressure between her thighs. She could hear his whispered words to the horse while he worked, even if it was only in her head.

*How am I going to be able to sit beside him in the truck all the way to town and then exchange pleasantries while we talk to the breeder, when all I want to do is ride his hips?*

"This is crazy. I need a man, and damn it, he's the one I want!"

Coming to her feet, she paced the bedroom like a caged animal. Back and forth in front of the window, stopping to peek out every few minutes to see what Travis might be doing. Watching him stroke the mare with his big hands sent her body into overdrive with a need so strong, she moaned.

"Tonight. If he doesn't have sex with me, I'll find someone who will."

*Yeah, like that would work. Knowing everyone in this town has its drawbacks and I already know one hundred percent of them aren't worth the effort of getting them in the bed.*

"I'm sure once we have sex again, this crazy attraction will dissipate. One thing I learned being married to John and living with my father, I can handle being alone and I can be a strong, independent woman in my own right. I don't *need* a man to take care of me. I want a partner, not an overbearing, takeover everything kind of man."

The grandfather clock in the dining room bonged one o'clock with a low, mournful sound. A heavy sigh rushed from her mouth as she stood and went out the door and down the stairs to meet Travis.

Two quick raps on the door announced his arrival.

"I got it!" she yelled, so Kelly wouldn't answer the door.

Her breath caught in her throat when she opened it to find him standing in front of her, big as life and devastating to her piece of mind. A sexy smile twitched on his oh-so-kissable lips, and his eyes twinkled in the sunlight.

*Damn.*

"Ready?" he asked, his gaze sweeping over her.

"Yeah. Let me get my purse," she replied, licking her suddenly dry lips.

"We can take my truck. I need gas anyway."

"Sure." Calling over her shoulder, she said, "Kel? I'm going to town."

Kelly came out of the den and quirked an eyebrow when she noticed Travis standing at the door.

"I should be back in about two hours or so. I have my cell if you need me. Ty is at Jimmy's for the afternoon."

"Travis going, too?"

"Yes."

"Have fun then."

She stepped out the door and pulled it shut behind her, bringing her up almost flush against him. The heat from his body puckered her nipples into tight balls of need. Warm breath flittered across her cheek, and she thought she might drown as she looked up into his eyes.

She cleared her throat and stepped around him. Not waiting for him to open the passenger side for her, she jerked it by the handle, slid inside and slammed it shut. Releasing a heavy sigh while he walked around the front, she fought the urge to calm her nipples by rubbing her palms over the tips.

"Where to?" he asked. when he settled behind the wheel.

"Rosie's on Main."

With a nod, he settled his sunglasses over his eyes and drove down the driveway toward town.

"Who are we meeting?"

"A guy out of Houston by the name of Landon Armstrong. He heard of Black through some mutual friends, and he has a mare he's interested in breeding."

"Without even seeing the animal?"

"I guess so. John made sure he talked about the stallion to whomever he came into contact with."

A frown pulled down the corners of his mouth.

"What's wrong?"

A quick glance at her, and he looked back out the windshield. "Nothin'."

"The frown on your face tells me something different, Travis."

"Any breeder worth his salt would insist on seeing the stallion, Ann Marie. That's all I'm sayin'."

"Maybe he will once we talk."

"I suppose."

"Let's give the man the benefit of the doubt, okay? We'll go from there."

One shoulder lifted in a shrug, and she ground her teeth together in frustration.

"It's your place. Your call."

"That's right. It is."

*Shit. I'm so tired of fighting with him. His opinion is important even if he's hired help.*

"Hired help. Yeah, right," she murmured.

"What did you say?"

"I appreciate your input. It means a lot to me."

They pulled up in front of the diner and he shut the engine off.

"I'll do the talking. You can observe for anything strange about him or the situation. Does that work for you?" she asked.

"Works for me, darlin'," he replied, flashing a smile that curled the toes in her boots.

The endearment slid over her like a silk negligee.

*Ah hell! He hasn't called me that in weeks.*

Clearing her throat, she popped open the passenger side and stepped out.

As she approached the front door of the diner, Travis held it for her and settled his warm palm on her lower back. Heat zipped from his hand, down her legs and back to settle between her thighs.

Sweeping the patrons with her gaze, she decided the gentleman sitting alone in the corner was probably Mr. Armstrong.

"Landon Armstrong?" she asked, approaching the table.

"Yes ma'am. You must be Mrs. Skolack."

"That I am, and this is the man who's been training the stallion, Travis Brooks," she replied, sliding into the booth with Travis next to her.

"Travis Brooks out of Amarillo?" Mr. Armstrong questioned.

"One and the same."

Landon held out his hand to Travis. "It's a pleasure to meet you, Mr. Brooks. I've heard a lot about you, and if Mrs. Skolack hired you, then I have very few questions. Your reputation precedes you."

"Thank you," Travis replied, shaking the man's hand.

"So, Mr. Brooks. What is your take on this stallion?"

*I guess I won't be talking.*

"He belongs to Ann Marie. You need to talk to her about him. I'm only training him."

*Well, I'll be damned.*

"All right then. Tell me about your stallion, Mrs. Skolack."

For over thirty minutes, she told him about the stallion, from coloring to speed and everything in between.

"Is he broke?"

"Not completely," Travis replied.

"Where does his training stand, Mr. Brooks?"

"I plan to run him this afternoon to see how he takes to a rider, saddle and bit. I've had him in the arena loaded down, but not in the open pasture yet."

"I'd like to see this."

"Sorry. Not open for observation."

"Why the hell not?" she asked, surprised he wouldn't let Mr. Armstrong watch when he said earlier the man wouldn't be a decent breeder if he didn't want to see the animal.

"This isn't open for discussion, Ann Marie," Travis growled low, keeping his gaze on the man across the table.

Her eyes narrowed into slits and she pushed against his shoulder. "Can I talk to you outside?"

Travis slid out of the booth and she followed him across the bench seat until she stood next to him. They reached the side of his truck moments later and she spun around and shouted, "What are you doing? If he wants to see the stallion run, then so be it."

"You hired me to be his trainer. I will *not* allow an outsider to watch my first run. If he wants to come over in a couple of weeks, then fine. Not today, Ann Marie and that's final."

"Excuse me?"

"Do I need to repeat myself? I really didn't think you were hard of hearing."

Exhaling a frustrated breath, she tipped her head back on her shoulders and stared at the blue sky above. "Fine, but if I lose this chance, I'm taking it out of your hide." She spun on her heel and walked back inside the diner to return to the table.

"Since Mr. Brooks is the stallion's trainer, I'm bowing to his expertise in this, Mr. Armstrong. You are welcome to come out to the ranch in two weeks to observe him run, but not today. Will that be all right with you?"

Landon rubbed his hand over his cheek and then across his chin.

*I'm going to kill Travis if this guy backs out.*

"That should work. I don't want to push things with Mr. Brooks. He's the expert, and if he wants two more weeks, I'm good." Retrieving his wallet, Landon pulled out a business card and handed it to her. "Call me when he's ready, and I'll make the trip out."

After the man left the table, she released the breath she hadn't been aware she'd held. "Let's go," she said with a nod.

On the way back to the house, he stopped for gasoline while she waited in the truck, grumbling under her breath about overbearing men, but she still couldn't keep her gaze from skimming over his broad shoulders and muscle chest. He glanced through the window at her and cocked an eyebrow in question. It only made her shift uncomfortably in her seat.

Silence enveloped them during the rest of the ride to the house. The moment he stopped near the barn, she said, "I want to see your files."

"Fine," he replied, leading the way inside and into the office. "The computer will need to be booted. I haven't been on there since yesterday."

Parking her butt in the rolling chair, she flipped on the power switch and waited until the files came up, then clicked on the one labeled Black. While she read Travis' entries, she could feel him standing behind the chair. Fingers brushed against her neck and she shivered at the touch, afraid he hadn't meant it and terrified he wouldn't do it again.

"Ann Marie?"

"What?" she asked in a whisper.

"I'm sorry about what happened a couple of months ago. You know, when you were gonna meet me out here, and I took off and went to town."

*Did I hear an apology? No. Couldn't have been, could it?*

"You're sorry?"

"Yeah. I wanted you so bad, and then you didn't show up... I got angry. I didn't even let you explain." One curl wrapped around his finger, and he tugged lightly. "Anyway, I wanted to apologize."

Releasing the curl, he stepped back several steps and rested his hands on his hips.

*I can't handle it anymore. I need this man.*

Coming to her feet, she pushed the chair out of the way and closed the distance between them. His butt hit the desk, and she wrapped her hand behind his neck to pull him closer. One tug and her lips latched onto his.

A low growl rumbled in his chest. His fingers tunneled through her hair and tilted her head to fit their lips better against each other. His tongue swept over her lower lip, and she whimpered as she opened her mouth.

Licking, stroking and sparring with their tongues brought her passion ever higher. His mouth left hers and blazed a trail across her cheek to her ear. Her breath hitched in her throat and released on a groan. Teeth nipped at the tender flesh beneath her ear, sending shivers rolling down her arms.

He stood and spun her around so she now sat on the desk.

One hand worked the buttons on her blouse until it lay open for him, while his lips continued to play along her skin and he whispered how much he wanted her.

Leaning back on her hands, she offered herself to him like the virgin on the altar.

The heat in his eyes when he lifted his head sent liquid seeping from her pussy to wet the piece of silk between her thighs.

The rough pad of one finger trailed down her cheek.

"Is this what you want?" he asked.

"Oh yeah."

"We should go to my room."

She nodded and grabbed his hand. Peeking around the corner of the office to make sure no one stood around and could see them, they ran down the short hall to his room, ducked inside and slammed it behind them.

The sexy-as-hell smile drifting across his lips almost made her come in her pants.

"Let me lock the door," he whispered. Two steps to the door and a turn of the lock, signaled they finally had their privacy.

"Good idea."

"You are so pretty," he murmured, pushing her shirt off her shoulders. "I could eat you up."

"Please do. The last time was downright amazing. I'm sorry we didn't get to finish."

"Me, too, darlin'."

Wanting to feel the warmth of his skin, she tugged at the bottom of his shirt until it was loose from his jeans and she could slip her hands underneath. Her fingers brushed against his nipple, and he inhaled a sharp breath and let it out on a moan.

"Take it off."

The piece of cotton material went up and over his head in a split second.

"Damn, you're one gorgeous man. All muscles and valleys." Fingertips danced over his flesh, and she smiled when his breathing hitched in his throat.

"Honey, you're killin' me here."

"Suck it up, cowboy. I wanna play."

A warm chuckle left his lips, but it turned into a tortured groan when she licked the hard tip. His fingers twisted in her hair, pushing her head harder against him as she sucked.

The tinkle of his belt buckle sounded loud in the room as she undid it and reached for the button at his waist.

"Wait." One finger lifted her chin before his fingers swept over her cheek.

"What? Did I do something wrong?"

"No, darlin'. If we don't slow down, this is gonna be over way too quick for me. It's been a long time, and you need to feel good, too." Taking her hand in his, he led her to the bed.

Her bra fell away with a tug of his fingers at her back.

"You're pretty good at that."

"Had a little practice here and there." The callus on his index finger felt heavenly as it rasped over her tight nipple, and she fought the moan in her throat. "Do you want my mouth here?"

"Yes, please," she breathed on a sigh.

One hand palmed the other breast while his tongue danced over her flesh, making it pull tight. A groan escaped her lips with the touch of his mouth.

"Travis."

He lifted his head, and his fingers swept over the button at her waist, undoing it with a sharp pull. Both his hands skimmed around the waistband of her jeans, and slipped beneath the material to cup her ass and pull her tight against him.

"You have a fantastic ass, darlin'."

The denim slipped down off her hips, along with her underwear, with an insistent push of his hands.

"I want you naked," he said.

"I think I am." A nervous chuckle left her mouth.

"I do believe you're right. And damn, but you are a sight to behold."

Heat crept up her neck and splashed across her cheeks.

"I…um…I'm not very good at this."

"There's nothin' you can do wrong, honey. Just the touch of your hands feels like heaven to me."

The praise in his words calmed her uneasiness. This need had been brewing between them since he stepped out of his truck the first day, and the tryst in her kitchen did nothing but remind her of the touch of a man. His body would claim hers in the most primal, passionate way possible between two people, and she couldn't wait to soar among the clouds on the high that comes with the ultimate climax.

A single step back, her knees connected with the mattress and she sank down on the soft surface. With one palm up, she invited him to join her. The wicked grin returned to his mouth as he followed her down and kissed her with such passion, she thought never be able to let him walk away.

Tongues entwined, teeth nipped and moans filled the air. Every sweep of his hands, every rasp of his fingers, brought her higher and higher.

He stood to shed his jeans, and she bit the inside of her lips to discourage the moan trying to break free at the sight of his impressive cock. She had almost forgotten the length and girth of him and how easily he had pleasured her. Coming to her knees, she let her hands wander over his chest, his arms and his abdomen until she hovered over the rock hard shaft between his legs. Fingers trembled with the need to touch.

"It's okay, honey. Touch me."

A low growl left his lips when she wrapped her hand around him.

"Not too much?"

"Just right, baby," he groaned, with a shift of his hips.

After a few moments, he forced her to stop with a kiss to her fingers and a sexy smile. "My turn."

He followed her back so they both reclined on the bed. His lips blazed a path from one nipple to the other, until he skimmed down her stomach, nipping and licking as he went. He settled between her parted thighs, and his warm breath flittered over her heated flesh. Anticipation rolled through her, and she shivered in need.

"Open for me, darlin' and relax."

Doing what he told her, she leaned back against the pillows, closed her eyes and waited with bated breath. The first stroke of his tongue almost sent her through the ceiling.

"Oh, God. Oh, God."

"Easy, baby." Hot breath blew across the wet surface of her clit. Nipples puckered tight, belly quivered with desire. Slick cream slipped from her pussy, and he lapped it up like a kitten after a bowl of milk.

Teeth nipped at the inside of her thigh, bringing her focus back to something other than the bundle of nerves between her legs.

Two fingers slipped knuckle deep inside her pussy and stroked slowly, in and out.

"Lordy, you are tight. I can't wait to fill you up. I've been dreamin' of this for weeks."

Wet, slick flesh met flesh as he stiffened his tongue and toggled her clit, alternating between spearing and licking until she couldn't stand it anymore. Heat crawled up from her toes, warming her legs, and prickling her flesh until it settled low in her belly and burst through her pelvis in a rush.

"Travis," she moaned, as stars flashed behind her eyelids.

Before she had even caught her breath, he licked his way up her belly, stopped for a moment to brush his tongue over each nipple, and then kissed her with so much passion, she wanted to wrap herself around him and never let him go.

He lifted his head and smiled. "Hold that thought. I need to get something out of the nightstand."

Within moments, he returned to her side, his cock safely wrapped in a condom.

"Now. Where were we? Oh yeah, I think I remember," he murmured against her lips while he settled between her thighs. Rocking his hips, the tip of his cock slipped inside her pussy, but he didn't go any farther.

She opened her eyes to see him staring at her with wonderment on his face.

"What's wrong?"

"Nothin', darlin'." He gritted his teeth. "I need to go slow. I'm sure it's been a while for you and you're tight."

"Is that bad?"

"Lordy, no. It's perfect. I don't want to hurt you. That's all."

"You couldn't hurt me, Travis. I trust you."

"God Almighty, Ann Marie," he whispered, slipping a little farther inside. "Hold tight, honey." Lifting his chest, he pulled her legs up and over his arms as he slid all the way in until she could feel his balls slap at her ass.

A whimper left her mouth, and he stopped.

"No, don't stop. Please, Travis, don't stop."

Her fingertips brushed across his nipples, and he shuddered. His hips rocked forward and he sheathed himself to the root. Another pull back had his cock almost out.

Sweat popped out on his forehead and she knew he fought to control the rhythm of their love making, but right now, she didn't want control. She wanted to come, needed to come.

"Travis?"

The movement of his hips stopped, and he looked down into her eyes.

"I don't want gentle. Fuck me."

"Are you…"

One finger pressed against his lips. "Yes, I'm sure. I need you. I need this. I want it right now."

With a tortured groan, he slammed his pelvis against hers and rocked his hips fast, bringing them both to the brink and pushing them over within seconds as she screamed his name and he groaned hers in her ear.

After several minutes, he shifted his weight and rolled onto the bed next to her as he sighed and murmured, "Holy hell."

A silly giggle bubbled in her throat.

*Oh my God. If that's what I'd been missing this whole time, it's a wonder I didn't jump every man who came around. John never made it like that. The quickie we had in the kitchen, can't even compare to what just happened.*

"Travis?" she whispered, sliding in next to him while he wrapped an arm around her shoulder and pulled her close.

"Yeah."

"Can I ask you a question?"

"Sure."

"Is it always like that for a man?"

"I hate to tell you this, but no, it's not."

"Oh," she whispered, laying her head down on his chest.

"Ann Marie, look at me." A second later, she looked into his eyes. "I say it's not like that always because it isn't. What just happened between us was amazing. I'm sure you made love with your husband on numerous occasions."

"Yes."

"Was it ever like that with him?"

She shook her head, almost embarrassed to admit to him and herself, John never satisfied her.

"Part of it came from knowing how to make sure you were satisfied, and I'm sure the rest came from it havin' been so long. Men are sexual creatures. They need sex on a regular basis. For me, it's been several months, except for what happened in your kitchen and I know it's been at least that long for you too."

"Are you saying if we did it again, it wouldn't be so good?"

"I don't know, but I'm sure hopin' so, and I would love to find out. What about you?"

Her gaze dropped to the tempting sculpture of his chest before she peeked at him through her lashes. "I hate to tell you this, cowboy, but now that I've had you for a second time, I want more."

# Chapter Seven

A silly grin played on Travis' lips while he walked out into the pasture to try to corral the stubborn stallion. Nothing would take him down this afternoon, nothing. The never ending case of blue balls he'd been sporting the last several weeks was gone, but the need to take Ann Marie to bed again remained.

*It's gonna be a long time before I get enough of her, I'm afraid.*

The soft whistle playing on his lips got the attention of the stallion.

"So, you like the whistle do you?"

The animal whipped his head around, throwing his long mane in the wind.

"Come on, big boy," Travis said, and then whistled a saucy tune.

The horse didn't move.

"No? You want something a little softer?"

The next song coming from his lips was a soft waltz, and the stallion perked his ears, flipping them back and forth while he listened and took several tentative steps in Travis' direction.

Travis slipped between the fence rails, continuing the soft song until he walked right up to the horse, slid the halter over his nose and hooked it around his ears.

"Well, I'll be damned. A song lover, are you?"

A quick scratch behind the ears, and the horse nudged against Travis' shoulder.

"Shall we go for a nice run today?"

The nicker he got made Travis smile.

*Maybe, this won't be so bad after all.*

Unlatching the gate, he led the horse to the barn to saddle him. He figured he'd do some work in the round pen first and then take him out for a run.

Once the saddle and bit were in place, Travis worked his way back outside, not the least bit surprised to see Ann Marie standing next to the fence with her arms crossed over the top.

The jeans she wore fit snugly over her ass and encased her gorgeous legs like a second skin. The tank top emphasized her breasts, and he fought the groan rumbling in his chest. Their romp earlier had done nothing but make him want her even more, but now that he knew what lay beneath her clothes... the soft skin, the pert nipples, the light brown curls guarding her sex...*shit!*

With a saucy smile and a tilt of her chin, she had him wanting to let the horse loose, throw her over his shoulder and run back to his bed.

"Hey."

"Hi. You come to watch?"

"Yep," she said, turning to face him. Without any warning, she stepped in front of him, wrapped her arms around his neck and planted her lips against his. Her tongue traced his bottom lip and then her teeth nipped softly.

*Holy hell, the woman is gonna be the death of me.*

The heat sizzling on her lips brought his cock to straining proportions within seconds.

A perfectly arched eyebrow rose when she broke the kiss. "Miss me?"

"Damn woman," he hissed, dragging her back against his chest. "Do you have any idea how hard I am?"

One palm skimmed over his straining cock. "Impressive."

"Fuck," he growled.

"Later, handsome."

"And I'm supposed to ride like this?"

The throaty chuckle that left her mouth made his hard-on even worse. "I'm sure you've done it before, cowboy."

"Not this damned hard, woman."

"Are you trying to tell me you're horny? Even after earlier?"

"We're just gettin' started, honey."

"Good. I sure hoped you'd say that."

Another quick kiss to her lips, and he stepped back to swing into the saddle. "Open the gate?"

"Sure."

Taking up her former position against the fence, she watched with a heated gaze while he took the stallion through his paces. The animal performed perfectly. Each nudge of Travis' heels or touch of the reins and there was no doubt the horse had been tamed.

"You've done an amazing job with him," Ann Marie said when he rode closer to the fence and pulled the stallion to a stop.

"Thanks," he replied, patting the strong neck beneath his hands. "The real test is coming. I'm gonna take him out in the pasture for a run, so I'll catch you in a bit."

Eyebrows furrowed in concern.

"Be careful, huh."

"Of course. I'll be back in about an hour."

She nodded, and he spun the animal around before he dug his heels into the stallion's side, sending them off toward the outer pasture in a pounding of hooves and a cloud of dust.

Muscles bunched under him and Travis had to be amazed at the speed. He'd watched when the stallion had taken off several times outside the main house, but leaning over the powerful neck with the wind whipping by him, the whole experience left him in awe.

*Man, this boy is fast!*

The horse began to wind, so he pulled back on the reins to slow him to a canter and let him rest.

"You are one amazing animal, Black. You'll be a fantastic contender in the Quarterhorse Races, buddy."

The stallion tossed his head and whinnied loudly.

"And you'll make some mighty pretty babies for Ann Marie."

Ears flicked back and forth at the mention of her name, and Travis had to wonder why the animal seemed so attached to the woman.

They rode for about thirty minutes while he worked with the stallion on more of the basics and so Travis could check out the property. Ann Marie had said she owned five thousand acres, give or take. The figured amazed him, but he supposed it shouldn't. His parents owned a similar spread outside of Amarillo.

"I need to call them. It's been a while since I've talked to Mom, and she'll be pissed at me."

Miles and miles of flat stretched in front of him, with an occasional mound that some would call a hill or mountain. He chuckled at the thought. The landscape was broken by a few trees here and there, but usually they hugged the stream he found. Ninety degree heat beat down on his head. Sweat tickled his back, and he blew out a puff of air in a sigh.

*Damn, it's hot, and the stream looks mighty invitin'.*

Swinging down from the saddle, he tugged the reins from around the horse's neck and led him to the water. Black sucked it up in wet, slurping sounds while Travis bent down and splashed some of the crystal clear, cool water over his face and neck. Sitting back on his haunches, he contemplated what he was going to do about the disturbing woman.

*We're good together. Damn good, but I can't get tied up in her life. Giving my heart away isn't an option. I guess we can have a good time together while I'm here and then part ways as friends when my six months is up.*

"Yeah. Like that's gonna happen."

*Maybe I can come back on occasion and see her. Kind of like a friends with benefits type thing.*

"Like she'd go for that."

Fingers cut a path through his hair while he stared out into the open pasture in front of him. The feelings she stirred disturbed him. Yeah, he wanted her. Beneath him, on top of him, all round him, but he didn't know how long he could keep up a strictly physical relationship with her. He had a feeling, over time, she'd worm her way into his heart and his soul, and he wasn't ready for that.

*I don't think I'll ever be ready to have a regular relationship with a woman again. Catherine took care of any chance of letting someone hurt me.*

His thoughts drifted back to the night Adam drowned.

"Call nine-one-one, Catherine!" he yelled, grabbing the boy from the tub and laying him out on the bathroom floor. "Come on, buddy, don't do this."

*CPR. Remember. Open the airway, check for breathing. Nothing. Damn it!*

Two slow, easy breaths. He checked for a pulse in the boy's neck while he vaguely heard Catherine on the phone in the other room. No pulse.

*Compressions. Start compressions.*

Placing the heel of his hand against his son's sternum, he pushed and winced when he heard ribs crack. One. Two. Three. Four. Five. Two breaths. And the cycle continued. He couldn't stop. His son wouldn't make it if he stopped.

*Keep going. Don't think. Breathe for him. I have to breathe for him.*

Moments later, someone came crashing through the door.

"Let us in, sir."

Travis looked up and saw the patch on the guys arm. Paramedic.

*Good. They'll know what to do.*

Tears streamed from his eyes while he watched them work.

*He has to be okay.*

Catherine wept in the corner in the chair, and he wanted to slap the hell out of her.

*Like she fucking cares, the bitch! She didn't want him in the first place.*

The paramedics continued to do what they could. They stuck a tube down his son's throat to help him breathe. Hooked him up to all kinds of wires and tubes, stuck him on a board and then placed him on the gurney.

"Where are taking him?"

"Orlando Memorial."

"I'm right behind you," Travis growled, following them out the door and to the rental car. It seemed to take forever for them to reach the hospital. He could do nothing but pace—back and forth in front of the registration desk, until the doctor came out and waved him to come in the back.

"Mr. Brooks. I'm sorry."

"What?" A broken sob bubbled from his lips.

"We did everything we could, but we couldn't revive him. I don't know how long he was in the water, but we never got a heartbeat."

"Oh God. My son. He's only three."

The doctor put a comforting hand on his shoulder, but he shrugged it off.

"Where?"

With a wave of his hand, he led Travis to a room in the corner with the curtain pulled across the doorway.

"Is there anyone we need to call?"

Travis shook his head and moved inside. Adam laid on the gurney, white as the sheet over him, tubes sticking out of his mouth, wires going everywhere and more tubes hanging from the metal poles. Hands trembled, tears rolled down his face and he thought he would be sick.

*My son's dead. How can that be? We were just playing in the surf a little while ago.*

Travis brushed the blonde curl off the boy's forehead.

"What am I gonna do, buddy? You are my life."

A wail of a female voice, sent shivers down his spine.

*Catherine.*

Moments later, she burst into the little room, threw herself over their son's body and sobbed hysterically.

"My baby!" she cried, and he wanted to fling her off. "No. No. No. He can't be dead!" Cold, pale blue eyes fixed on him. "Why didn't you save him, Travis? You let him die!"

*What the fuck?*

"You left him in the bathtub alone. He died because you weren't watching him like a mother should."

"This isn't my fault. It's yours! If you hadn't gone downstairs and drank away our problems in the bar, he'd still be alive."

*Your fault. Your fault.*

The words echoed in his mind as his thoughts came back to the present. After the arrangements had been made to send his son's body back to Texas, he'd gotten on the same plane and gone home. For several months, he drowned his sorrow in anything alcoholic he could find. Catherine never came back, and he was almost thankful. She filed for divorce, and he pulled himself out of his drunken stupor long enough to go to court and stop her from taking what little he had left. But with his son gone, he didn't have much, and he didn't care.

The stallion snorted and pawed at the dirt.

"You ready to go back, big boy?" he asked as he stood and brushed his hand over the horse's nose.

Taking the reins, he tugged enough to bring the horse a little closer to a row of boulders. An ominous sound cut through the air, and Travis turned around to see a huge rattler sitting on the rocks not five feet from him.

The horse panicked, whinnied and reared back on his hind legs, pulling the reins from Travis' hand before he spun around and took off like a shot, leaving Travis to stare down the deadly snake.

* * * *

Ann Marie paced the carpet in front of her window. The tip of her fingernail disappeared between her teeth.

*He knows what he's doing. He's a professional, so calm down.*

Shivers rolled down her arms, and she rubbed them with her palms.

"He'll be fine. I have to keep telling myself that and not worry."

The next sight she caught when she looked out her window sent chills down her back. The stallion slid into the pasture, reins dangling and saddle empty.

Terror gripped her heart as she sped down the stairs.

*Please let him be okay.*

Yanking the front door open, she yelled at the men and ran toward the animal that now stood, sides heaving from exertion, foam on his withers and sweat pouring down his neck.

She grabbed the reins and ran her hands over the animal to calm him while she checked the saddle for blood or any other sign of what might have happen. Manuel and several other hands ran from the barn at her call.

"What happened? What's wrong?"

"Travis took the stallion out in the pasture for a run. The stallion came back a few moments ago, empty. Saddle me a horse, Manuel. I'm going to look and pray nothing bad has happened."

"Yes ma'am."

Within minutes. she was astride her mare, ripping across the countryside with several of the ranch hands on her heels.

*I have to find him.*

Not knowing which way he went, she tried to discern if there were any tracks that seemed fresh, but she wasn't a tracker.

Manuel reined up beside her, and she asked, "Any idea which way?"

"I thought I saw him ride toward the north. We can try there first."

With a swift nod, she kicked her mare and took off for the stream. Hopefully, with this heat, he'd, stopped there and they might be able to get a gauge on which way he went.

As she got closer to the tree line, her heart leapt into her throat when she spotted what she hoped was Travis walking toward them.

The horse skid to a stop, and she jumped from the saddle to throw her arms around his neck and plaster herself to the warmth of his chest. Her body shook with relief he settled his hands on her waist.

"Easy, honey," he whispered in her ear.

"Damn you, Travis! You scared the hell out of me!" she yelled, pulling back in his arms and punching him in the chest.

"Ouch! Knock it off, woman."

Hands skimmed over him from chest to arms, while her gaze sought out any damage.

"Are you all right?"

"I'm fine, darlin'."

"What happened? Black came running hell-bent-for-leather into the yard."

"I went down by the stream for some water, and as I went to remount, one of the rocks shifted. A rattler must have been sunnin' itself nearby and got spooked by Black. Scared the stallion so bad, he reared up, pulled the reins from my hands and took off."

"You weren't bit?" Her gaze searched over him again to make sure. "Do we need to get you back?"

"No, I wasn't bit. The rattler took off back under the rock when I backed away."

"Thank God," she whispered, framing his face with her hands. "I thought I'd lost you like John. All I could picture in my mind was finding you like we found him." The others faded from her consciousness as she stared into his eyes. "Are you sure you're all right?"

"Yes, Ann Marie. Don't worry your pretty little head anymore."

On a soft whimper, she fastened her lips on his and wrapped her arms around his neck. A tortured groan spilled from her mouth, only to be swallowed by his when he deepened the kiss and tongues entwined. Warm hands skimmed down her sides and pulled her tight against his chest, squashing her breasts flat.

The soft clearing of a throat behind them brought her attention back from the passion-filled fog. Disengaging herself from him, she stepped back and smoothed an invisible wrinkle from her jeans.

"You can ride with me," she said, grabbing her mare's reins. Seconds later, his hands encircled her waist and lifted her into the saddle. He grabbed the pommel, stuck his foot in the stirrup and swung up behind her.

*This is a mistake. How the hell am I going to keep my hands off him, if he's pressed against my back the whole ride home?*

"Mmm... I think I'm gonna like this," he murmured in her ear. "Just don't be rubbin' your tight little ass on me, or I might explode before we get home."

*Like hell, buddy. You put me through the wringer the last couple of hours.*

"You mean like this?" She wiggled her hips, grinding her butt into the cradle of his pelvis.

A warning hiss erupted from behind her, and she fought the giggle in her throat.

"Ann Marie," he growled. "I'm gonna beat your ass."

His forewarning sent trepidation down her back. Those were the words her father grumbled many a time when he would beat her black and blue. Back ramrod straight, she shifted forward in the saddle to get as far away from him as possible.

"I'm sorry, honey. I didn't mean it."

Her father said the same thing over and over.

The mare halted with a tug on the reins in his hands. "Ann Marie, look at me."

She shook her head and closed her eyes.

"I would never lay a hand on you, darlin'. It was a joke on my part, and a bad one at that. I didn't think. That's all."

A brush of his lips on her neck, sent shivers down her arms, even though she continued to pull away from him.

"Son of a bitch," he grumbled and then kicked the mare into motion again.

The rest of the ride back to the house was made in silence...stiff, uncomfortable silence.

They rode back into the yard a short time later, and she quickly threw her leg over the pommel and slid to the ground. She needed to get away from him and think. His words frightened her—terrified her, actually, and she needed distance between them to get her ragged feelings under control.

"I'll take the mare and put her away," he said, once his feet were on the ground.

He gently grabbed her hand and tugged her back when she turned to go into the house.

"We need to talk, darlin'. I'll be up at the house when I'm finished getting the mare settled."

"I—" The lump in her throat grew bigger, forcing her to swallow hard. "I need some time, Travis. Leave me alone for now."

"I can't do that, honey. I need to make you understand I wasn't serious back there."

"It doesn't matter," she whispered, tears burning her eyelids and clouding her vision.

"Yes it does, damn it! I don't like you afraid of me."

"I'm not afraid."

"I can see the terror in your eyes, and it breaks my heart."

His words calmed her some, but not enough to control the fear or the almost violent shaking of her body.

"Go on in the house, honey. I'll be right back."

The mare followed complacently behind him as Ann Marie watched from her spot. She hadn't moved, couldn't move. All she wanted to do was throw herself into his arms and beg him not to hurt her like her father.

* * * *

*Fucking stupid! I couldn't have said anything more insane in this lifetime!*

The saddle and bridle fell from the mare with a tug of his hand. The brush smoothed her coat as he ran it over her, to dry some of the sweat from her hide. The poor animal had worked hard to get them back to the ranch. She wasn't built to carry two people for any length of time, but she had without complaint, and he had to be thankful.

"What the hell am I gonna say to Ann Marie?"

Fingers cut a path through his hair in his frustration.

"The stiffness of her body was like a knife twisting in my gut. How could I be so damned stupid? I have to make her understand."

Tossing the brush in the bucket, he threw some grain in the feed bin and made sure her water was full before he secured the stall door.

Quick strides took him back toward the house, through the backyard and up to the kitchen door. Female voices met his ear, and he stopped to listen.

"I can't, Kel."

"Why the heck not? You're attracted to him, right?"

The hesitation in her voice sent chills down his back. "Yeah."

"Then what's the problem? You can't tell me John's death is still making you pull away from any man."

"No. It's not that."

"Okay, so what?"

"It's daddy."

"That son of a bitch is making you afraid still, isn't he?"

"Mom called several weeks ago and said, he'd put her in the hospital again."

"Fucking bastard! Why doesn't she just leave?"

"She'll never leave, Kel. You know that. He'll have to kill her first, and I'm afraid for her."

"Why did she call you? She hasn't talked to you in years."

"I know. It was the night we had the barbeque out back and Travis cooked. She couldn't have picked a better time," she said, sarcasm clear in her voice.

Travis kicked himself.

*That's why she didn't come out to the barn after I left. God, what an ass I am.*

"Is she all right?" Kelly asked.

"For now. Until the next time."

"So what's this all got to do with Travis and what's going on between you two?"

Silence met his ears even though he moved closer and tried to hear.

"Ann Marie?"

"I'm afraid, Kel. What if he's like daddy?"

Her words broke his heart.

"He's not like dad. You've seen how gentle he is with Ty and how he treats the animals. No man can fake that kind of behavior. Ty looks up to him."

"I know," Ann Marie whispered. "Did I tell you he had a son?"

"No. What do you mean, had?"

"He died ten years ago."

"Wow," Kelly murmured.

"Yeah. I can so see him with a little boy riding on his shoulders, laughing and carrying on."

Tears stuck in Travis' throat. Her vision nailed his relationship with Adam to a T. It tore his heart out when his son died, but lately, being around Tyler and Ann Marie, made it beat again.

"So how can you possibly think he's like dad?"

"He said something today."

"What?"

Travis knocked on the screen, interrupting their conversation. He didn't want Kelly knowing what he'd said until he could convince Ann Marie he wasn't serious.

"Come in."

The screen opened under his hand, and he stepped into the kitchen, but her eyes held him spellbound. The wary look, didn't sit well with him. Not one bit

"I'll…um…talk to you later, Ann Marie. Travis," Kelly said, nailing him to the floor where he stood with a look that told him he'd better tread lightly.

"Kel," he answered, nodding in her direction before she scooted through the doorway leading into the living room.

Ann Marie's bottom lip disappeared between her teeth, and a smile quirked at his lips.

He stepped closer and she shuffled back.

"I'm not gonna hurt you." Lifting his hand to her cheek, his heart stopped when she flinched.

*Damn. This terror goes deeper than I thought.*

One finger traced the path of a tear on her face.

"I'm sorry. I know you don't trust me anymore, but I'll earn that trust back, honey. I promise. I will never, ever hit you, Ann Marie. I give you my word as a man and you know I live by my word."

A watery snort left her mouth, and her gaze shifted around the room, refusing to meet his. "I've heard that line before."

"Have I given you reason to doubt my word?"

A frown settled between her eyebrows, and she lifted her gaze to look him in the eye. "No."

*I'll kill that son of a bitch! Her father has made her so scared of men, it's a wonder John ever got close to her.*

"Will you sit with me?"

She nodded, and he laced their fingers together before he tugged and led her outside to the back patio. The sun had started its descent into the night sky and one or two stars were visible. With a little pull, he brought her down on the swing with him and set the double seat in motion with a push of his boot.

"Tell me about your relationship with John. What did he do to make you comfortable enough to trust him?"

Exhaling swiftly, she said, "John didn't have a mean bone in his body, I don't think. His eyes were always soft, never hard. I could always tell when my father was about to go off, because his eyes got hard like stone, and they would narrow into agitated slits. I tried to avoid my father if he was like that, but sometimes there wasn't any way." A heavy sigh left her mouth, and she leaned against his shoulder.

"Thank you, God," he mouthed, looking up.

It was a step, and one he wanted to cherish and not push.

"I guess I could just tell John would never do anything to hurt me. Maybe it was because he wasn't a handsome man by most people's standards, and I didn't get that heady rush when we first met. He helped me get something off a high shelf at the feed store. A new bridle, I think."

Her fingers slid over the back of his hand in little circles and he wasn't sure she knew she did it.

"We didn't have a long courtship or anything. No multiple dates, no intimate dinners. You know, things normal dating people do. Things seemed to click with him. There was several years' difference in our ages, so I guess I looked up to him. I knew he would take care of me, and he did. I never wanted for much, and my father taught me money didn't buy love or companionship. John was my companion, but he never developed into the love of my life. I didn't need the mind-boggling feelings or any of that."

Pulling her hand from his, she stood and walked toward the fountain in the corner of the backyard. Her gaze stared off into the distance, and she rubbed the bare skin of her arms.

He stopped behind her and hesitated a moment before he laid his hands on her shoulders.

Her body leaned into his, settling back against his chest.

"You scare me, Travis," she whispered.

"Why?" he asked, almost afraid of her answer.

"Because of the way you make me feel. This need I have to be in your arms, to be near you, to have you make love to me, terrifies me."

*Ah hell!*

She stepped out of his embrace and turned toward him. The look in her eyes sent his heart to his toes, but her next words had him running scared.

"I think I'm falling in love with you."

# Chapter Eight

"Ann Marie, I—"

One finger on his lips stopped his words.

"Don't, Travis. I don't want to hear how you don't want to be in love again. I know how you feel about relationships. You've told me. I needed to tell you because these feelings scare the hell out of me, too. You'll leave in a few months, and I'll probably never see you again. But I have to ask you one thing."

He kissed her fingers and pulled them away from his mouth. "Anything."

"Don't upset Tyler. He looks up to you."

"I won't. I pray I never hurt either of you."

She stepped back and said, "You will. There's no way around it, because you'll leave. I can't stop you, but I can cherish every moment we have together until then. I'm sorry about what happened earlier. Your words brought back memories I never wanted to relive."

"I'm sorry, honey. I wish I could take them back."

"It's okay. I understand now it was said in a teasing manner when I wiggled against you. It was my fault, but I was joking."

Grasping her hand, he replied, "No, it's not. Don't ever think those kinds of words or behaviors are your fault. Not from me and not from your dad. Nothin' you said or did brought them on. I knew what you were doin', honey. Makin' love to you earlier did nothin', but whet my appetite for more, and the feel of your pretty little butt against me sent my need for you through the ceilin'." He pulled her against his chest and wrapped his arms around her. A heavy, thankful sigh left his mouth as her hands settled on his back. "I care about you, but I can't let myself fall in love again. It hurt too much the first time. Catherine walked away from me, and when she blamed me for Adam's death, it couldn't have hurt more. The worst part of the whole thing was I blamed myself. If I hadn't been downstairs drinkin', I would have been there."

She lifted her head from his chest and looked into his eyes. "It's not your fault either."

*God, he is in so much pain from this.*

"But, I—"

One hand wrapped behind his neck and pulled his mouth down to hers as she whispered against his lips, "It's not your fault. You loved your son and would never do anything to hurt him, just like I'd never do anything to hurt Tyler."

Her tongue brushed over his bottom lip, and he moaned softly as he pulled her tighter into his embrace.

"I need you to hold me, Travis."

"Anythin' you want."

Stepping back, she took his hand and led him into the house, up the stairs and into her bedroom.

Bright eyes watched while she stripped her shirt off, unsnapped her bra and shimmied out of her pants. The long filmy nightgown she normally wore slipped over her form and settled around her thighs.

"You're killin' me, darlin'."

"I know," she answered with a smile that turned into a frown. "I want you to make love to me, but for tonight, I need you to hold me. That's all. Okay?"

"Let me get rid of my boots and socks. I'll leave my clothes on."

"No."

"No?"

"I want your skin next to mine. Well, at least some, anyway. I like how it feels to lay my head on your chest and feel the crisp hair tickle my cheek." A soft groan left his lips, and she had to smile. "You'll be fine, cowboy. I'm sure you can handle it."

"You'll pay for this in the morning, because I'm gonna fuck to you until you scream, right there in your bed and maybe again in the shower."

"Promise?"

"Oh, hell yeah. You have my word."

"And I know I can trust it."

His T-shirt went flying and jeans slipped down his muscular thighs, revealing the boxer shorts he wore and the impressive tenting in the front.

*Maybe I should rethink this no sex tonight thing.*

Chewing her lip, her gaze wandered down his sculpted chest, washboard abs and the happy trail disappearing into the elastic at his waist.

"You need to quit lookin' at me like that. Otherwise, I won't be gettin' any sleep," he growled as he pulled her into his arms. "I wanna lick you all over. I love the little sounds you make. You sound like a kitten when I stroke you."

A heavy sigh left her lips on a rush, but she shook her head, grabbed his hand and led him to the bed. He slipped beneath the sheet on one side and she slid in beside him. One arm wrapped around her shoulders and tucked her in next to his side. Closing her eyes, she relished the feel of his warm skin beneath her cheek as she laid her hand on his chest, letting the hair slide through her fingers.

His hand gripped hers and laced their fingers together. Tears burned her eyes.

*What am I going to do when he leaves? God help me, I'm already in love with him.*

* * * *

Lips whispered over Ann Marie's bare shoulder, pulling her from the best night's sleep she'd had in as long as she could remember. A small smile, played across her lips, and a moan bubbled in her throat.

"Are you gonna play possum?" he asked, his hand palming her breast under her nightgown.

Sometime during the night she'd rolled away from him, but he must have spooned himself against her back. His pelvis was intimately pressed against her butt, his hard shaft cradled in the crack of her ass.

"Are you saying you have something in mind, cowboy?" she asked, rolling onto her back to meet the heat of his gaze.

*Oh, man. It's even better waking up next to him. I'm so screwed.*

"I do believe I promised somethin' last night, and I never go back on my promises."

Looping her arms around his shoulders, she pulled his head down so their lips almost touched.

"Good. Shower or right here first?"

He threw back his head and laughed.

"I've created a monster."

"Suck it up, buddy. You promised."

Tossing back the sheet, he rolled out of bed and she frowned, wondering what he was up to. He walked around to her side as she leaned up on her elbow. A squeal left her mouth when he scooped her up in his arms and headed for the bathroom.

"What are you doing?" she asked with a giggle.

"I'm gonna have you in the shower, honey. Problem with that?"

"You can have me any way you want me. But does that mean you won't...um..."

"What?"

Heat crawled up her neck and splashed across her cheeks as he set her feet on the floor. She couldn't meet his gaze. Embarrassment kept her gaze locked on the hair on his chest until he tucked one finger under her chin and forced her face up.

"Tell me what you want, Ann Marie. I'm not a mind reader. I need to know what will make it good for you."

Chewing the inside of her lip, she shook her head, unable to ask him to lick certain spots.

*Good lord, I've become a slut, wanting him to do that all the time.*

His nose brushed against her ear, and his tongue slid along the soft skin beneath it, sending shivers down her body. Her hands brushed over the muscles of his chest.

"It's okay. Do you want my tongue?"

A whimper left her mouth.

"Where, honey?"

She couldn't breathe...couldn't think...only feel.

The rough pad of his tongue slipped down her throat, over her shoulder and then his teeth nipped at the nipple through her nightgown.

"Travis," she breathed, grasping him harder to her chest.

Both of his hands pushed the material up her thighs until she could feel the calluses of his fingers on her flesh. Around to her ass, he slipped inside her underwear to grasp her butt cheeks in both palms and pull her belly flush against him.

"Damn, you're so pretty."

The gauzy material muted the fluorescent light of the bathroom for a second as she lifted it over her head and let it float to the floor at their feet.

Hooking her underwear with his thumbs, he peeled the silky material down until it dropped joined her nightgown.

"Turn on the shower and I'll grab some supplies," he said with a wicked grin creasing his lips.

"Supplies?"

The grin got bigger and she sucked in a ragged breath.

He disappeared out the door and she turned on the water with a flick of her wrist. The warm spray touched her hand when she leaned in and tested the temperature.

*Oh God.*

The silky steel of his erection pressed against the crack of her ass. She wondered for a moment what it would feel like to have him there. She'd heard about anal sex, but never imagined ever wanting to try it, but with Travis, she wanted everything.

Crispy hair tickled her back. Desire curled in her belly. Fingers traced along the curve of her waist, moved around the front and slid one between her thighs to glance across her clit. Shivers rolled over her flesh and she moaned.

"Shall we?" he whispered over her skin.

With a minuscule nod, she stepped out of his embrace and into the shower, with him right behind her. She turned to face him, but he stopped her with hands on her shoulders and a whisper in her ear. "I get to play."

"But I can't touch you this way."

"I know." Lips skimmed over her shoulder and his hands cupped her breasts. Two fingers plucked at one nipple while the other hand dipped down her abdomen and between her legs. "Put one foot on the side." Her slit now open to his fingers, he slipped two into her waiting pussy. "That's it, honey." A low whimper left her mouth and she rocked her hips with the motion of his fingers. "Ah, yeah. Feel good?"

"I want your mouth," she murmured.

"Where?"

She shook her head.

"You have to tell me, Ann Marie, or no go, darlin'," he whispered against her neck

*Damn man!*

"On my…on my…"

*Breathe. Breathe.*

His fingers were doing wonderful things, but it wasn't enough.

"I need your tongue on my clit, Travis, please."

Those fingers disappeared from her cunt, leaving her gasping for breath when he turned her around to face him.

"See. You can say it."

"Bastard."

A warm chuckle left his lips, and his eyes sparkled. In seconds, his mouth settled on hers, and she forgot everything but his tongue between her lips, stroking the inside of her mouth just as she wanted him to do between her thighs.

He finally lifted his head and said, "Stand right there, with your foot on the side."

Not knowing how he would accomplish what she wanted, she watched with heavy eyes. He dropped to his knees inside the shower and wiggled between her legs.

"What are you...oh my God," she whimpered when his tongue licked from vagina to clit.

Legs wobbled and quivered as he toggled the tiny nub of nerves. Luckily, he gripped her hips with both hands to hold her up or she knew she would have sat right on his face. Not that it would be a bad thing with what he was doing.

Warmth crawled up from her toes to burst through her stomach. She moaned his name and climaxed so hard she saw stars.

Moments later, he stood in front of her again, and she wanted to smack the smirk from his lips. Instead, she decided payback would be a bitch.

Soaping her hands, she skimmed them over his chest, tweaked his nipples between her fingers and smiled while he groaned low in his throat. His abs quivered under her touch and his breathing sped up to a soft pant. The length and girth of his cock amazed and delighted every part of her senses. Silk over steel. Hard and tempting. She wanted ever part of it deep inside. Her slippery hands rode his cock, slid between his thighs to cup his balls and simply torture him like he'd done to her.

"Ann Marie."

"Yes?"

"You're a witch."

"You don't like?"

"I love it."

"Then hush."

She pushed him back so the shower washed away the soap, and then dropped to her knees to take him in her mouth. One hand cupped his balls and rolled them between her fingers as she swirled her tongue around the tip of his erection.

"Mmm."

His hands tangled in her hair, and guided her movements. The soft whimpers from his lips, spurred her on. He tried to pull back, but she grabbed his butt cheeks and held on, giving him all the pleasure she could before he grabbed her shoulders and forced her to stop.

"I want to come inside your sweet heat, darlin'. Turn around," he said.

His soapy hands slid over the bunched knots under the skin of her shoulders when she presented him with her back.

"Damn you're tight."

"That feels fantastic."

Fingers kneaded her flesh and skimmed down her spine, tracing each vertebra until he reached her butt.

"You have such a nice ass. Perfect. Rounded just right."

A small laugh erupted from her lips. "Glad you like it."

Water washed away the soap as he dipped one finger between the cheeks and teased her back hole. Breath hitched in her throat, and a small groan slipped out.

*Did he know her secret desires?*

"Ever had a man in your ass, honey?"

"No," she moaned and leaned back.

"Want to?"

"Maybe. I've thought about it."

"Not tonight then, but soon."

*Wow. What a thought.*

"Bend over."

His warmth disappeared for a moment, but then he returned, his cock encased in a condom and nudging at her pussy from behind.

"Easy."

Whimpers spilled from her mouth as he pushed inside and she stretched to accommodate his girth.

"God, you feel perfect. So tight. So warm."

"Now, Travis, please," she groaned, pushing back against him.

The tortured growl spilling from his mouth as he rocked his hips made her smile. He obviously wanted her. There would be no denying the raging desire between them from now until he left at the end of racing season.

Tears sprang to her eyes at the thought. *How am I going to let him go?*

* * * *

"You okay?" Kelly asked when Ann Marie walked into the kitchen two hours later.

"Yeah. I'm fine. Why?"

Kelly sipped at the coffee cup in her hand and looked over the rim at her. Her sister could read her like a book. Right now, she didn't want Kelly to read too much into anything going on with her.

"You look well loved, but pensive."

"Well loved?"

"I saw Travis leave about ten minutes ago. His departure wasn't very discrete."

"Forget it, Kel. It's meaningless sex. That's all."

"You? Meaningless sex?"

A smile twitched her lips. "I've come realize there's more to two people making love than what John taught me."

"Making love, huh?"

*Shit.*

"Sex. I meant sex."

Her sister set her cup down, grabbed Ann Marie's hand and pushed her onto the stool next to the bar. "Forget it, sis. You won't be able to convince me it was only sex with Travis."

A sigh escaped her lips. "What am I going to do, Kel? He'll leave in a few months, and I'll never see him again."

"Maybe."

"There's no maybe. He's already told me he won't fall in love again. It hurt too much and he refuses to do it."

"We can't control who we fall in love with. I've seen the way he looks at you. If he's not in love with you, then he's damned close and is confused."

She hugged her sister and sniffed back a tear. "I wish that were true."

"You're in love with him, huh."

"Afraid so. At least I think I am. I've never been in love before either. I wasn't with John. My relationship with him consisted of comfort." She tipped her head back on her shoulders and sighed.

"Everything will work its self out, Ann Marie. If you and Travis are meant to be together, then you will be."

She walked to the refrigerator and pulled out the pitcher of lemonade, pouring herself and Kelly a glass. "I thought I could sleep with him and enjoy his company until he left. You know, walk away unscathed, but I don't think that's going to happen now."

* * * *

Hooves pounded the dirt like thunder as the stallion sprinted across the open pasture. Wind whipped by Travis' ears like the roar of a tornado and a smile spread across his face. It had been a long time since he'd been on a horse that could thrill him with the power between his legs, but this animal had done it.

*Maybe it wasn't the stallion that brought me here, but Ann Marie.*

Pulling back on the reins, he slowed the horse to a walk.

"Bullshit. I don't need a woman, any woman, not even Ann Marie."

*Yeah, then why does my heart race when she's near? Why do I yearn to be buried in her sweet heat every minute of the day? Making love to her might have been a huge mistake.*

"Damn it! This is crazy. I need to get this horse ready for the races in a couple of weeks, get him to win and then be on my way."

*And what about Tyler?*

The kid had a serious case of hero worship from where he stood. Tyler spent every waking hour with him in the barn, working with the horses, asking questions and just hanging out. Unfortunately, the boy needed a father.

*I can't be that for him.*

"Not even if he is helping my heart heal, too. I can't get involved in their lives."

*Maybe I already am.*

About an hour later, he rode back into the yard to find Tyler perched on the fence, waiting for him. Tyler waved and jumped down.

"How come you didn't tell me you were going riding, Travis? I wanted to go."

"I know, buddy, but I needed to let the stallion stretch his legs. Misty couldn't keep up with him."

"My dad said he's fast."

"Yep, he is."

"Momma wants to race him. Is that why she asked you to train him?"

"Yeah. That's the plan, I'm thinkin'." Swinging down from the saddle, he grabbed the reins and walked toward the barn with Ty on his heels. "Where's your mom?"

*Shit. I have to quit thinkin' about her and askin' about her.*

The kid smiled like he had a secret, and Travis felt like kicking himself.

*So much for not gettin' involved.*

"She went into town to get something, she said."

"Oh?"

"Yeah and Aunt Kelly went along too."

*Two women together shoppin'? Bad idea. They might not be back for a while.*

"Well, I guess it's just us men then, eh?"

Tyler puffed up his chest and pulled back his shoulders. "Yep, just us men."

Travis smiled. He liked the kid and he hated the thought of leaving and making him miserable again, but he didn't have any choice in the matter. Staying here with them wasn't in the cards—wasn't what he saw in his future. A very lonely future, it appeared.

* * * *

The sight meeting Ann Marie's gaze when she walked inside the house made her smile. Travis sat on the couch with Tyler right next to him. A huge pizza box between them, soda cans on the table and football on the television across the room.

"Hi Mom," Ty said, grinning from ear to ear.

"Hi yourself. What are you two doing?"

"Eating pizza," her son answered, giving her a look that said, "well duh."

"I see that."

"Did you and Kelly have fun shopping?" Travis asked, and then sipped from the can in his hand.

"Yes we did," she answered, shuffling the bags in her hands so she could set them on the table nearby. "I'll be back in a minute." The last thing she wanted him to see was the bright pink bag with big black letters spelling out the name of the adult toy store she and Kelly found. Scurrying up the stairs and into her bedroom, she breathed a sigh of relief and set the bag on her dresser.

A screamed ripped from her throat when she turned around and saw Travis lounging against the doorjamb with a wicked grin on his face.

"God, you scared the hell out of me."

The grin got bigger as he pushed away from the doorway and sauntered toward her with his slow, easy glide.

Plucking the bag from the dresser, he asked, "What's this?"

She grabbed for it, but he held it up so she couldn't reach it. "It's nothing." Explaining to him right now wasn't at the top of her list. Sure, she planned to show him what she bought, and even let him use a few of the things on her like the little vibrator and the flavored lubricant, but right this minute, she was embarrassed.

"Mmm…doesn't look like nothin' to me, darlin'. I believe this is from the Pink Lady."

Her quick exhale blew the curl falling over her eyebrow off her forehead. "Well, yes it is. And exactly how do you know about the shop?"

"I saw it when I drove through town."

"Uh-huh. You wouldn't know what the bag looks like, if you only drove by it."

Eyes twinkled and white teeth flashed as he stepped closer. "I went there myself yesterday."

"Oh?"

"Yeah. See, there's this beautiful woman I've been with, and I wanted to help her expand her horizons."

Her heart dropped into her toes, and she focused on the tips of his cowboy boots. He obviously had been seeing someone else besides her, and the thought made her miserable. "I see."

One tanned finger slipped under her chin and forced her gaze to his. "I'm talkin' about you, Ann Marie."

"Me?"

His hand slipped into the hair at her temple, and she closed her eyes at his touch. He didn't have to do anything but brush against her, look at her or say her name and she was ready to push him back on the bed and ride his hips.

"Honey, open your eyes," he whispered.

She did and the look in his eyes set fire racing up her arms, across her chest to settle low in her belly.

"I don't want anyone else. For as long as I am here, I want no one but you. I want to rock your world, darlin', and make you think of only me."

"I can't think of anyone else. I haven't been able to since you walked into my life, Travis Brooks. I'm not sure what I'll do when you walk out of it."

"Let's not think of that right now. I wanna love you."

*If that were true.*

"Where are Ty and Kel?"

"Busy."

"Good," she said, sliding away and shutting the door before she turned back to catch his movements. "Did Ty see you come up here?"

"No. I went out the back like I was goin' to the barn. He went up to his room. I'm glad it's on the other side of the house."

"Yeah. Me, too," she breathed.

He stopped in front of her and pressed her against the wooden panel behind her trapping her efficiently with one broad hand on either side of her shoulders.

"Lordy, I want you woman."

"I know the feeling. It seems like it's been days and days instead of this morning."

"I want to taste you all over."

"Ooh, I like the sound of those words," she whispered, bringing their lips close. "Kiss me."

"My pleasure."

Her eyes closed again, and he brushed his lips over hers as she whimpered, wanting more. His tongue slipped over her bottom lip, and she opened her mouth to take him deep inside, wanting all of him. Tongues swirled and danced, stroked and licked, until they were both breathing hard.

"What kind of toys did you buy?"

"Want me to show you?"

The grin lifting his lips, sent shivers down her back. He grabbed her hand and walked her back to the side of the bed.

"Mine are in the barn, so we'll have to play with yours tonight."

*Oh my.*

"I have one thing I want to try if you're willing," she said in a shy, low voice.

"What's that darlin'?"

Chewing her bottom lip, she moved toward the bag and air rushed from between her lips. It took a minute or two for her to get her nerve to pluck her prize from the bag and then turn to face him again.

His eyes widened and one eyebrow shot up in surprise.

"Handcuffs?"

# Chapter Ten

*I think I'm gonna like this.*

"Who's handcuffin' who here, darlin'?" he asked as all sorts of decadent thoughts ran through his mind.

"Um…I thought we could take turns."

A tortured groan slipped from his lips. Tying her up and having free rein to her body sent his desire soaring out of control.

"I want to have my way with you, Travis."

"What might that mean?"

"It's a surprise. Will you let me?"

"Anything you want, honey."

She grasped his hand and snapped one cuff around his wrist.

"Lie down on the bed and put your hands over your head."

"Do you want my clothes off first?"

The wheels turned and her eyes brightened. "Your shirt, yes."

Fingers tugged at the hem. She had it loose a second later, and her warm palms slipped up under his T-shirt. He sucked in a ragged breath when she brushed them against his nipples. *Damn, her touch does things to me I haven't felt before.*

"Sorry," she whispered."

"No you aren't."

A small, sexy-as-hell smile lit up her face. "You're right. I'm not."

The shirt bunched under his armpits, and her wet lips closed around one hard nipple and sucked.

"Damn, honey," he grumbled and then whipped the shirt off.

"Mmm," vibrated against his chest.

Seconds later, she took his hand to lead him to the bed. Once, he was stretched out, he place his hands near the headboard and watched while she captured her lip between her teeth. The other cuff snapped around his wrist. He tugged lightly, and the cuffs clanked against the metal.

"Now what?"

The wicked gleam in her eyes made his cock hard as a rock. He couldn't wait to see what she had planned.

"I get to play all I want." A frown pulled down the corners of her lips. "Are you okay? Not too tight or anything?"

"I'm fine. Have your way with me, darlin'. I can't wait to see what you have in store, but remember, turnabout is fair play."

The soft tips of her fingers played over the muscles of his arms, across his chest and tickled down his abdomen, making his skin quiver. Watching through hooded eyes, he was mesmerized by the concentration on her face, the pink tinge of her skin and how her hands trembled when they moved over him.

"You are magnificent. All hard, sculpted angles that take my breath away," she whispered. Lips brushed over his chest, her tongue skimming down, following the path of hair to the edge of his jeans at the waist. "No gym can make muscles like these. Only a hard working man."

"Glad you approve."

"Oh, I more than approve."

The belt buckle at his waist clanked loudly as she worked it loose. Her fingers skimmed over his erection and his balls drew up tight at her touch.

"A little horny are we?"

A warm chuckle left his mouth. "A lot horny."

"Good. Me, too." Palms flittered over his abdomen again and back up his chest. "You make me feel things I never knew existed. I didn't know a man could make me feel all gooey and warm inside from a look, or make me want to strip off every stitch of clothing between us, to feel the crisp hair against my skin."

She took his nipple between her lips and pulled it into her mouth, sending electricity zinging straight to his cock.

"Does that do the same thing to you as it does to me when you suck on my nipple?"

"If you mean, does it make my cock feel like it wants to explode if I don't get inside you soon, then yeah."

"It makes me throb and tingle."

"Undo my hands and I'll make you throb, tingle and come."

"Uh-uh. I'm not done yet."

Harsh, ragged breaths escaped his lips.

"Lift your hips," she murmured, her tongue dancing over the skin of his abdomen.

He complied, and she swiftly pulled his jeans and his boxers off his hips and down his legs, freeing his already painful erection to her gaze.

"My, my. What have we here?" Her warm breath flittered over his heated skin. "Looks painful."

"Only because you haven't touched it yet."

"Oh, I intend to touch, lick, suck…"

"Aw fuck!"

"Mmm…that too."

Her hand cupped his balls and he fought the moan in his chest, without success. He closed his eyes and strained upwards at the touch of her wet, warm tongue skimming down his cock. A whimper of need left his lips when she finally opened her mouth and took him inside.

"Ann Marie…"

He bumped against the back of her throat and he felt it close around him as she swallowed.

"Ah, God, honey."

She sucked, swallowed, licked and caressed, and he lost all train of thought beyond what her mouth felt like until he hung on the edge of the abyss by his fingernails.

"Darlin', you …" Deep breath. "You need to stop."

Her murmurs vibrated down his cock and zinged through his balls.

"If you don't, I'm gonna come in your mouth and I don't want to do that."

She lifted her head, releasing his erection with a pop.

"Release me."

"Nope."

"Ann Marie," he growled.

"This is my party, remember?"

Moving back from the bed, her fingers slowly started to undo the buttons down the front of her shirt.

*I'm going to die before this is over.*

Inch by inch, her creamy skin appeared through the gap in her shirt. The blue and white plaid bra she wore played peek-a-boo with him, and he had to lick his suddenly dry lips.

"You're killin' me, woman."

The smile that spread across her face looked almost evil as she continued with her little strip tease. Two fingers undid her jeans and skimmed them over her hips to drop to the floor at her feet, leaving the little scrap of silk between her thighs in place. One hand reached around behind her to undo her bra. She held the cups with her palm while the fingers of her other hand slid the straps off her shoulders.

His chest rose and fell with his rapid breaths and his stomach clenched with need.

*God, she's beautiful.*

The bra fell from her chest, revealing her exquisite breasts, and saliva flooded his mouth.

"Want to taste?"

"God, yes."

She straddled him and leaned in so her breasts dangled over his face. The tempting flesh beckoned, and he lifted his head to suck one pert nipple between his lips.

*Ambrosia.*

The sweet scent of her arousal floated to his nose, and he could feel the dampness of her panties on his skin.

A tortured whimper left her lips as he sucked, pulling the tight little nub deep into his mouth. Swirling and flicking it with his tongue, he could hear her breathing speed up and her hips started to move.

"I need…"

"What, honey?"

The key appeared between her fingers, and she unlocked his wrists.

"Touch me," she whispered.

"My pleasure." He flipped her over on her back and did a slow exploration of her body. "You are so soft. Like silk. I can't get enough of you."

Each breast in turn was given his utmost attention until she squirmed under him. Palms slipped down over her sides. He licked his way to her belly button, swirling and nipping every inch of skin he encountered.

"So sweet," he murmured, settling between her thighs. "You smell like heaven."

One swipe of his tongue against her quivering center, and she almost came apart in his arms.

"Easy, darlin'."

Two fingers slid into her hot pussy as his tongue worked her clit.

"Oh God. Oh God." Her head swished back and forth on the pillow, and her fists clenched the sheet beneath her palms.

"Come for me, honey."

With a loud cry, she climaxed and cream spilled from between her pussy lips to coat his tongue. When she finally stopped trembling, he kissed the inside of her thigh and licked his way up her body until he reached her lips.

"This was supposed to be about making you want me so badly, you can't hold back," she said.

"You have no idea how much I want you. Making you feel good makes it that much better for me."

"Yeah?"

"Yes." His thumb skimmed over her nipple and she inhaled a sharp breath. "All I can think about every day, every minute, is getting you somewhere we can be alone. You are like a drug, and I can't get enough."

"I want you inside me, Travis."

"Hold that thought," he said, sliding off the bed to grab his pants and retrieve the condom he kept nearby all the time these days.

Once he had his cock covered, he moved between her thighs and nudged at her opening.

"Open for me, darlin'. Wrap your honey sweetness around me."

They both moaned when he slid inside her until he couldn't go any farther, his cock buried to the hilt, inside her warm, wet pussy.

Her hands danced down his spine. Fingernails scratched over his heated skin, until he thought he'd go crazy with need.

"Hang on, honey," he growled and lifted his chest off her, pulled her legs up and over his elbows and rocked his hips.

*Slow. I need to make this good for her, too. Slow and easy.*

"Travis?"

His movements stopped and he looked down into the smoky eyes staring back at him.

"If you don't hurry up and make me come, I'm going to take matters into my own hands, and then I'm going to torture you, like you are torturing me."

"But, I want this to last."

"We can do it again slow if you want. Later. Right now, I need hard."

Control disappeared. Desire zinged down his spine, straight to his toes and back up the inside of his legs to grip his balls so tight, he thought he would explode. The growl erupting from his lips didn't sound like anything he'd heard before, but he didn't care. His need for her bordered on insane.

Whimpers left her mouth. Vaginal walls clamped down on his cock. Her legs shook as she lifted her butt off the bed and forced him so deep, he thought for sure he felt her heart wrap around him and squeeze.

* * * *

"Are you sure it's okay, Ann Marie? I don't want to impose by bringing Tucker here," Travis asked a week later while they sat on her couch and watched a movie.

"It's fine. I'm sure there's plenty of work for him to do around here if he's not afraid of hard work."

"He's a good kid."

"Not much of a kid if he's twenty-five, Travis."

"Yeah, well, he'll always be a kid to me."

A warm bubble of laughter burst from her lips and he smiled. This domestic kind of thing with her felt good…for now.

"He can stay in the bunk house with the rest of the men, unless you want him bunking with you."

He trailed his fingers down her arm and smiled as goose pimples dotted her flesh. They'd come to an agreement. Hot, heavy lovin' and no talk of later, and he liked it that way.

"Since I'm spendin' lots of nights elsewhere, he could take my bed," he whispered against her ear.

The sharp edge of her elbow met his midsection.

"Ouch!"

"You deserved that."

"Just sayin'."

"You could be banished back to your lonely bed there, cowboy," she said with a wicked gleam in her eyes.

"You wouldn't do that, would you, darlin'? I thought you kind of liked havin' me in your bed."

"I do," she murmured as he sucked her earlobe into his mouth. "Don't get too comfortable. Your sinful tongue will get you into trouble."

"I'm countin' on it. It's been almost a damned week since I got to make you scream."

"I don't scream."

"Yes you do. Kelly's even heard you."

Her eyes widened, and she pulled away.

"Did she tell you that?"

"Not in those exact words, but she did say something like, 'Wow, there must have been one huge spider in Ann Marie's room last night. I'm sure you had to save her, too, huh, Travis.'"

Color rushed into her cheeks, and he had to laugh.

"Shit. My sister knows we are having sex."

"I didn't think we'd made it a secret. And she is over the age of eighteen. I'm sure if she hadn't figured it out before then, she knew it well and good after last week."

"I need to talk to her," Ann Marie said, coming to her feet until he grabbed her hand and tugged her back down on the couch with him.

"Later, honey."

"But—"

Stopping the flow of words with his lips became a pleasurable diversion. He nibbled at the corners of her mouth and when she moaned, he slipped his tongue between her lips to stroke the inside.

Hand wandered down his chest and slipped around behind to pull him closer.

"Oops. Sorry."

Kelly's voice snapped her head up so fast, she hit him in the nose.

"Son of a bitch."

"Oh my God, Travis, I'm so sorry. Are you all right?"

"Other than a busted nose, yeah," he answered, his tone nasally. Blood start to drip and he tipped his head back to slow the rush.

"I'll get some ice," Kelly said, racing for the kitchen.

"Do we need to call an ambulance?"

"I'm fine, Ann Marie. It's only a bloody nose."

"I'm sorry," she whispered, tears choking her words.

Grabbing her hand, he brought her fingers to his lips and kissed them, trying to reassure her.

Kelly returned with a plastic bag full of ice, and he leaned back against the cushions of the couch in order to balance the bag over the bridge of his nose. "It's not my first bloody nose, honey, and I'm sure it won't be my last."

A high-pitched whinny reached their ears and the three of them looked at each other.

"The stallion?" Ann Marie asked, and he nodded.

"Sounds like it. I wonder what's got him in such an uproar," Travis replied, sitting upright again. He brushed his finger over his nose and realized the bleeding had stopped for the most part.

"I've never heard him make a sound like that," Ann Marie said.

"Let's check it out. Somethin' has him upset."

The sun had begun to set behind the hills, bathing the entire area in a soft orange glow. Black ran back and forth behind the pasture fence. Every few seconds he would stop, twirl on his hind legs, rear back and paw at the air.

"What's wrong with him? He's acting crazy."

Travis' whistled and the horse stopped on his rear haunches, peering over the fence. Ears flicked back and forth for a moment before he took off again.

"Somethin' isn't right, but I need to get closer to find out," he said, stepping through the fence rails.

"Be careful. He's wild-eyed."

Travis began to whistle. The soft tune he'd come to realize the horse enjoyed. The stallion stopped again, sides heaving, foam gathering on his sides and hide quivering.

*Something's got him all wound up.*

"Easy boy," he murmured, reaching his hand out and letting the animal sniff his palm. "Easy. You know me. We're buddies now." Without a halter on, he wouldn't be able to keep the animal next to him if he decided to take off again.

"Travis?" Ann Marie whispered, but he held up his hand to quiet her. The last thing he needed was her coming inside the pasture and getting hurt.

The stallion didn't move. Just stood there, continuing to quiver as he approached.

"Good boy. Let me see if we can figure out what the trouble is, huh?"

Palms up, he let the horse sniff him before he started to rub his hands down the soft hair. Slowly he worked his way from front to back, feeling for any abnormalities or anything he thought might be making the horse act like he got a hold of a batch of locoweed. When he reached the horses flank, he found the problem.

"Ann Marie, call the vet, honey."

"What? Why?"

With a sharp tug, he pulled the three-inch dart out and walked toward her.

"Someone is trying to drug this horse."

"What the hell?"

"It's a tranquilizer dart. Whoever shot him must have been a bit of a distance away because it didn't go in that far. Not far enough to give him the full effects of the drug, but enough to send him into a tizzy. Go call the vet, and I'll see if I can get a halter on him and get him stabled."

She nodded and ran for the house as he walked toward the barn. All kinds of thoughts ran through his mind.

*Who would want to try to take the animal down? Were they trying to steal him, kill him or what?*

The qualifying runs for the Quarterhorse Races were coming up soon. Word was getting around about the stallion, he knew, but was it enough for someone to try to keep the animal from running? Stakes were high and money flowed freely when it came to good horseflesh, and he knew Black could bring some serious cash to Ann Marie's ranch if he won.

Travis ran a hand through his hair in frustration.

*Damn it! This is all I need. I'd planned on taking off after the first races, but now I need to stay and make sure Ann Marie, Tyler and Kelly are safe. Now that Tucker is coming here too, it could be so much more dangerous.*

"You are gettin' more and more tied up in this place, Travis old boy," his logical side said. He cussed under his breath and continued to the barn.

Within the hour, Travis had the stallion in a stall in the barn, even though the horse continued to pace.

"Is he going to be all right?" Ann Marie asked, worriedly chewing her bottom lip.

"He'll be fine, honey."

"Yes he will, Ann Marie," Rhett Blackstone, aka Dr. Blackstone, said as he approached from the doorway.

"Thanks for coming, Rhett."

"No problem. What happened?"

"Not sure what drug, but it appears someone tried to tranquilize him," Travis answered, holding up the dart.

"Mmm. Not good. He's agitated all right."

"Yeah. Wound up tighter than a spring," Travis replied.

"I'm sorry. You are?" Rhett asked.

"Travis Brooks. I've been training him for Ann Marie."

"Ah." Rhett's gaze swept between him and Ann Marie, and Travis didn't like the look on the man's face at all.

"Problem?"

"No. Just curious." Rhett walked inside the stall and did a quick exam of the horse. "I'm going to have to put him down for the night, Ann Marie. His heart is racing way too fast, and if I don't, it could kill him. He needs to rest and let whatever drug was in that thing work itself out of his system."

"Do whatever you feel is necessary, Rhett," she replied. "We'll keep an eye on him tonight."

Once the veterinarian gave the horse the shot, they helped the stallion lay on his side so he wouldn't hurt himself and then left the stall.

"I'll come back in the morning to check on him, but he should be fine."

"Thanks again. I sure appreciate you coming out this late."

"No problem. You know you are one of my favorite customers."

*Is that a blush I see staining her cheeks? Did Ann Marie and this guy have something going on before I got here? If so, they hadn't slept together by the way she's been with me.*

Travis cleared his throat and brought Ann Marie's attention back to him.

*What the hell difference does it make to me who she's seen or who she'll see after I leave?*

The clench of his belly and the ache in his chest, didn't sit well with him at all.

# Chapter Eleven

Once the vet left, Travis rounded on her and growled, "What's goin' on between you and the veterinarian?"

"Rhett?" she asked, tipping her head to the side and bracing her hands on her hips.

"Yeah."

"Nothing. Never has been." *Interesting. He almost acts...* "Why? Jealous, Travis?"

"Hell no."

*Oh, yes he is. He's jealous.*

Stepping in front of him, she laid her palm on his chest and looked into his eyes. "You are the only man in my bed and in my thoughts."

The look in his eyes spelled trouble when he raked his hand through his hair and stepped back. "I don't have a right to feel this way."

"Sure you do."

"No, I don't. We aren't in a relationship or anythin'."

*Okay, that stung.*

Lowering her eyes, she stepped back several feet.

"I'm sorry, honey. I'm makin' a mess of this." He moved close again, backing her up against the stall behind her. One finger trailed down her cheek. "We are good together, Ann Marie. You drive me crazy wantin' you, and thinkin' of you with him and not me doesn't sit well. Jealous? Yeah, maybe, but it doesn't matter. There can't be anythin' more between us than we have right now."

"I'm good with that," she murmured, knowing she lied. The feelings he stirred bordered on love. and they scared her to death. With John it had been a comfort level, not this crazy, gotta get close to you kind of a feeling.

"Are you sure, honey?"

"I'll take what I can get, Travis, and right now, this is all I can have." One hand wrapped around behind his neck and pulled his mouth down to hers. Her tongue swept over his bottom lip, and she smiled at the tortured groan that left his mouth.

His hands wrapped in her hair and tilted her head to the side.

Horses nickered and stomped in the late evening light, and she vaguely heard a door slam in the distance, but having Travis' mouth on hers, his hands all over her, made her not care.

"Travis," she whispered, pulling her mouth from his. His lips wandered down her neck, and his fingers plucked at the buttons on the front of her blouse.

"I want you, Ann Marie."

"I know. I want you, too, but we need to take this somewhere more private.

Breath hissed through his teeth as he placed his forehead against hers. "My room?"

With a smile, she nodded.

Grasping her hand in his, she fought the giggle bubbling in her throat while they rushed down the dirt walkway toward his door.

Before they could disappear inside, Manuel stepped out of the office a few feet ahead of them and said, "There you are, Ann Marie. I need to talk to you."

"Now?" she asked, trying not to sound aggravated as Manuel stopped next to them and Travis dropped her hand like it burned.

"Yes. We need to discuss the cattle."

"What's wrong with the cattle?"

"I've left you several notes. You didn't get them?

"I haven't seen any notes. Where were they?"

"In the office, on the desk. We are missing several cows and their calves, but the bull went missing this afternoon. We can't find him anywhere."

"Damn it!"

*Great! Shit is falling apart and all I can think about is getting Travis into bed with me. I need to pull my head out from between my legs and get busy or this ranch will cease to exist. I'll be damned if I'm losing this place over a man.*

"Did you see any notes in the office, Travis?"

"No. Are you sure you left them on the desk?" Travis asked, his eyes narrowing.

"I'm sure."

"Well, nothin' we can do about it this evening. It's too dark to track anythin' now. We'll have to go out tomorrow and see if we can locate where they might have disappeared and where the bull might be," Travis said.

"I'm going into town. I'll keep my ears open for anyone talking smack about anything going on out here," Manuel replied.

"Good and let me know if you hear anything at all," she said.

Manuel shot a distrusting look at Travis and then disappeared back down the aisle.

News of the missing cattle had a cooling effect on her desire, like an icy shower.

"I need to take a look at the books."

"Right now?" he asked. The shocked expression on his face had her smiling.

"Yes, now."

"But, we were goin' to…"

One finger pressed to his lips, and she shivered when he sucked on it.

"I know what we were going to do, but I need to check the totals on the cattle. I can't afford to lose a lot of them, and if the bull is indeed missing, it could cost me this ranch. I refuse to let go of it. I've worked too damned hard to keep it."

"Let's take a look together then," he replied, taking her hand in his.

"It's okay, Travis. I can handle this. You don't need to get involved."

A frown wrinkled the skin between his eyebrows.

*I don't want to become too dependent on him. I need to do this myself. Eventually he'll leave, and I'll be here alone.*

"I want to help you."

"I know and I appreciate it," she said, placing her hand on his chest and rising up on her toes to kiss him lightly on the lips. "I'll see you in the morning."

With one last parting look, she walked toward the house and her office.

Once inside, she pulled out the journal with the tabulations on the cattle numbers and spread it open on the desk.

*I'll have to find out from Manuel the exact number missing, but this isn't good. A few cows we can handle, but the bull will hurt this place. The races are coming up soon, too. I think Travis has the stallion ready to run. If he wins, he could be the saving grace. The beef market sucks right now, but the Double S was built on it, so I need to keep it going.*

Thoughts of Travis returned to her mind and she fought the despair. *He will hurt me in the end, when he leaves and never returns.*

"I can't think about that part. It will happen, and I need to be prepared, but for now, he's here to help. He said so."

A quick exhale blew the hair off her forehead.

"I'm going to take a nice warm bath and try to relax. This whole mess has me wound up tighter than a pogo stick."

Moments later, she stood in the bathroom and waited for the tub to fill. Bubbles bounced on the surface of the water and glistened in the fluorescent lighting, while the scent of honeysuckle lifted to her nose. She dropped her clothes to the floor and slipped into the warm water with a sigh.

Within seconds, her mind wandered to Travis for the umpteenth time.

*What's he doing right now? Is he thinking of me?*

"This is crazy," she grumbled, trying to relax. Resting her head against the back of the tub, she closed her eyes.

* * * *

"What the hell just happened?" Travis asked himself as he stood in the barn and watched Ann Marie leave. "One minute we were going to my room to have a rousing bout of sex, and the next she's heading back to the house alone." His fingers cut a path through his hair while he continued to grumble.

"Cold shower." He pushed open the door and then slammed it shut. "Damn it! I thought I was done with these once I got her in bed."

Icy needles of water hit his skin.

"Fuck. That's cold," he said and shivered.

The water finally managed to cool his ardor, so he stepped from the shower and dried off. He grabbed a pair of jeans and slipped them on as his cell phone rang from where it lay on the nightstand.

A smile spread across his face when he saw the caller ID.

"Hi, Mom."

"What are you up to, Travis?"

"Nothin' in particular. Just workin'. Why?"

"Did you check with your employer about Tucker coming there?"

"Yeah, and she said it was fine. I'm sure there's plenty of work for him here."

"She sounds very nice. Is she pretty?"

He chuckled. It was like his mother to play matchmaker. "Yeah, Mom, she is. And she's also widowed, with a son."

"A ready-made family then."

"Don't start. I'm not interested in hookin' up with Ann Marie."

"Ann Marie, huh. Have you slept with her?"

"Mom!"

"Come on, Travis. You are a man, after all, and around a pretty woman. You would find it hard to keep your hands off her."

He pinched the bridge of his nose. "All right, yes, we've had sex, but that's all it is, Mom. Sex. She's not interested in a relationship, and neither am I."

"Are you going to let Catherine ruin you for any other woman?"

"Catherine doesn't have anything to do with this."

"Yes, she does, Travis. Honey, please. Don't turn your back on the possibility of finding love and being happy with another woman because of that witch."

"Did you know she found me here in Bryan?"

"She what? You can't be serious."

"Yeah, actually she did. Had the gall to even say she still loved me."

"Where is she? I'm going to put her in the hospital myself."

"Easy, Mom. I showed her the door. I guess she got wind of my good fortune and thought she could cash in on it. I wouldn't touch her again with a ten-foot pole."

"Good. If you did, I'd have your head examined."

*Leave it to my mother to make light of all of this.*

"Sorry, Mom. I need to go. There's a stallion I need to keep an eye on tonight."

"Okay. I'll talk to you again soon. I think Tucker is planning on driving down there in the next couple of days. I wanted to make sure there weren't any problems with your boss lady. By the way, how is it working out for you, being employed by a woman? I know you have issues with taking orders from a female."

Her bubble of laughter made him smile.

"We worked it out."

"Oh?"

"Yeah. When I told her I wouldn't work for a woman, she called me a male chauvinist pig and threatened to sue me for breach of contract."

The roar of laughter from his mother had him chuckling in return.

"I need to meet this woman. She's perfect for you."

"Bye, Mom."

"I'll talk to you later, son. Let me know when Tucker gets there."

"Sure. Night."

The phone clicked in his ear after she said her goodnights. A soft cotton T-shirt slipped over his head before he tucked it into his jeans, pulled on a pair of socks and his boots so he could check on the horse.

A light shining near the stall surprised him, but it shouldn't have. *So much for the cold shower.*

* * * *

*Damn, he looks good. And the soft look in his eyes has me wanting to ride him right here in the stall.*

"Did you take a shower?"

"Huh?"

"Your hair is wet."

"Uh, yeah. Cold one."

*So he's not immune to me. That's good to know.*

"What are you doin' in here? I thought you were lookin' over the books."

Her gaze dropped to the horses head in her lap as she stroked his forelock. "I wanted to check on him."

"You shouldn't be sitting there like that. What if he spooks and comes up fast. You could be hurt."

"He'd never hurt me."

'Maybe not intentionally, but he's still a horse. A very big horse, too."

A palm appeared in her line of vision, and she looked up to see Travis holding out his hand to help her to her feet. She let him pull her up, and she wasn't prepared for him to tug her into his arms.

"No bra?" he asked, his voice dropping an octave.

"I took a bath and didn't put one back on before I came out here," she whispered, loving the way his hands moved down her back and how her breasts were pressed against his chest.

"You do realize it wasn't very nice of you to leave me hangin' earlier and go into the house."

"Don't you think I suffered, too?" A quick glance at his face and she could see the desire smoldering in his blue eyes. *I love the way his muscles feel under my hands. All hard plains and valleys. Yummy.* "But the ranch has to come first," she whispered, slipping her hands up around his neck. "It bothered me when Manuel said there were so many cattle missing and now the bull, on top of Black being drugged. Something's going on here, and I don't like it."

"I know."

"Strange thing. It all started since you've been here."

He stepped back as if she'd slapped him.

"Are you suggestin' it has to do with me?"

"No. Not necessarily, Travis, but it does seem coincidental."

"Let me tell you something, lady. If I wanted to take your ranch, I would. I've got enough cash in the bank to buy this place three times over if I wanted to. I'm a damned good trainer, and that's how I make my money. Not by beddin' the widow and taking it from her. The sex between us is fantastic, but that's all I'm after. I don't want your place. I don't need you or your ranch."

Her mouth hung open as he spun around, stomped down the walkway and slammed the door to the office.

* * * *

"Son of a bitch! I can't believe she just accused me of wanting to take this place from her. What the hell gave her that idea?"

He paced back and forth in front of the desk for several minutes before he sighed, sat down in the chair and switched on the computer.

*Something gave her the idea. I'm going to comb these files and find out what her husband was up to.*

For the next two hours he went through every file on the computer.

"Damn," he whispered, finally closing the last one. "He was up to his eyeballs in debt. I wonder if she has any idea he borrowed from almost everyone to keep this place afloat."

*I can't get involved.*

"It would kill her to lose this place."

*It's a bad idea.*

"It would be a loan."

*Hello? Getting involved here.*

"Shit. Might as well jump in with both feet. I've always been a sucker for a woman in trouble. I hope she knows how much trouble she's in."

The door opened with a sharp tug before he made his way down the aisle. He almost expected to see her still with the stallion, but when he reached the stall, she was gone.

His steps beat a path across the yard, and he heard thunder in the distance.

*Great. She'll be a bundle of nerves with a storm movin' in.*

Boots clunked on the wooden porch as he stepped up. A quick couple of raps on the door and he waited.

Within moments, the door creaked open.

"Travis?" It opened farther. "I thought you were pissed at me."

"I am."

"Then what are you doing here?"

"I need to talk to you about somethin'. Where are your books?"

"The ranch journals?"

"Yeah. I need to see them."

"Listen, Travis, the journals aren't your concern. You made it clear you don't want anything to do with this place or me other than in bed. I'm done being used."

"Did you have any idea John was in debt up to his eyeballs, Ann Marie? You are going to have notes coming due. Unless you have twenty thousand in the bank, honey, you're going to lose this ranch."

"What? Twenty thousand? You aren't serious."

"I'm dead serious. I pulled up the computer files in the office in the barn. He obviously didn't want you knowing he'd borrowed so much against this place and the money the stallion *might* bring in. I can show you, if you want. I have a feeling he kept this a secret from you and on the computer in the barn rather than in here."

She left the door open as she walked into the living room and sank down on the couch.

"Twenty thousand," she whispered in awe.

"I hope that's all," he said, sitting down next to her and taking her hand in his. "I'm not sure, because the files were so jumbled. That's my best guestimate."

"What am I going to do, Travis? I don't have that kind of money." Jumping to her feet, she paced in front of the fireplace. A loud crack of thunder rattled the windows and she stopped and looked at him with terror-filled eyes.

"Come here, darlin'." Without preamble, she slid into his embrace and he pulled her close. "It will be okay. I have money—"

"I'm not taking money from you, Travis."

"It's a loan, Ann Marie."

"I still can't borrow your money. It's not right. I'd feel like you are paying me to sleep with you. Like a whore or something."

"You aren't a whore. That thought never crossed my mind."

Her fingers brush against the cotton of his T-shirt and he sucked in a ragged breath. They'd been trying to have sex for a week now, but kept getting interrupted, and it was driving him crazy. His cock swelled behind the fly of his jeans, and he grabbed her hand to forestall her downward path.

"You don't want me to touch you?"

"It's not that, sweetheart. I want to fuck you so bad, my balls ache."

"So what's stopping you?"

"I'm still pissed off that you think I want to take this place from you, and I want to know what brought it on."

"Someone is behind the cattle disappearing and trying to drug Black. I'm trying to sort it all out in my mind."

"I'm not involved, Ann Marie. I don't know what you want me to say to convince you."

"You don't have to say anything. I believe you," she murmured while her hand snaked up the tail of his T-shirt to whisper across the skin of his abdomen. "I want you."

"Because you believe me, or because you want me to make love to you?"

She jumped to her feet and scowled even though sadness swam in her eyes. "Forget it, Travis. Get your rocks off somewhere else. I'm not interested in playing your games anymore."

The sadness in her eyes tore at his heart. "Ann Marie."

"Get out. I'm done. Do your job, and as soon as the stallion is ready, you can leave. In the meantime, keep your hands to yourself and I'll do the same. If I need a man, I'll find someone else."

*Okay. A kick to the nuts wouldn't have hurt this bad.*

Bile rose in his throat when she turned around and raced up the stairs. The door slamming on her room, made him jump.

*I managed to fuck everything up.*

His feet took him to the office downstairs, and he slowly opened the door. The journals lay across the top of the desk.

*Her anger will see new heights if she finds out I'm in here.*

"It doesn't matter. I'm going to make sure she doesn't lose this place no matter how damned stubborn she wants to be."

An hour later, he shut the light off and closed the door behind him. He fought the urge to go upstairs and take her in his arms, but he knew she wouldn't allow it. Not after what he'd said earlier.

*A trip to the bank tomorrow will be needed. It appears most of the notes are being held by the bank and a couple of local ranchers. I hope they are hospitable enough to take the money.*

* * * *

Morning light burned through the window of the barn. He'd spent the night in the stall with the stallion, leaning against the wall, sleeping fitfully. The horse began to stir and try to stumble to his feet.

"Come on boy. You can do it," Travis said to the horse while he tugged on the halter, trying to help the animal to his feet. "Good boy."

Wobbly legs and quivers over the horse's flesh had him wondering how much more drug might be circulating through the stallion's system.

"You need to stay inside today, boy."

A weak knicker met his ears.

"I know buddy, but it's best. I have a couple of errands to run."

Travis ran his hands down the horse's coat and patted his sides.

"I'll be back in a little while."

The stall door opened with a push, and then he latched it again. He walked to his room to change clothes and a have a quick shower. The business in town might take a bit, and he wanted to be fully prepared.

An hour later, he headed to his truck. He glanced up at Ann Marie's window, wondering if she slept still.

*Damn it! Right now she's not going to let me touch her, and she might never again when she finds out what I'm about to do. I have to make damned sure she doesn't lose this place no matter how stubborn and bullheaded she wants to be about it.*

The engine on his truck turned over with a growl, and he drove down the driveway toward town.

An hour later, he stood and shook the hand of the bank manager.

"I appreciate your business, Mr. Brooks."

"Call me Travis."

"All right, Travis. I'm sure Ann Marie will be thrilled to know the notes have been cleared on her place. John had me concerned when he borrowed so much."

"I'm not sure how thrilled she'll be," he grumbled under his breath.

"What did you say?"

"Nothin'. I would appreciate it if you would keep this under wraps for now. I want to tell her myself."

"Sure. I guess I'll be seeing you around here more. You've got an investment in the Double S and it will probably require your firm hand."

*Damn it! I hadn't thought of that.*

"Yeah. Thanks again, Mr. Aslind."

Once he'd slid inside his truck, he drove out to the two ranches and paid the ranchers off too. With the notes in his hands, he drove back to the ranch to tell Ann Marie.

*She's not going to be happy about this, I'm afraid. I know. I'll tell her once the stallion wins, she can pay me off with the money he'll earn. Maybe that will pacify her.*

"Who the hell am I kiddin'? She's gonna be madder than a wet hen."

Stopping the truck in front of the house, he blew out a steadying breath and popped the door open. When he slammed it behind him, he jumped and laughed out loud.

*Ann Marie can tie me up in knots and make me jumpier than a cat in a room full of rocking chairs.*

"Travis," she said, bringing his thoughts back to her, sitting on the porch.

"Can we talk?"

"Do I have a choice?"

"You always have a choice, Ann Marie." The forced exhale made him think how ornery she could be.

"Shall we take this inside?"

"After you," he said, sweeping his hand wide.

He couldn't help but watch her ass and admire how her jeans fit tight across those cheeks that begged for his hands.

"Stop watching my ass, Travis," she grumbled even though she didn't turn around.

"Why? You have a nice one. No harm in watchin', even if you won't let me touch anymore."

"Your choice."

"So you say." They walked inside the living room, and he saw Kelly and Tyler watching television. "Can we go in the office?"

She shrugged her shoulders and continued down the hall. Once they were behind closed doors, he opened the papers he held in his hands and gave them to her.

"What's this?"

"The payoff on the notes."

"You can't be serious. All of them? I thought you said there was something like twenty-thousand owed?"

"Actually the total came to twenty nine thousand four hundred and twenty six dollars."

Her butt hit the chair behind the desk, and her mouth hung open.

"You paid them in full?" she asked in a whisper.

"Yes."

"Why?"

"Because I refuse to let you lose this place. It means everything to you."

Tears welled up in her eyes, and one fell in a watery streak down her cheek. "I don't know what to say."

"Nothin'. I know you'll pay me back in time, and I ain't worried about it. The money was just sitting in the bank anyway."

She sniffed, wiped her cheek and then pulled out a piece of paper while he wondered what the hell she was up to as she scratched something across it. A few moments later, she handed him the sheet.

"Now you can't leave. You have purchased one quarter share of the Double S."

# Chapter Twelve

"You can't be serious, Ann Marie. A quarter share of this place is worth a lot more than thirty thousand."

"It doesn't matter. You've purchased it. It's yours to do with as you wish. If you want to sell it, then go ahead. I'll have the surveyor's out here next month so they can section off a piece for you. That way if you want to build a house or whatever, you can." She squared her shoulders, and braced for the explosion she knew would come. Staying here wasn't what he wanted. Forcing his hand like this would piss him off.

"I'm not takin' this." He tried to push it back into her hands, but she refused, holding up her hands so he couldn't.

"Yes you are and I'll hear no more about it. I'll have a deed drawn up with the lawyer next week."

"I'm not takin' your land, and I'm not stayin' here."

Her gaze dropped to the desktop, and she chewed her lip for a moment, trying not to let her heart break in her chest with his words.

*Not staying. Not staying.*

She lifted her face and met his eyes again. "It doesn't matter, I guess. It's still yours. Whether you stay or not is your business."

*Okay, change the subject while he's speechless.*

"When is Tucker supposed to be here?"

"In a day or two, accordin' to my mom."

"Good. We could use the help. Are you riding out to look for the bull this morning?"

"Yeah. You?"

"Yes." Coming to her feet, she said, "Kelly is going to keep an eye on Tyler."

Her jeans bunched at her hips, so she pulled at the seams to tug them back into place Hunger reflected in Travis' eyes as their gazes met. His pupils were dilated, and his breathing had sped up a little.

"Shall we?"

The question hung in the thick air around them, and she wasn't sure if she meant to find the bull or run upstairs and jump his hot body for a few hours.

*I'm the one who made the hands off stipulation.*

"Find the bull," she clarified, and he nodded stiffly before he turned and strode for the door.

For the next several hours, they rode side-by-side while they looked for any sign of the bull or the missing cattle. They didn't talk much, only a few words here and there. The low baritone of his voice drove her wild with every word. Awareness zipped along her nerve endings with each look, every shift of his powerful thighs in the saddle and every change of position he made. They ate in the saddle, drank in the saddle and only stopped to look at tracks or take small breaks.

The sun was setting behind the hills when they rode for home.

*Home. Only my home, at least for now. How am I going to feel if he builds a house on the property I gave him and brings home another woman to share it? I don't think I'll like it at all, but what to do. What are my feelings for Travis anyway?*

"What are you thinking about?" he asked, tilting his head to the side.

"Do you want the truth? I'm afraid you won't like it."

His eyes narrowed into slit. "Never lie to me, Ann Marie, and we won't have a problem."

"All right then. I was thinking about you."

"Me?"

"Yep and how I wouldn't like it if you built a house on the land I gave you and brought another woman there to live."

"Oh?"

One shoulder lifted in a shrug, and she avoided his gaze.

The rest of the ride back to the house was made in uncomfortable silence. At this point, she didn't know what to do. Having Travis in her bed seemed like a great plan to start with, but now her heart wanted more. She wanted more. The thought of him leaving broke her heart, and she didn't know how she was going to handle it.

As they rode up to the house, she spotted a vehicle she'd never seen before.

"I wonder who that is?" she asked.

"Tucker."

"Oh?"

"Yeah. That's his truck."

"Good. I'm glad he made it. If nothing else, I'm sure you could use some help with the horses, so you can concentrate on the stallion, get him ready to run and then be on your way to the next job. I won't even hold you to the six months."

\* \* \* \*

*Well, that's a relief. I can leave when the stallion's ready, and she won't hold me to the six-month agreement. Then why do I feel like shit?*

"Hey, Tucker."

"Hey, brother. You look good. This place must agree with you. I don't think I've seen a smile on your face like that in years." Tucker held out his hand to Ann Marie. "Hi. I'm Tucker Brooks."

"Nice to meet you. I'm Ann Marie."

"You didn't tell me she was gorgeous, Travis."

"Tucker, mind your manners," Travis growled.

"What? Just sayin'."

"Aren't you the charmer, Tucker," Ann Marie said, looping her hand through his arm. "Why don't you come inside the house and we'll get something cool to drink while Travis puts the horses away."

*I'm pretty sure I just got the brush-off.*

"Damn women," he grumbled, grabbing the horse's reins and making tracks for the barn.

Once the horses were brushed and settled, he walked back for the house. Tucker and Ann Marie getting cozy didn't sit well with him.

Kelly answered the door at his knock and ushered him inside.

"They are in the kitchen."

"Thanks."

"No problem." When he started to brush past her, she asked, "Can I ask you a question?"

With a shrug of his shoulders, he said, "Sure."

"What's going on between you and my sister?"

"I don't know what you mean, Kel."

"You two were sleeping together and getting along great. Now, I don't know what to think."

"Things are kind of tense between us at the moment."

"You could say that again. She's in there with Tucker, acting like she's all into him."

"Really," he murmured, his gaze shooting to the doorway of the kitchen with the sound of Ann Marie's light tinkle of laughter.

"Yeah. I don't begrudge her being happy. She put up with a hell of a lot of shit from our dad, and then John. Don't get me wrong. John was a good guy and did a wonderful thing by marrying her and getting her out of our parents' home, but he wasn't the love of her life. I've told her not to settle for anything less than fireworks when she settles down again." Her head cocked to the side, and she gave him a penetrating look. "You know. I thought the two of you were good together, and I thought you were beginning to care about her."

"I do care."

"But you aren't in love with her."

"I won't fall in love again."

"Sometimes our hearts don't listen to our brains very well, Travis. By the look in your eyes, I'd say you are already there."

Without another word, she turned and left him standing in the foyer, her words ringing in his ears and making his heart dance to its own tune. One he wasn't sure he liked.

*In love with Ann Marie? I can't be. I refuse to allow those emotions again.*

Squaring his shoulders, he walked toward the kitchen. He stopped in the doorway, and his heart dropped to his toes when he saw Ann Marie's hand on Tucker's arm. The first thought running through his mind was to rip Tucker's head off.

*I won't let a woman come between me and my brother.*

"Hey. Why don't I show you around a little so you can get settled," he said, schooling his expression into one of indifference.

"Sure, bro." Tucker stood and leaned down to kiss Ann Marie on the cheek. "Thanks for making me feel so welcome."

The kiss felt like a punch to the gut for Travis.

"Come on. We've got work to do."

Tucker grinned and winked at Ann Marie, and Travis growled low in his throat. He knew his brother could wrap a woman around his little finger with that smile if he wanted to, and Travis was sure Ann Marie would be no exception to the rule.

He rounded on Tucker once they reached the barn and said, "Keep your hands off Ann Marie."

"Why? She's a pretty woman, all alone out here. This spread is big enough to keep even the biggest wanderer busy. I bet she's a firecracker in bed, too. And, she seems to like me."

"I'll fucking kick your ass if so much as lay a hand on her. Brother or not."

"Whoa! That sounds a little possessive there, Travis. Are you sure you ain't tied up with the little woman? You're looking might green around the gills."

"She's too old for you."

"Too old? If she's a day over twenty-eight, I'd be surprised."

"Thirty-two, to be exact."

"Ah. More up your alley then, hey brother?"

"Playing games isn't her thing. She needs a husband, not a boy-toy."

"Like you?"

*Like me?* Kelly's words came back to haunt him, too. *Am I already in love with her?*

\* \* \* \*

Over the next several weeks, Travis kept Tucker busy running the stock animals while he worked the stallion. The races would be starting soon, and he needed to make sure Black was ready.

*Not that I'm trying to keep Tucker and Ann Marie apart.*

"Yeah, right," his heart said.

The perpetual hard-on he sported these days drove him nuts and he couldn't seem to bed any other woman, either. No matter how sexy, pretty, funny or whatever they were, his dick didn't respond in the normal manner, except when he smelled the sweet scent of honeysuckle or experienced the innocent brush of Ann Marie's body.

"The woman is going to slowly drive me insane. That's it. She's made it her mission to send me to the funny farm," he grumbled as he slipped the bridle over Black's head.

Today, he'd take the stallion through his paces.

"Travis?"

*Ah, hell. Ann Marie.*

"Yeah?"

"I need to talk to you in the office. Can you leave him for a minute?"

"I'll be right there," he answered and she nodded before she walked back toward the house.

The forced exhale from his lips did nothing to calm the blood rushing in his ears while he watched her pretty little ass in those jeans.

Several minutes later, he walked into the office and shut the door behind him.

"You wanted to see me?"

"Yes. When will the stallion be ready to run?"

"Couple of weeks, why?"

"No particular reason. There are a few qualifying runs coming up and I didn't know if he would be ready to go." She pulled open the middle desk drawer. "And, I needed to give you this."

"What's that?"

"The deed to your land."

"We had this discussion. I'm not takin' your property."

"Take it or leave it, Travis. One thousand acres has already been deeded to you and transferred with the county," she replied, shrugging her shoulders and laying the paper on the desk.

"Why are you insisting on this? You could have paid me back after Black won."

Her eyes narrowed, and a single tear single down her cheek.

"Because even though I didn't want it to happen, and I know you don't feel the same, I'm in love with you, and I don't want you to leave. If you own part of this ranch, I'm hoping maybe someday you'll come back here."

They stared at each other for what seemed like an eternity, and he was sure she felt the same.

"I can't give you what you want, darlin'."

Coming to her feet, she walked around the desk and stopped in front of him.

"I don't want promises you can't keep. You've shut your heart off to everyone because of Catherine. Truthfully? I wish I could hurt her right now for doing this to you." A small chuckle left her mouth. "I wish I'd met you first. Before John, and before Catherine, because I think we are amazing together, and I don't want these feelings to end."

Standing on her toes, she wrapped her hand behind his neck and pulled his mouth down to hers in a searing kiss.

*Good Lord, she tastes fantastic.*

A tortured groan left his mouth to be swallowed by hers when she swept her tongue between his lips. His hands were everywhere. Clothes disappeared under seeking touches and bold strokes until she stood naked in front of him. One palm cupped her left breast while he thumbed her already hard nipple.

"Yes. Touch me," she whispered, bowing her back to push the soft, round flesh further into his hand. "God, I need you."

"You have no idea how bad I want you, Ann Marie. I ache for you. It's been hell staying away."

"I know, and I'm sorry."

Spread out on top of the mahogany desk like an offering to the pagan gods, her hooded eyes called to him, begged him, and he could do nothing but give her what she wanted. It wasn't in him to deny her.

"Love me, Travis."

The words echoed around in his mind while he watched her. The same words sent an arrow straight to his heart. *I can't love her.*

"Your heart belonged to her the minute she shed tears for you because of your son," his heart whispered, taking him beyond thought or reason.

Refusing to listen, he shook his head.

His tongue blazed a trail from her left nipple to the right, and then he flicked it.

A low moan rumbled in her chest.

Licking his way up to her ear, he nibbled the spot below it and then took the lobe between his teeth, tugging lightly. The moment his lips touched hers, he lost all thought. The warmth of her mouth pulled him in and scattered his control to the wind. One hand slipped down her flat stomach and then dove between her opened thighs.

Whimpers left her throat while their tongues dueled and sparred inside their mouths.

Two fingers pushed inside her and her hips arched toward his touch.

"I need to taste you, darlin'. I love your sweetness," he said, trailing his mouth down her chest and across her stomach until he reached the swollen center of her desire.

His cock ached with need. His balls pulled up tight against his groin with a want so strong, he wasn't sure he'd be able to stand it until she had at least one orgasm, but he had to. Making her feel good had to be a priority.

One swipe of his tongue against her clit and she almost came off the desk. Her heels hung on the edge of the top as she splayed her legs open for him. Each swipe of his tongue, she lifted her butt up and he knew it wouldn't take much to throw her over the edge into completion. Stiffening his tongue, he speared her pussy several times and then went back to toggling her clit.

"Ah, God," she moaned as she came apart.

Lapping at her pussy until she stopped trembling, he took everything he gave him.

He stood and positioned his hard shaft at her opening, and then he pushed inside with a tortured slowness.

"Hard, Travis. Please. It's been too long. I need hard and fast," she murmured.

Control snapped. He pushed into her with enough forced to scoot her back on the desk. Two hands anchored her hips and pulled her back toward him.

"Yes. Yes. Yes," she panted, as he rode her hard, his own grunts of satisfaction slipping from between his lips.

When his orgasm slammed into his nuts and zipped to the end of his cock, he spilled everything inside her hot center. She moaned his name and climaxed again.

Breathing hard, he slumped over her chest and buried his nose in her neck, allowing himself to inhale her sweet scent.

"I hadn't planned on doing this so fast," he grumbled.

"Yeah, well. I think we were both a little horny."

A chuckle left his lips. "A little?"

"Okay, a lot horny."

They both moaned when he pulled from her warmth. She sat up on the desk and scooted off to grab her clothes. With slow almost jerky motions, she pulled everything on and tried to straighten her hair.

"Are we okay, Ann Marie?"

Her eyes widened and she went back around the back of the desk. "Okay how, Travis? Am I going to let you back into my bed? Yes. I don't like being apart from you. I know you don't love me, and there isn't anything I can do to change the facts. They are what they are. But I'll take what I can get."

"I don't know what to say."

"What I want to hear is I love you, Ann Marie, but it won't happen," she said with a shrug.

"I wish…" his words were cut off by a loud banging on the front door of the house.

"What the hell?"

A quick glance in his direction and she raced for the door.

She got into the hall and stopped so suddenly, he almost slammed into her back.

"You aren't welcome here," Kelly screamed and tried to shut the door.

"You'll let me in right now, Kelly."

"Who is that?"

Ann Marie turned tear-filled eyes to him and started to shake.

"Honey?" he asked, his arm going around her shoulders to steady her.

"My father."

"I'll take care of this," Travis growled, moving from her side and approaching the man standing in the doorway arguing with Ann Marie's sister. "Is there something I can help you with?"

"Yes. Get this girl out of my way. I need to talk to Ann Marie."

Hands on his hips, he faced the man who abused the woman he'd come to care for and her sister. "She doesn't want you here."

"I don't care. She's my daughter, and I need to talk to her."

Leo Boyd must have seen Ann Marie standing behind him because his gaze went over Travis' shoulder. "Ann Marie."

"What do you want?" she asked in a voice Travis had never heard before, and it broke his heart to see her so vulnerable.

"Your mother."

"What about Mom? What the hell have you done to her now? Did you finally kill her?" Her voice escalated to the point she almost screamed.

"She's fine or at least I think she is. I don't know."

"You don't know?"

"She left me."

"She left you?" Ann Marie started giggling. Her soft bubbles of giggles turned into loud peals of laughter, and she slid to the floor.

"It's not funny," Leo spat, his face turning redder the louder her laughs got.

"It's hilarious. She finally got tired of your abuse, and it only took thirty years."

"Where's John, Ann Marie. He'll understand."

"John died a year ago. This is my home, so get out and don't come back."

"Sir, you need to leave. You aren't welcome here," Travis said, taking the man's arm, but Leo pulled it out of his grasp.

A snarl curled Leo's lip, and then he turned his attention back to Ann Marie. "Hooked up with some other stud? I always figured you were like a bitch in heat."

"Don't. If you say one more word, I'll kill you," Travis growled stopping nose-to-nose with Leo.

"Who the hell are you?"

"Ann Marie's fiancé."

# Chapter Thirteen

*I didn't just hear what I thought I heard. Fiancé?*

"You're getting married again?"

"Uh, yeah," Ann Marie replied, glancing quickly at Kelly, who stood openmouthed.

"This isn't over. I'll be back, and if I find out you know where your mother is, I'll take it out of your hide."

Travis grabbed Leo by the front of his shirt, twisting the material in his hands, and got right in her father's face.

"You won't touch her or Kelly ever again or you'll answer to me. Got it?"

"Do you know who I am?"

"Yes I do and I don't give a flyin' fuck. If you don't want your dirty laundry aired to the whole fucking country, you'll leave them both alone. You are a wussy of a man if you beat up on women."

Travis pushed Leo back against the wall, and Leo brushed the front of his skirt as if to tidy the wrinkles.

"You'll be sorry you got in the middle of this."

"I don't think so. If you ever come back here again, Mr. Boyd, you'll be sorry you got between me and the woman I love. I won't tolerate you layin' a hand on either Ann Marie or Kelly. I've got a bull whip, and trust me, I know how to use it."

"I'm not done with you or you, Ann Marie."

"Yes, you are," Travis said stepping closer while Leo moved toward the door. "If you put one tire tread on this property in the future, I'll have you arrested for trespassing."

Leo grumbled under his breath, but didn't say anything else as he walked out the front door and slammed it shut behind him.

Ann Marie leaned against the doorframe with her mouth hanging open, staring at Travis.

A moment later, she said, "Kelly, can you leave us alone for a minute."

"Sure." Kelly hugged Travis and then stepped back. "I guess congrats are in order." She kissed him on the cheek, winked at Ann Marie and then walked into the living room.

"Would you like to explain?"

"Can we go back into the office?" he asked, running his fingers through his hair.

When they were behind closed doors, she braced herself against the desk and folded her arms over her breasts. "Correct me if I'm wrong, but I'm pretty sure I don't remember you saying you loved me, and I'm sure I would have remembered a marriage proposal."

"He pissed me off."

"I'm aware of that, but getting you mad gets an 'I love you' and a marriage proposal? Because obviously I've been doing this all wrong for the last few months." A rush of air from between her lips came out in a sigh. "I'm sorry. I guess I'm giving you a rough time over this. I know you didn't mean what you said, but it caught me off guard. You didn't expect to see my father, and neither did I. It was a shock to both of us. I'm glad Tyler didn't hear what you said. Kelly, I can deal with. Disappointing Tyler is a whole different story."

*Knock. Knock.*

"Who is it?" she asked.

"Me, Mom—can I come in?"

"Sure, Ty."

Her son pushed open the door, and the beaming smile on his face had her heart dropping into her toes.

"You and Travis are getting married?"

*Oh, hell!*

* * * *

"Listen, Ty. There's been a mistake," she started, but Travis interrupted her.

"That's right, buddy."

"When?"

"We don't know for sure yet, Ty. I asked her a little bit ago. We haven't had time to talk about it."

*Okay, I haven't asked her, but he doesn't need to know that. But wait! What the hell am I doing? I don't want to get married again.*

"Your mom and I need to talk right now though, okay? Can you leave us alone for a little bit?"

Tyler nodded, threw his arms around Travis' waist and hugged him. "I'm glad you're going to be my new dad."

*Holy shit!*

The boy pulled away and disappeared out the door.

"Now what are you going to do?" she asked, tapping her foot on the floor. "You told my son we are getting married."

"So we will."

"Wait just a damned minute here, Travis. You don't love me, and you don't want to get married. Why are you doing this?"

"I wish I knew." He stopped in front of her and took her face between his palms. "Listen, darlin', it's not that I don't care about you, because I do. In love with you? I don't know. The words came awfully easy out there in the hall. And right now, the idea of spending the rest of my life with you doesn't sound so bad. At least we get along."

"What are you saying, Travis?"

"Maybe we should get married."

She twisted out of his hands and paced in front of the window. "You have lost ever lovin' mind."

"Are you saying you don't want to marry me?"

"This is crazy, Travis. You don't want to get married again. You told me as much."

"Yes, I do."

"No, you don't. Listen to yourself. You are trying to rationalize it in your mind that it's something you need to do to protect me and Kelly. I can take care of myself."

"Against him? I don't think so. Let me help you."

"You've already done enough. You paid off the loans, you trained the stallion..."

"The stallion is my job, Ann Marie."

"I know, but taking care of things with the finances isn't. It's my job, and I'm doing a really piss poor at it."

"You didn't even know about the loans."

"But I should have. Why didn't I get any statements or anything from the bank to let me know? Can you answer that?"

"Mr. Aslind said they were balloon loans, which means you wouldn't have known about them until the final payment came due in about three months—if I hadn't found them on the computer in the barn office."

"It doesn't matter. John didn't share it with me. Do you have any idea how this whole thing makes me feel? He must have felt I couldn't handle it. Incompetent is the word coming to mind here. I thought we ran this place together, Travis, but he didn't want me to know how financially in trouble we were." She threw up her hands, and he could tell she was becoming irrational with everything going on.

"Ann Marie," he whispered, pulling her to his chest and trapping her arms to her sides. Wetness seeped through the material of his shirt, lodging a large lump in his throat. "It's in a man's nature to take care of a woman. I'm sure John didn't want you to worry."

"You are defending him," she murmured against his shoulder.

"I know."

"Why? Would you have done the same thing?"

"Not fair, darlin'. Your question is loaded." A watery smile lifted the corners of her mouth when she leaned back, and he brushed the tears from her cheeks with his thumb. "You know I would have."

"I'm sure you would. That's why I said it." She stepped out of his embrace and rubbed her arms as if she wanted to ward off chills.

"So what's it gonna be, Ann Marie?"

Her eyebrow rose in question.

"Are you gonna marry me, or not?"

"Is that supposed to be a proposal? Because if it is, you need work, buddy."

"I'm thinkin' this way. We could be partners in the ranch and stuff."

"A marriage of convenience? They don't do those anymore, Travis."

"I realize that, but having a man around would keep the wolves at bay. You wouldn't have to worry about men dating you or trying to get you in bed for the ranch. I have the financial resources to keep this place running until Black gets his feet in the races." A chuckle bubbled from his lips. "I won't be bringin' another woman home to a house I built on the land you deeded to me. In fact, you could tear up the piece of paper."

"And you would have access to half of everything on this place," she murmured, her eyes showing nothing of the emotions running through her.

"True, but we can draw up a pre-nup if you want. I don't want your ranch, darlin'."

"I suppose it would mean you could and would come and go as you please."

He ducked his head a little sheepishly. "Depends."

"On?"

"You. If I'm gettin' lovin' at home, why should I go anywhere else?"

"So you would expect this to me a real marriage, to some degree."

"You said you loved me."

"Yes, I did, but you also said you didn't love me." She stared at the ceiling for a moment before she leveled her gaze on him again. "I'll have to think about this, Travis. I don't want to be in a loveless marriage."

"All right. Put it this way—if in five years we can't say 'I love you' to each other, then we split up. You'll still have your ranch because we'll have the pre-nup, which will say we both leave this marriage with what we came in with. Agreed?"

"I don't understand you. Why are you so willing to give up your freedom for me? It appears I'm getting the better end of this deal. What are you getting out of it?"

"You."

* * * *

"Hey, Mom."

"Travis? This is a surprise. You never call home."

"I know, but I needed to tell you something and give you a quick invite."

"Invite? I don't understand."

"Can you and dad get to Bryan two weeks from now?"

"I suppose. I'd have to check the calendar and make sure we don't already have an auction or something going on, but why?"

"I'm gettin' married."

"You're what? I didn't just hear you say you are getting married again, did I?"

He chuckled. "Yeah, Mom, you did."

"To who?" A bubbly laughter erupted on the other end of the phone. "Oh! I know, to that woman on the ranch. What was her name? Ann Marie? The one who put you in your place the first time you met. This is rather sudden, though, isn't it?"

"I'll fill you in on the details later, Mom. The weddin' will be two weeks from this coming Saturday. Not a big thing—a few friends from around here, my family, so spread the word to the sisters. Tucker's already here, so he'll be there. Her sister Kelly and her son Tyler."

"What about her parents?"

"Bad blood there. They won't be here. Well, maybe her mom, but it depends on if Ann Marie can get in touch with her."

"Don't worry, Travis. We'll be there. Come hell or high water."

"I knew I could count on you. One thing."

"What?"

"I need you to help make Ann Marie feel welcome. She's had it pretty rough with her family and all."

"Of course. She'll be your wife. Why wouldn't we make her feel welcome?"

"You'll understand when I give you the details, but for now, I need to go. I have to find a jeweler in town."

"Don't do that, honey. Watch for a special delivery in the next day or two."

"Why? What are you up to, Mom?"

"Nothing. Just watch for them and give me the address there."

Travis shook his head. His mother was up to something and he wasn't sure he would like it. Once he rattled off the address to her, they hung up and he whistled softly as he went to find his bride-to-be.

* * * *

The day of the wedding dawned bright. Ann Marie hadn't slept a wink the night before, and her stomach felt like a thousand butterflies had been let loose in there. Her silky robe swished around her legs when she moved from window to window. It had been one of her bridal gifts from Travis. One hand went to her belly while she tried to calm the nervous jitters and watched the busy activity going on in the backyard.

Shelia Brooks directed people like a drill sergeant from the patio below. Travis' sisters were nowhere to be found at the moment, but Ann Marie knew they weren't too far behind. Travis' father, Walter Brooks, sat on the low wall and watched his wife with a grin on his face. Ann Marie certainly could tell where Travis and Tucker got their looks. The color of their eyes came from their father, but their hair color and complexion came from their mother.

Her breath caught in her throat when her husband-to-be strolled from the barn, his long legs eating up the distance between there and the patio. The roar of his laughter reached Ann Marie above and made her smile, before a worried frown pulled down the corners of her mouth.

*What in the hell am I doing? I'm supposed to marry Travis today, and I'm scared to death. I pray I can trust him.*

The bull had been located at the neighbor's ranch and brought home, but they never figured out where the missing cattle went.

*God, please don't let Travis be mixed up in this.*

The beautiful diamond on her left hand twinkled in the morning sun streaming through the window. His mother's.

The day it arrived, he'd insisted on taking her out for a romantic dinner in Houston, at one of the most expensive restaurants in town. A small, intimate table for two. Champagne, roses, and soft candlelight greeted her at the table. He'd gone all out. Had she ever thought of Travis as not romantic? She wasn't sure. Even if she'd teased him about needing work on his proposal, he had definitely made up for it during their dinner. Soft kisses on her neck, holding her hand, and when he proposed properly, it was down on one knee, with a twinkle in his blue eyes and a sexy smile on his mouth. She couldn't help but say yes. The yellow, marquee cut diamond appeared in his hand, and when he slipped it on her finger, she almost died, but he wouldn't take no for an answer. He insisted on her wearing it and told her it would hurt his mother's feelings if she didn't.

His family had arrived at the house the day before and had taken over. Women bustled around, his mother ordering everyone to their places, his sisters making her feel like part of the family from the beginning, and she couldn't help but love him for it.

*Not that I wasn't already in love with him anyway, but I'm sure he said something to his mother about making me feel welcome. It would be just like Travis to do something like that.*

A soft knock sounded on the door, and she called for the visitor to come in.

Kelly poked her head around the corner, and smiled as she came inside and shut it behind her.

"You okay?"

"Other than scared to death, yeah."

"You'll be fine, sis. You love him."

"I know. I wish I didn't. I wish I wasn't getting into a one-sided marriage. I didn't want it to be this way, Kel, but the last thing I wanted was for him to walk out of my life and never come back."

Kelly wrapped her in a hug and squeezed. "I know, Ann Marie, but even if he doesn't love you now, he will in time. I think he's already there. He's being stubborn about it, that's all."

"I hope you're right. We've made a deal. If within five years he can't tell me he loves me, then I'll let him walk away."

"You're serious?"

"Yeah."

"Wow. That's pretty harsh."

"It's the way it has to be. I won't trap him into this marriage if he doesn't want to be here."

"Well, today is your wedding. What do you say we get your hair and makeup done? Travis' sisters are chomping at the bit to get up here and help you."

A nervous laugh bubbled from her mouth. "I can imagine." With a sigh of resignation, she said, "Get them up here, so we can get this over with."

"You act like you are going to your own hanging, Ann Marie. It's a wedding. You should be happy."

"I am. See?" She forced a bright smile and Kelly shook her head.

*I don't want to think about what tonight will bring. The last time we made love was on the desk in the office the day dad showed up and caused all kinds of ruckus. The day Travis said he loved me, but didn't mean it.*

Laughter bounced off the walls as Travis' sisters and mother filled the room with their chatter.

"Come on, Ann Marie. Sit. We need to get you ready," Sheila said.

"The wedding isn't until one, and it's only ten," she replied.

"Doesn't matter, dear. We have work to do. The cook we hired to cater the reception is going to be bringing us up something to eat in a few minutes."

"I'm not sure I can eat."

"Bridal nerves?" his sister, Jessica, asked.

"A little."

"It's normal to be nervous. Travis is a great catch though," Jan, another sister, added.

"Not that all of you aren't a little partial," Ann Marie said.

"Not us," Jess replied as the rest of them laughed.

"Enough girls. We need to get busy on your make-up, your hair and your dress. You'll be a beautiful bride."

Ann Marie laughed. "How can I not with a hairdresser in the family?" She indicated his sister, Charlotte with a wave of her hand and a smile.

"Okay. Out of the way, ladies, and let me work," Charlotte insisted with a smile, waving her siblings and her mother aside and pushing Ann Marie down on the chair in front of the vanity.

Her hair ended up on top of her head with several tendrils hanging down around her ears and neck in soft curls. Charlotte did her make-up, and when she finished, Ann Marie gasped at the sight.

"Something wrong?" Charlotte asked.

"No," Ann Marie whispered, touching her hair and face. "It's… beautiful."

"You're beautiful," Shelia said, standing behind her. "Travis is a lucky man."

"I hope I can make him happy."

"He's already happier than I've ever seen him," Jess added. "He smiles and laughs more than he has in years. You are good for him, Ann Marie, and I'm glad he fell in love with you."

*Fell in love with me. Don't I wish?*

The two of them had come to an agreement before his family arrived; they would play the loving couple for them. He didn't want them worrying about him getting into another bad marriage. Not a problem on her part— she loved him anyway, but the way he'd treated her over the last couple of days, she could almost believe he loved her back.

"I know your own mother couldn't be here, Ann Marie, and I'm honored you've chosen to wear the engagement ring I sent to Travis."

"It's gorgeous, Shelia. How could I not?"

"Thank you. It was my first ring, and I always swore I would give it to my eldest son's wife, but I couldn't give it to Catherine. She wasn't right for him." She cleared her throat, and then she continued. "There's one more thing I want you to wear today as something borrowed." Shelia opened a long, slim box and pulled out a perfect strand of gray pearls. "Would you do me the honor of wearing these? They belonged to my grandmother, and each of my girls wore them when they got married. Well, the ones who have gotten married so far."

A round of giggles twittered through the room while the other four stood behind their mother and nodded.

Ann Marie choked back a sob and agreed. His mother placed the strand around her throat and connected the clasp.

"They are amazing," she whispered. "Thank you."

The lone tear slipping down her cheek quickly disappeared with the swipe of a handkerchief.

"No crying," Charlotte said, dabbing at her face. "You'll ruin my make-up job."

A watery chuckle left her mouth. "Sorry."

Breakfast arrived, and they all picked at the wonderful display of fruit, cheeses, croissants, fluffy eggs and meats, while they chatted. Jan and Sheila talked about their own weddings and even Kelly added how she wanted her wedding to be when she finally found the man of her dreams.

"I'm sure he's out there somewhere, Kel," Ann Marie said.

"Oh, I know he is, and I even have an idea of who he is."

"You do? Who?"

"Just a fantasy guy, sis. He's way out of my reach, but I can certainly look for someone like him."

Jessica grabbed the off-white satin dress and held it up. "It's going on noon."

"Really? Wow. Where did the time go?"

"Yep, and you need to get dressed."

Satin material slid over her slip as she stepped into the gown and pulled it up her abdomen and over her shoulders. Kelly zipped it up in the back and hugged her.

"You look beautiful, Ann Marie. I hope I look that good at my wedding."

"Go on with you," she murmured, sniffing back the tears threatening to fall.

Kelly adjusted the small veil on Ann Marie's head, kissed her cheek and stepped back. The woman in the mirror looked nothing like her. The gown hugged her curves and fell just above her knees in the front with the back falling to her heels. The sleeves brushed seductively against her shoulders and felt like heaven on her skin. A scooped neckline lay soft against her chest, covering her breasts, but leaving enough cleavage to tempt any man, even her husband-to-be.

A soft knock at the door brought her attention around as Tyler poked his head through the portal.

"Wow. You look pretty, Mom."

"Thanks, buddy." He walked to her side and hugged her. "What have you been up to this morning?"

"Keeping Travis company while he walked back and forth in the barn."

The women laughed.

"Sounds like our brother," Jan replied.

Shelia stood by the window and pulled the curtain aside. "The seats are filling up nicely."

"They are?" Ann Marie asked, walking over to peer outside. "Wow! Where did all those people come from?"

"News travels fast among our family. I'm sure, even though they weren't officially invited, Travis' uncles, aunts, cousins and every other relation we have, are out there. In fact, I recognize most of them." A worried frown settled between her eyebrows. "You aren't upset are you?"

"Oh my, no, of course not." She hugged Sheila. "This day is for him, too, not just me. If he wants his family here, then so be it."

"You are totally opposite in temperament from Catherine," Jessica added from the other side of the bed. "But from what I've heard, you have a bit of temper, too."

Ann Marie blushed.

"We heard about your little speech when Travis said he wouldn't work for a woman," Charlotte added with a little laugh.

"I'm glad you put him in his place, Ann Marie," Jan said. "He knows better than to cop an attitude like that around home. We girls would have kicked his ass."

The imagine of his sisters giving him shit brought a smile to her lips that lasted until the music started to play outside and her stomach flipped over.

"I think it's about time," Shelia chimed in. "Shall we go?"

Ann Marie shook her head.

"You aren't changing your mind now, Mom," Tyler said, taking her hand and tugging softly. "Travis is waiting."

She allowed Tyler to pull her out her bedroom door and around to the front of the house. Her son would be walking her down the aisle to meet her new husband. Sheila and all the sisters kissed her on the cheek, smiled encouragingly and disappeared out the front door to take their places. Kelly stayed behind because she was maid of honor, but when the music started, she too left Ann Marie standing in the foyer with Tyler.

"Do you love him, Mom?"

"Yeah, Ty, I do."

"Like you loved, Dad?"

"In a different way, Tyler. Your dad meant everything to me, and he'll always hold a special place in my heart, but Travis makes me feel different in ways you'll understand someday."

Ty nodded and slipped her hand through the crook of his arm as the bridal march started to play beyond the door.

After a small, forced exhale, she walked out into the bright sunlight. At first, the glare blinded her, but she blinked several times and the whole scene came into focus.

White and pink flowers lined the chairs spread out on either side of the aisle. Faces blurred with the tears in her eyes, but the smiles remained. Everyone seemed so happy to see her marry Travis. A trellis near the front was draped with flowers cascading over the top and down the sides. Kelly stood to the left of the trellis and, oh God, Travis stood on the right, with Tucker beside him.

A black jacket enhanced his broad shoulders, with a small tie at his throat and his black Stetson on his head. A smile twitched at the corners of her mouth the moment her gaze skimmed down his frame and she saw the black jeans on encasing his powerful thighs and trim hips.

Breath hitched in her throat as she met his eyes. The smile gracing his lips and the twinkle in his gaze stopped her heart.

*He almost looks like he's in love.*

* * * *

*Holy shit!*

Tucker elbowed him and he wondered if he'd said it out loud.

"Damn she's pretty," Tucker whispered behind him while they watched Ann Marie come toward them, holding onto Tyler's arm.

*And she's all mine.*

She finally reached his side, and he leaned down to kiss her on the cheek. "I'm one hell of a lucky man."

A pretty pink blush stained her cheeks and she dropped her gaze to the green carpet of grass under their feet.

"Shall we begin?" the minister asked when they faced him.

The warmth of her hand in his made him ache for her. Not crawling into her bed with her over the last week just about drove him past crazy, but the surprise he'd set up for their wedding night would be the crowning glory to their wedding. A couple of times over the time they'd spent together, she had revealed the lack of vacations since she left home. She and John never felt comfortable leaving the ranch for any length of time during their marriage, but Travis knew his father and mother would be staying until they returned, to watch over the place. If they didn't get away now, they wouldn't for a while.

The stallion was ready to run, and the races started in a little over a week.

The minister's voice brought Travis back to the task at hand.

"I do believe the two of you have vows you wish to say to each other?"

"Yes," he answered and turned to face Ann Marie. "I, Travis Walter Brooks, take you, Ann Marie Skolack, to be my lawfully wedded wife, my constant friend, my faithful partner and my love from this day forward. In the presence of God, our family and friends, I offer you my solemn vow to be your faithful partner in sickness and in health, in good times and in bad, and in joy as well as in sorrow. I promise to love you unconditionally, to support you in your goals, to honor and respect you, to laugh with you and cry with you, and to cherish you for as long as we both shall live."

*Okay, that's was easy.*

Ann Marie frowned, and he didn't like the look on her face. Yes, he'd changed the vows a little from what they discussed, but he meant them— every word.

"Ann Marie?" the minister asked, concerned when she didn't immediately speak her vows.

She cleared her throat and said, "Travis Walter Brooks, I take you to be my lawfully wedded husband. Before these witnesses I vow to love you and care for you as long as we both shall live. I take you with all your faults and your strengths as I offer myself to you with my faults and strengths. I will help you when you need help, and I will turn to you when I need help. I choose you as the person with whom I will spend my life."

They exchanged rings, and then the minister said, "You may kiss your bride". Travis lifted her veil and leaned toward her. The crowd disappeared with the touch of her lips.

When he finally lifted his head, he smiled and brushed her ear with his nose and murmured, "God, I can't wait to get you alone."

"May I present to you, Mr. and Mrs. Travis Brooks," the minister said, announcing them to the well-wishers around them.

The crowd enveloped them in hugs and kissed until his mother broke through the throng of people and led them to the tent side aside for the reception and formal pictures.

As the music started, he swept her up in his arms and pulled her out into the middle of the makeshift dance floor.

"What's wrong?" he asked, seeing the frown on her face.

"You changed the vows."

"Yes, I did. I think the new ones said more of what I felt than the old ones."

"Why didn't you tell me you were going to change them?"

"I found those this morning on the web. I never saw you to tell you."

"We agreed on the others."

"Why is this such an issue, darlin'?"

"It's not, I guess. The ones you said were beautiful. I'm sorry you didn't mean them."

"I did, Ann Marie. Every word."

# Chapter Fourteen

"Ann Marie!" a bellowing voice yelled from near the house.

"I don't believe this," she whispered turning away from Travis.

"That son of a bitch has balls showing up at our wedding," Travis answered, following behind her. "Let me get the two deputies."

"No, let me talk to him first," she replied, touching his arm.

"He has no business here, darlin'. I told him not to come back here."

"By the tone of his voice, I'd guess he's drunk."

"All the more reason to have him arrested."

They walked into the sunlight as Leo Boyd yelled again, "Ann Marie! Goddamn it girl, get out here."

"What do you want?" she asked, approaching the staggering man on her front lawn.

"Where's your mother? I know she's here. She wouldn't miss this."

"I have no idea. Momma didn't come."

"Bullshit. Where the hell is she?"

"You need to leave, Mr. Boyd," Travis said, stepping up to her side.

"Get the hell away from me. I'll do as I please. I'm a fucking senator. You can't tell me what to do."

Travis nodded to the two deputies standing off to the side.

"I want him off this property and charged with trespassing."

"No problem, Travis. We'll take care of it," Deputy Jackson replied. They grabbed Leo by the arm, but he managed to slip out of their clutches and approach her.

"You fucking slut!" Leo screamed, and slapped her hard enough to jerk her out of Travis' hold and throw her to the ground.

A possessive growl left Travis' mouth as he pulled back his fist and hit her father, knocking him unconscious. He hit the ground with an almost audible thump. The deputies pulled Leo's arms behind his back and handcuffed him tightly before they picked him up and shoved him in the back of the squad car.

"Trespassing and assault," Travis told the officers as he helped Ann Marie to her feet.

"Got it," the officer answered, and then shut the door. "We'll need a statement."

"Not a problem," Travis replied, taking her hand in his and leading her into the house. "You need ice on that, darlin'." He rummaged through the drawers for a plastic bag, filled it with ice and pushed it into her hand. He made her to sit down on one of the dining room chairs. "Stay there while I deal with our guests."

"We still need to cut the cake and things."

"We will. Right now, I need to take care of you. I'll be right back."

Moments later he disappeared out the door, and a tear slid down her cheek.

*Why do I let him get to me like this? Leave it to that son of a bitch to ruin my wedding day.* A soft laugh left her mouth. *I can't believe Travis hit him! My knight in shining armor.*

"What are you giggling about, Mrs. Brooks?" Travis asked, returning to her side.

"You."

"Me? What did I do?"

She grabbed his hand and examined his knuckles. Two of them were scraped and had a miniscule amount of blood on them. "You punched my father."

"He deserved it. I don't tolerating anyone hitting my woman."

"Your woman?"

"If I remember correctly, and please tell me if I'm mistaken, didn't you agree to be my wife about an hour ago?"

"Yes, I did."

"Well then, it makes you my woman." He leaned in and kissed her. "Don't worry about him. I'm calling in a few favors, and since he decided not to heed my warning and stay off our property, I'll take care of him."

"What do you mean?"

"Just what I said, darlin'. I'll take care of him, and he won't bother us again. He had his chance." His finger traced the spot on her cheek. "You might have a bit of a bruise. I'm glad we took all the formal weddin' pictures before he showed up. Let's go cut the cake and get all the niceties out of the way so we can leave. I want you naked in my bed in short order."

"Leave? Where are we going? I thought we were staying here tonight."

"Nope. I've got a surprise for you, and it means leaving here for the next week."

"Week? We can't leave for a week, Travis."

"Yes we can. My parents are staying to take care of the ranch and Ty, while we're gone. They will have him spoiled rotten."

Excitement zinged down her back as he traced her ear with his tongue and then slipped down her neck to the hollow between her shoulder and neck.

"God, I need you. We can't go this long again. It's driving me crazy, not having you," he growled against her skin. "I can't wait to hold you, taste you, kiss you and make love to you."

With a playful push, she disengaged his mouth, took his hand and led him outside. The reception seemed to go on forever. They danced, laughed, cut the cake, opened presents and drank until her head began to swim. Time came for them to leave, and she went upstairs to pack a few things. Since he wouldn't tell her where they were going, she wasn't sure what to take, but he'd told her she could buy anything she needed at their mystery honeymoon spot.

*How did I get so lucky? He might not love me, but I have a feeling this is going to be a happy union, and with a little luck and a few prayers, maybe he will come to love me in time.*

Suitcase in hand, she stopped at the front door to wait for her husband with a smile on her face. The party still blared in the backyard, and she hoped everyone was having a good time. From the laughter and the shouts, she figured they were.

A couple of minutes later, Travis walked in the door and said, "Ready?"

"Yes. Are you going to tell me where we are going?"

"No. It's a surprise."

"Brat," she grumbled.

He smiled and brushed his lips against hers.

When they walked outside and around the side of the house to where his truck was parked, they weren't at all shocked to see it decorated with streamers, cans and shaving cream.

"I'm going to kill my sisters."

"You'll have to kill mine too," she replied, spying the groups peeking around the edge of the house. "You are all so busted!"

Giggles and laughter met her ears, and then they disappeared.

"Do you have any idea how hard it is to get shaving cream off paint after it's dried?"

"Well, they can scrub it. Kelly can, anyway, since your sisters will be gone by then."

"You bet she will."

Travis opened the door and she slid inside, while he stuck her suitcase in the back seat. She couldn't help but admire his chest and arms as he moved around the front of the truck. The width of his shoulders and the bulge of his biceps made her want to force him to make love to her right this minute.

*I can't wait to get him between my thighs.*

"Damn, I've turned into such a hussy," she murmured.

Within moments, they were driving down the driveway as guests laughed and waved behind them until they couldn't see anyone anymore.

"Did you enjoy yourself today?" he asked, keeping his eyes locked on the pavement in front of the truck.

"Yes. Well other than getting hit by my father."

Glancing across the truck, he grabbed her hand and kissed her knuckles. "I'm sorry I didn't protect you."

Shock zipped down her back. "Don't be sorry, Travis. It wasn't your fault. I didn't expect him to pull something like that, but he gets drunk, and does crazy things."

"I shouldn't have allowed him to get that close to you."

"Please, don't blame yourself."

"Come here. You're too far away," he said in a low voice, tugging her arm.

With her seatbelt unlatched, she scooted into the middle of the bench seat and buckled the middle belt around her waist.

"Much better." One arm went around her shoulders, and he tucked her in close to his side.

They drove on through town and out onto the highway leading toward Houston. The compatible silence inside the truck warmed her heart while he traced little circles on her shoulder.

When they approached the outskirts of Houston, he asked, "Are you hungry?"

"Heavens no. All the food at the reception, and then you stuffing my mouth with cake…"

"But it was fun licking it off. Too bad we didn't bring any with us."

"Wicked man."

"I'm sure the hotel could bring us up some ice cream. I would love to lick some sweet, chocolate cream off your breasts."

"Hotel?"

"Damn. I gave it away."

"We're going to a hotel? Where?"

"I have reservations at a place on the beach in Galveston. We'll stay there for the next week. We have the honeymoon suite."

"Wow," she breathed, shocked at what he'd done to make their honeymoon special.

Two hours later, they pulled into a fancy resort, and he drove right up to the valet parking attendant.

"Can I help you sir?"

"We have reservations tonight. Can you park this for me?"

"Of course, sir," the valet said, taking down their information, pulling out their bags and waving to a bellhop to help them inside.

The man opened the door to their room several minutes later, and she gasped at the sight that met her eyes. Gold accents, plush carpet, wet bar, separate kitchenette and a view of the bay from the windows.

"My God, Travis, this is beautiful."

Wide glass windows graced one whole wall, reflecting moonlight as it sparkled on the water below.

Travis wrapped his arms around her waist and buried his nose in her neck from behind. "We'll take a walk on the beach after a bit. Right this minute, I need you to kiss me, wife."

"My pleasure, husband."

He swept her up in his arms and sat down with her on the leather sofa so she could straddle his hips. With a low growl in his throat, he fastened his mouth on hers, and his tongue swept between her half-parted lips.

They came up for air several moments later and she said, "How about we stay in tonight. I seemed to be feeling a little bereft."

"You are, huh."

"Yes. It's been an entire week since I've made love with you," she replied, working the buttons on the front of his shirt. "I really was beginning to think you didn't wear shirts with sleeves, you know."

A roar of laughter left his lips.

"I had to dress up for my weddin' didn't I?"

"You still managed to wear jeans though."

"I wondered if you noticed."

"Mmm…yes, I did. But I do have to say, Mr. Brooks, you look damn nice in a tux shirt, black dress jacket, jeans and your boots."

"Quit talkin', woman. I want your mouth."

"Where?" she asked against his lips.

"Ah hell, honey, anywhere you want."

"Sounds promising."

The shirt parted, and she sucked in a ragged breath as she slid her fingers through the hair peeking out.

"Have I told you I love your chest hair?"

"I don't think you have," he replied in a murmur.

"I do. It's so soft."

Scooting back, she dropped to the floor between his knees and gave him a wicked grin. She tugged the rest of his shirt out of his pants and pushed it off his shoulders. She started at the base of his throat where his heart fluttered rapidly against his skin. Nipping softly with her teeth, she smiled at the moan that rumbled in his chest. Next, she worked her way to his left nipple and grazed it before she sucked it between her lips.

He buried his hands in her hair, pulling out the pins his sister had placed so strategically.

"You're killin' me," he whispered.

Two fingers rolled his other nipple and tugged, forcing another moan from between his lips. The line of hair from his chest to his groin called to her, and she couldn't resist following the path down his flat stomach to the waistband of his jeans.

The clank of his belt buckle sounded loud in the quiet room. Nothing broke the silence except their breathing while she undid his buckle and slipped it free of the belt loops. She unsnapped his jeans and pulled the zipper down with a small tug.

"Oh my goodness. I've miss this terribly," she whispered looking up into his face only to find his head back against the rear of the couch and his eyes closed in ecstasy.

"Lift," she instructed, wanting his jeans off.

His butt came up off the couch, and she tugged until they were down around his ankles and his cock was free to her touch.

"Much better."

Wrapping her hand around his girth, she worked from tip to base several times and then her tongue began to follow the same path. His hips came up off the couch the moment she took him inside her mouth.

"Baby, please," he groaned.

"Mmm."

She sucked for several minutes, loving the salty taste and the silky feel of him in her mouth, until he grabbed her and forced her up in front of him.

"Too many clothes, darlin'."

One hand skimmed under the skirt of her dress to caress her thigh, sending shivers racing down to her toes and back up to settle between her legs.

"No underwear you wicked girl and what's this?" he asked, sliding one finger across her bare pussy as he glanced up. "You shaved?"

"I thought you might like it."

"Holy hell, woman. You have no idea how sexy this is. But next time, I get to do it."

Her skin quivered where he touched, and she moaned as the rough pad of his finger slid across her clit.

"Touch me, Travis. I need you."

"Oh I plan to do more than touch. I'm gonna eat you up, honey."

Clothing flew in several directions while they raced to get undressed.

"Bed?" she asked.

"Nope. Right here. Open for me," he said, lying her back on the couch.

Her breath caught in anticipation, until his mouth settled on her clit and she released it in a sigh.

*God, I love when he does this.*

Soft licks, small sucks and quick flicks had her hovering on the edge of climax within moments. Two fingers drove inside her pussy, and she tossed her head from side to side with each push in and out.

"Oh, God, yes."

The pressure eased and she almost cried, she was so close.

"Easy, darlin'," he whispered, kissing the inside of her thigh and licking the skin from her knee to her clit, and then went down the other side.

"Travis, please."

"Do you want to come, honey?"

She couldn't answer. The words tied her tongue to the point all she could do was whimper.

"I'll take that as a yes," he answered. He stiffened his tongue and speared her vagina several times.

Warmth built from her toes to sweep up her legs and center on her clit until she came apart at the seams on a scream.

His wicked tongue continued to torture her until she stopped trembling.

"I want you inside me," she whispered, tugging at his shoulders to bring him up and over her.

One swift movement and his cock filled her.

"Perfect."

"Hold on, honey," he said, pulling her knees up and over his forearms. "Too deep?"

"No. Amazing."

His hips rocked, slowly releasing his hard length from inside her until he shifted forward again and encased his cock to the hilt.

"Do it again," she murmured.

"Slow?"

"Yeah. For a little bit."

They both moaned while he slid in and out for a couple of minutes, until she couldn't stand it anymore.

"Hard. Oh, God, Travis, please harder."

The sounds of flesh slapping flesh and hearty groans of pleasure filled the room while he brought her to the brink of satisfaction and pushed over into the abyss. His own climax hit soon after hers with a roar of satisfaction from his mouth. For several minutes, he relaxed against her chest with his nose buried in her neck.

"Better?" he murmured.

"For now."

"Insatiable."

"Your fault. You started this," she giggled.

When he went to move off her, she sighed.

"How about we call for some of that ice cream?" he asked, waggling his eyebrows.

"I like how you think, Mr. Brooks."

"I'll be right back," he said before he headed for the bathroom.

Crossing her legs beneath her, she grabbed the remote for the television and flipped it on to the news.

"Breaking news."

"This just in from the small town of Bryan Texas. Senator Leo Boyd has been arrested and charged with trespassing and assault of one Ann Marie Brooks. We were unable to get a statement from Mrs. Brooks today. We were informed it was her wedding day, but Mrs. Brooks is the daughter of Leo Boyd and his wife, Lily. The information we have received indicated that Mrs. Lily Boyd recently left Senator Boyd in the midst of abuse allegations spanning over a long period of time. Approximately thirty years if our source is correct."

"Travis!" she yelled. "Come quick."

"Ours sources report the former vice president of the United States, Joshua Collins is involved in the investigation of abuse. We have been unable to reach the former vice president to ask about his connection to this case, but we have it on good authority Mr. Collins is related to the new Mrs. Brooks by way of her new husband Travis. We will bring more as it develops. Back to you in the studio."

She turned to find out where he was and found him standing behind her with his arms across his chest.

"Damn it. They weren't supposed to leak that."

"The former vice president is related to you?"

"Yeah. Remember those favors I told you I was calling in?

She nodded.

"Joshua Collins is my mother's brother. I didn't even have to call him. Mom did when she found out what your father had done and who he was."

"This is unreal," she whispered as he wrapped his arm around her and tucked her next to him. "I'm related to a vice president?"

"Former vice president, but yeah. He's a great guy. You'll like him."

"Wow."

"It's not that big of a deal."

"This all blows me away. I never thought my father would face any kind of legal ramifications over this."

"I don't want your father getting away with the abuse anymore, honey, but if you want me to let it go, I will."

Her fingers danced on the naked skin of his chest.

"I'm not sure, Travis. I mean, he's done it for so long, and we never thought he would ever be punished for it. My mother finally left him, both Kelly and I are gone…I don't know how far I want to take this."

"The media has it now, so he's ruined no matter whether you bring charges or not."

"I know, and I feel bad."

"You can't be serious, honey. If what I saw him do to you at the weddin' was only a small portion of what he's done over your lifetime, I'd kill him myself if I didn't think it would take me away from you."

The anger in his words brought her gaze up to his, and she could see the frustration and rage he held in check.

"I know you would. I love you, Travis."

Thinking he wouldn't answer, she laid her head back on his chest.

Her heart soared when his whispered words met her ear.

"I love you, too, Ann Marie."

"What did you say?" she asked, afraid she'd misunderstood.

He leaned away and looked her in the eyes. "I love you. Don't ask me how it happened, or when. All I know is I could have killed your father when he slapped you today. I don't know any other way to explain these feelings I have, except that I love you."

Tears burned behind her eyes, and one slowly slipped down her cheek.

"Don't cry, honey."

"I never thought you'd ever say those words."

"Get used to it. You'll be hearing it every day, several times a day, for the rest of our lives."

\* \* \* \*

Their honeymoon was spent lounging on the beach, making love in the sand and loving every minute of every day they spent together, but home called and they needed to return. Travis needed to finish the stallion's training, her father would be going to court and they still needed to give statements to the police and find out who was trying to sabotage the ranch.

"You're back. How did the honeymoon go?" Kelly asked when they walked through the front door.

"Fabulous. I'll tell you all about it, but later," Ann Marie said.

"Ah, there they are," Sheila called, coming in from the kitchen. "You two look well rested."

"How is everything here, Mom?" Travis asked and he kissed her on the cheek. "Did Tyler behave?"

"Of course. He's an angel."

Ann Marie's eyebrow lifted in astonishment. "Boy, does he have you fooled."

Sheila laughed. "He's a boy. He got into trouble and all that, like boys do. I raised two of them. I know how they think."

"Hey son," Walter added, joining them. "That stallion you've got is a pistol, ain't he."

"Yes, he is. I take it you had a run-in with him?" Ann Marie asked.

"Nah. Not really. He's a stallion. They are ornery."

"But he's fast, and he'll be a winner once we enter him in the American Quarter Horse Races," Travis replied.

"I think you are right there, son. From what I've seen of him, he's quick. Which race do you plan to start with? I know there are several coming up soon."

"I registered him late last year, so we're good there, but I'm not sure which one would be best as a qualifying race for him," Ann Marie added.

"I'm glad you were thinkin' ahead, darlin', with the registration. We can look online and see the best place to start," Travis said as he wrapped his arm around her shoulders and brought them both down on the couch. "But he's ready."

"You think so?"

"Yep. I can't do much more with him. He'll run his heart out for you, honey."

Thoughts of the problems going on around the ranch, made her frown.

*I need to figure out what's going on. Who wants to hurt Black, and who wants to take down this ranch?*

"What's wrong, Ann Marie?"

"Mmm. Nothing I guess."

"You guess."

"I was thinking. Trying to figure out who would want to pull the shit that has been going on around here like drugging Black and stealing the cattle."

"Someone tried to drug the stallion?" Walter asked.

"Yeah, Dad. We found him one night with a tranquilizer dart stuck in him with some kind of drug in it. It made him kind of crazy until the vet put him down for the night."

"Maybe you need to hire a private investigator to get to the bottom of this, while you focus on Black's training," Walter said.

"That would be a good idea, Travis," Ann Marie said. "I can center my attention on the books, you can worry about getting him ready to race and the investigator can do the poking around. We can make him out to be a new hand, so the others around here wouldn't get suspicious in case one of them is involved."

"I agree, darlin'. I know of a good guy from up around home who would fit the bill. I'll have to call him and see if he's available."

*Oh, I love when he calls me darlin'.*

The front door slammed as Tyler ran inside. "Mom? Travis? Something's wrong with Misty."

# Chapter Fifteen

"What is it, Ty? Is she hurt?"

Tears streamed down his face and he sobbed. "I dunno. She's breathing hard and lying on her side. Help her, Mom." Ty grabbed her hand and pulled her to her feet before he tried ushering her outside. "Come on, Travis!" Tyler yelled behind them, while he kept moving.

Glancing at Travis, she tried to give him a pleading look and followed her son out.

Everyone else trailed behind, but Tyler ran ahead.

"Any ideas," she asked Travis.

"Not a clue, honey. I hope it's not colic or somethin'."

"Me too."

They reached the barn, and Travis moved inside the stall with the mare to look her over while Ann Marie waited for him to give her any indication she needed to call the vet.

Travis looked up and smiled.

"She'll be fine, Ty."

"What's wrong with her?"

"Nothing a few hours won't fix, buddy. She's gonna give you a new foal to handle."

"A new foal?" Tyler asked.

"Yep. It appears the stallion got to her at some point," Travis replied.

"Will she be all right, Travis?"

"She'll be fine. You might want to check on her off and on throughout the night, but my guess is, her baby will be here around daylight."

"Can I stay out here with her, Mom?"

"I don't see why not. You can even sleep in Travis' old room if you want."

Tyler hugged her and whispered, "Cool. Thanks, Mom. You are the best."

"You're welcome. Just don't stay up all night, okay? You can come out and check on her, and don't get in the stall with her at any time. If you think something's not right, you come and get me and Travis."

"I promise."

With one arm around her shoulders, Travis led her and the rest of the adults back toward the house.

"Are you two goin' home in the morning?" he asked his parents.

"Yeah. We can't leave our place for much longer. The foreman can handle it for a week or two, but we have an auction coming up and need to get ready," his dad replied.

Travis nuzzled her ear and whispered, "Good. I need some alone time with my woman."

"We just had alone time."

"Not sufficient in my book. A lifetime won't be enough."

A soft giggle left her lips, attracting the attention of his parents and Kelly. "Stop. You're embarrassing me," she whispered, blushing at the sly look the others gave them.

"What? We're newlyweds. We can act crazy in love if we want to."

"In love?" Kelly mouthed, and she smiled and nodded. Her sister gave her two thumbs up.

"I'm going to make a couple of phone calls, honey," Travis said giving her a light squeeze when they stepped into the living room. "I'll be back in a few minutes."

"Sure. I'm getting kind of hungry. Anyone else want something to eat? I'll even cook," she asked the group.

"Uh, it's great you want to make something, darlin', but how about we order pizza."

Hands on her hips, she gave him a pretend fierce scowl and said, "I can cook." When he cocked a questioning eyebrow, she added, "All right, so I can't cook very well."

With a quick kiss on her nose, he smiled and handed her the phone. "Call for pizza."

"Pizza's a good idea," Kelly replied.

"Thanks, Kel. Way to back up your sister."

Kelly shrugged and smiled, while Ann Marie grumbled and dialed the phone.

* * * *

"Thanks, Mark," Travis said. "I'm sure we can make you fit in around here while you investigate. I'm thinkin' there is someone on the inside feeding info to a competitor or something."

"Sounds like it, Travis. Will this weekend be soon enough for me to get there? You're down in Bryan, right?"

"Yeah. It's the Double S. My wife's place."

"Wife?"

Travis chuckled. "Sorry. I didn't tell you I got married again about a week ago."

"That was kind of fast wasn't it? I mean, you swore you would never get married again after Catherine."

"I know, but Ann Marie wormed her way under my skin like a burr under a saddle blanket. I couldn't shake her loose even if I wanted to."

"You sound like a man in love."

"I am."

"Wow. I never thought I'd ever hear those words come from your mouth, but I'm happy for you. I'm glad you found someone to get over the shit with your ex."

"Me, too. And, she has a son who I love. He's about the age Adam would have been. He's a great kid."

"Ready-made family."

"You could say that. Listen, I better go. We ordered pizza in, and I can smell it. I'll see you in a few days."

"No problem. Take it easy, and kiss your wife for me."

"Got it covered."

"I bet. Talk to you later," Mark replied with a laugh.

After he hung up the phone, he walked down the hall and into the living room to find the rest of his family chowing down on the pizza.

*My family. Wow. I never thought I'd have one of those again. much less one I love so much it hurts.*

"Hey. Did y'all save me some?"

"Of course. We can't have the man of the house going hungry. How did it go?" Ann Marie asked.

"Good. Mark will be here in a couple of days. He can have my old room. That way, he'll have the privacy to do the investigation and access to the computer files in the barn office."

"Sounds perfect."

The rest of the evening, the five of them talked about ranch life in general and the issues with her father. Ann Marie thanked Sheila for getting involved. Travis knew his mother, and his instinct to protect came from her.

"I'm sorry if I butted in where I shouldn't have, Ann Marie, but the one thing I never would tolerate from a man was abuse, whether it be physical, emotional or whatever. When I found out what happened out in the front yard, and who your father is, I took matters into my own hands."

"And I love you for it, Sheila. During my entire life, he made us think he would never pay for what he did. Untouchable, in a sadistic sort of way, but sometimes you have to go above someone like that to get things accomplished."

"Exactly, sweetheart," he murmured against her ear, pulling her in close.

"I'm going to be sorry to see you leave tomorrow," she told Sheila and Walter. "You two have become a very important part of my life."

"Trust me, we will be back. I can't wait to see the children you two produce," Sheila said.

"Mother," Travis growled, but a smile graced his lips.

Ann Marie laughed. "We'll see. No rush."

"Practice makes perfect," he added, kissing her hair.

Pink rushed up her neck and splashed across her cheeks. "You are impossible, husband." A frown pulled down the corners of her mouth. "I thought you said you didn't want any more children?"

"I didn't want to be in love again, either, but a certain blue eyed siren changed my mind and lassoed this stubborn heart of mine in short order."

"Such a cowboy. All tough on the outside, but like a blob of gelatin on the inside."

"Blob of gelatin?" he asked with a chuckle.

"Yep. Squishy and moldable."

"Well there are certain parts of this cowboy that get hard and achy only for you," he murmured low near her ear.

The pretty pink blush returned, and she elbowed him in the ribs.

\* \* \* \*

"Welcome to the Double S, Mark. We are certainly glad you're here," Ann Marie said, when Travis' friend stepped out of his truck.

"You must be Ann Marie," Mark replied, pulling her close for a hug.

"Hands off, buddy," Travis' growled with pretend fierceness as he came to stand behind her.

"I can certainly see why you feel in love with her, Travis."

"Oh, a charmer. Great! Just what I need, another one of those around here," she grumbled with a smile.

The two men shook hands and laughed.

"Let me show you the barn, office and your room," Travis' said, tipping his head toward the barn. "I'll be inside in a minute, darlin'."

A quick brush of a kiss to her lips by her husband and the two men walked toward the structure in the distance.

Ann Marie went inside the house and into the kitchen to make up some fresh lemonade and sandwiches for lunch. She wasn't sure if Mark would be hungry after his drive, but the noon hour fast approached. A dust devil whirled in the front yard, and her thoughts turned to the troubles on the ranch as her hands stilled.

"Damn it! I wish I knew who was behind this crap. I hate distrusting people."

"Hey, honey," Travis said, coming into the kitchen with Mark right behind him. "Can we feed this pain in the ass? He hasn't eaten yet."

"Of course. Sandwich okay? As my husband and my son like to remind me, I don't cook worth a hill of beans."

"Sandwich is fine. I'm not much of a cook myself," Mark replied with a chuckle.

"Take a seat there and I'll make some. It's about lunchtime around here anyway, and I'm sure Kelly and Tyler will be looking for food soon."

"Kelly and Tyler?" Mark asked, sipping from the lemonade she placed in front of him.

"Kelly is my sister, and Tyler is my son," she replied, slathering the bread with mayonnaise and adding ham and cheese before she set one plate each in front of the two men. Travis grabbed her around the waist and kissed her.

"Thanks, darlin'."

Once she'd made one for herself, she slid into the seat next to Travis. "How about you bring me up to speed on what the plan is?"

"We'll introduce him as a new hand and bring only those we have to, into the loop, like Tucker, Kelly and Tyler."

"What about Manuel?"

"No. I don't even want him to know. The fewer people aware of why Mark is here, the better."

"True," she said.

"I'll make friends with the hands and see what I can learn without causing too much suspicion. You know, dig around a little."

"Did you tell him everything that has happened, Travis?"

"Yeah, I already filled him in on the problems with the stallion and the missing cattle."

A moment later, Kelly walked into the kitchen and stopped in her tracks. "Well hello."

Ann Marie about choked on her food at the tone in her sister's voice and the sexy hello that came from her lips.

"Kelly, this is Mark Grissom. Mark, this is my sister, Kelly. Mark is here to do some investigating for us."

"Nice to meet you, Kelly," Mark replied, standing up and taking her hand.

"You, too, Mark."

Red swept up Kelly's neck and painted her cheeks as Ann Marie frowned. Her sister didn't need to get involved with someone who would only be here for a short time.

"Mark's here for a little while, Kel," Ann Marie said with a warning in her voice.

"Great. I guess I'll be seeing you around then."

"You sure will," Mark said, his voice dropping an octave, making Ann Marie leery of his motives.

"Can I talk to you a minute, Kel."

"Sure."

"In the other room?"

"I was going to get—"

"Now," Ann Marie said, taking her sister's arm and pushing her ahead.

"What's gotten into you, Ann Marie? You're acting like a mother hen."

"I'm trying to. Don't get involved with Mark."

"I hadn't planned on it, but now that you brought it up…"

"He'll only be here for a short time, so I would suggest staying away from him."

"I don't want to get married right now anyway. If nothing else, he would be a nice diversion."

"Kelly!"

"What? I have needs, too. I'm not a virgin, Ann Marie. I lost that a few years ago, and I haven't been with a man in several months. I'm sure you know how that feels."

"Yes, I do."

"Then stop trying to deny me the same opportunities. If I hook up with Mark, it will be for sex, nothing more."

"Yeah, I said the same thing with Travis, and look where I am."

"Happily in love. Don't knock it. You've hooked up with a great guy." Kelly walked toward the window. "Besides, I know what I want, and Mark isn't it."

"Oh?"

When she turned back around, Ann Marie could see the sadness in her eyes. "Forget it, Ann Marie. The guy I really want is gay."

"Well, damn."

"Yeah, so lay off, okay? Anything between me and Mark would be a little sexual release."

They returned to the kitchen a few minutes later to find Mark gone and Travis sipping his lemonade.

"Everything all right?" he asked.

"Yeah. Ann Marie is trying to be the big sister and warn me away from your friend."

Ann Marie raised her hand to silence him when he opened his mouth. "We'll talk about it later, Travis."

One eyebrow cocked and he stared at her for a moment with a sexy-as-hell grin spreading across his lips. His gaze traveled down her body and then back to her face. The shiver rolling down her back made her want to drag him upstairs for a rousing couple of hours of sex.

*I've become a terrible hussy.*

"We can always go upstairs and *discuss* it now," he said with grin.

"All right you two. Talk about me!" Kelly exclaimed with a smile.

"We're married. We can do whatever we want in our own kitchen," Travis grumbled. "But, I'll behave and go outside to work." Backing Ann Marie up against the counter, he lifted her and set her on the granite behind her. "Kiss me, woman. I need fortifying before I go back out in the heat."

With a hearty laugh, she skimmed her hands up his chest and wrapped them around his neck. "I think I can do that." A few quick nibbles to the side of his mouth had him sighing. He captured her face between his palms, tilted her head and locked his lips with hers.

Moments later he said, "You are a witch and a tease, lovely wife. I'll extract punishment later tonight. I think those handcuffs are still around."

"Mmm. That they are."

The wicked smile spreading across his face had her panties wet inside seconds.

"I'm looking forward to later then."

One quick peck on the lips and he went outside. .

"What?" she asked, eyeing Kelly as she stood on the other side of the room with a huge grin on her face.

"I'm so happy for you. That's all. Travis is a great guy, and I hope someday I find someone like him. Well, maybe not a cowboy, but you know what I mean."

"Yeah, I do, Kel. I'm not sure how I got so lucky."

* * * *

The day of Black's first race approached and Ann Marie was scared.

*Does he really have a chance to win? I think he's fast, but up against the others born and bred to race, I'm not so sure.*

The whole family had hooked up the horse trailer, climbed into Travis' truck the night before, and left for New Mexico for the first race. The drive had been long, and they had to stop several times to let the stallion out to stretch, but they finally arrived at the racetrack where they were to board him.

"He'll be fine, honey," Travis said as she stood stroking the horses nose, unwilling to leave him.

"I know, but I feel bad leaving him here."

"We'll be back in the morning to stretch his legs. All the other horses are here already. He won't be alone. They'll be nickering back and forth half the night, I imagine."

To prove his point, the stallion let out a loud whinny that was answered in kind by several of the others nearby, and she had to laugh.

"I see. You don't need me anymore, do you, big boy?"

The stallion nudged her shoulder and bobbed his head.

"See."

"Okay fine. We'll go to the hotel."

Travis draped his arm around her shoulders and steered her toward the truck.

"A nice bed, and maybe a warm bath, will relax you, and then maybe you'll let me have my way with you," he said.

"I'm glad you thought to get two rooms."

"Do I look stupid, woman?"

A warm bubble of laughter left her lips. "Not at all, husband. You're a pretty smart cookie. You married me, after all."

"Very true. And fell head over heels in love with you."

"Come on, Mom. I'm hungry!" Tyler yelled from the back seat of the truck.

"When aren't you?"

"He's a growing boy. Trust me, it'll only get worse. Ask my mom." Travis chuckled and smacked her on the butt as they approached the vehicle.

"We will have to compare notes. She's got a couple up on me."

When they'd eaten and settled in for the night, Travis filled the big bathtub with steaming water, lots of bubbles and her favorite honeysuckle fragrance.

"Go. Relax, honey. You need it," he said.

"All right. It will be nice to kick back in those warm bubbles. I don't think I've ever seen a bathtub that big before."

"Maybe I'll join in a bit, but first, you take your time. I'm going to call the ranch and check in."

"Good idea. I know Tucker and Mark can handle the place for a few days, but it still worries me, Mark hasn't been able to get much closer to who is behind the trouble."

"Me, too, but he's good. It takes time to build trust. He's considered a new hand on the place and face it, you've brought in several for the last six months."

"Very true." Thoughts drifted across her mind, and she pulled her bottom lip between her teeth.

"What's wrong?"

"You do realize your contract is about up."

"What contract?"

"The original one that said you had to stay six months."

Wrapping his arms around her shoulders, he pulled her in close and whispered, "The new contract supersedes the first one."

She tipped her head back and looked into his eyes. "New contract?"

"Yeah, the marriage certificate on the wall at home. I'm pretty sure I remember the vows, and they didn't say anythin' about leavin' after six months. You're stuck with me, darlin', for the rest of your life."

"I kind of like that idea."

"Good," he murmured and then his lips fastened on hers and coaxed her to open for him as he swept his tongue inside her mouth.

Low moans of desire echoed in the room while she pushed her aching breasts against his chest, begging for his touch.

A quick swat on her butt and she yelped. "What was that for?"

"For temptin' me. Go take your bath, and I'll be in there in a few minutes to join you," he replied with a wicked grin and a waggle of his eyebrows.

"Promise?"

"Definitely. Why do you think I booked the room with the giant tub?"

"Wicked. I like it."

Giving him a quick kiss to the lips, she turned and headed for the bathtub. A dimmer switch on the wall slid under her fingers, bringing the lights down to a romantic, soft glow. The scent of honeysuckle drifted to her nose. Tank top and jeans hit the floor in quick order, before she skimmed her underwear down over her hips, letting them join the rest of her clothing. She quickly piled her hair on top of her head in a loose, messy bunch of curls. A groan of satisfaction left her lips when she sank beneath the bubbles and laid her head back against the rim.

* * * *

"Everythin' quiet around there?" Travis asked when Mark picked up his cell phone.

"Yep. Not much is happening at the moment although I got a tip on one or two of your hands."

"Really?"

"Someone left a message on the desk in the office about, 'watch Cody and Jinx'."

"Well, maybe it's a tip. Have they done anythin' that would make you suspicious?"

"Nope. Not yet anyway, but I'm watching everyone, not just those two."

"Good."

"The trip to New Mexico go okay?"

"No problems at all. Black is settled in at the racetrack, ready to go in the morning. We met with the jockey we contacted, and he's ready to ride."

"Sounds like you're all set then. I'm sure the stallion will do great."

"I hope so. Ann Marie has pinned so many hopes on him, not knowing the money I have in the account could keep us going for several years before we ever had to worry."

"At least you know she didn't marry you for your money, Travis."

"True. She doesn't even know about it. We did sign a pre-nup though, more for her peace of mind, than mine, but that was before she knew I loved her."

"You got yourself one fine woman."

"Don't I know it. The great thing is, I know she would never cheat on me like Catherine did."

"I hope you never judge her on the same terms as your ex."

"I'm pretty sure I'll never have the reason to."

"Keep that in mind, if there is ever a doubt."

"Oh, I will. Listen, I'd better go. That fine woman of mine is waiting in the tub for me."

"In the tub?"

A small chuckle left his mouth. "Yeah. There's a huge bathtub in this room, and I aim to take advantage of it."

"Have fun."

"I intend to. I'll call you tomorrow after the race."

With a decisive click, he hung up and raced for the bathroom.

"It's about time. I thought you'd forgotten about me," Ann Marie said, opening one eye when he walked inside.

His gaze swept over his wife while she relaxed against the porcelain. Her creamy skin glistened in the dim lights, her honey blonde curls were piled on top of her head in a messy array of hair that looked sexy-as-hell, and her pouty lips begged for his kiss. "Oh, hell no, honey. I've been lookin' forward to this since we left home."

"We need to put one of these in our bathroom."

"I like that idea."

"What are you waiting for, cowboy?"

"I'm admirin' the view."

"I might want to admire the view myself, but right now, I need your lips against mine, so get your sexy ass in here."

Quickly stripping off his clothes, he groaned when he slipped beneath the warm water, but stifled a whimper as she wrapped a hand around his already stiff cock.

"Keep that up and I won't be able to wait."

"Good. Waiting is a bad thing," she whispered, and then she fastened her lips around one erect nipple.

"Damn woman."

"Are you complaining?" she asked and then nipped at his chest.

"Hell no."

He let her torture him for several minutes before he took control of things and pulled her on top of him, to straddle his hips. One swift plunge and he sheathed himself inside her sweet heat.

"God, you feel good," he murmured, lifting her hips only to thrust in again.

Water sloshed onto the floor.

"We are getting water everywhere," she whispered, her eyes closed and her head back.

"Do you care?"

"No."

"Me either. We'll clean it up afterward."

"Afterward?"

"After I love you until we can't breathe."

"You're working on it, husband."

A hearty groan rumbled from deep in his chest as he thrust his hips over and over, pulling her along with him until they both cried out in ecstasy.

"I love you," Ann Marie whispered against his neck.

His hands wandered down her back and up again as he murmured, "I love you, too."

\* \* \* \*

Dawn brightened the sky with streaks of purple, then pink and orange, as the sun peeked over the horizon. The morning light found Travis, Ann Marie, Kelly and Tyler at the racetrack watching while the jockey took Black on a few trial runs. Travis timed him with each start, still amazed at the times the stallion put up.

"So?" Ann Marie asked.

"Eighteen point zero six," he answered.

"That's good."

"Damn good, honey. If he does this well during the actual race, we'll be all set."

One hand grabbed his and squeezed. "He will."

"The real test is when he's runnin' with the others. It's hard to run a stallion."

"I know, but he's focused."

"And we have one of the best jockeys in the country."

"That, too," she said with a smile.

"Let's go back to the hotel for a while. It will be a few hours before the race."

"Okay. Maybe we can try out the tub again."

"Hopeless woman."

Travis wrapped an arm around her shoulders and walked toward his truck.

"Ann Marie!" the jockey yelled, leading Black toward them.

"What is it, Jacque?"

"We have a problem."

# Chapter Sixteen

"Problem?" Ann Marie asked as Jacque approached.

"Black's limping," Travis replied, noticing the stallion favoring his front hoof.

"No, this can't be happening," she replied.

"Did he stumble or anything out there, Jacque?" Travis asked.

"No," the jockey replied. "He wasn't favoring it until I started to bring him back to the barn.

Travis grabbed the hoof pick out of his pocket and lifted the stallion's front foot. After several tense moments and a few passes of the pick over the hoof, he released it and frowned.

"He may not be able to race today, Ann Marie."

"What? Why?"

"I can't see any reason for him to be limping. His hoof is clean. The leg doesn't appear to be swollen or hot. I'm not sure why he's favoring. We'll have to wait and see how he is in a couple of hours. Let him rest in the stall, and we can check him again before the race."

Tears rolled down her cheeks. *I can't believe this. What if he can't race?*

Travis took her face between his palms and wiped her tears with his thumbs. "It will be okay, honey. If he can't race today, we'll get him ready for another one."

"You don't understand. We need him to race. He has to win."

Travis took her hand, and they walked toward the truck. "Is there somethin' you haven't told me, darlin'?"

"No, I—"

*How can I tell him we could lose the ranch if he doesn't win?*

"Ann Marie, please tell me what's troublin' you. We are partners. You have to trust me."

Pressing her lips into a thin line, she tried to decide if she wanted to tell him the whole, ugly truth of John's debts and the threatening phone call she'd received.

"We need the money, Travis. I found more loans John had against the ranch."

"More?"

"Yeah, but they weren't with any bank or anything. He had some stuff out with some loan sharks. Apparently, on his trips into Houston, he'd been gambling and not winning."

"Shit," he growled, running his hands through his hair. "How much?"

"Ten thousand."

"How do you know?"

"They called."

"And you didn't tell me? I thought we had trust between us, Ann Marie."

"We do."

"Obviously not, if you didn't tell me."

"I only found out a few days ago, and I thought if Black won, I could just pay them and be done with it. I didn't like the thought of John doing this kind of stuff, and I didn't have a clue. I felt it was my problem, not yours."

"Listen, darlin', anything to do with the ranch is *our* problem. Do you understand? I love you. We're in this together, the two of us. Not you and not me. Both of us."

"I'm sorry." She wrapped her arms around his waist and pressed her face to his shoulder. "I didn't want you to worry."

"I'll pay them off if Black doesn't race and win," he said, running his hands down her back.

"No. You've already paid off thirty-thousand of his debt. I don't want you paying more."

"I have the money, Ann Marie."

"It's not fair to you."

"It doesn't matter if it means saving our home."

"I can't ask you to use the rest of your savings for that."

"Honey, ten thousand hardly touches what I have in the bank," he replied, leaning away so he could look into her eyes. "I know we signed an agreement, but what's mine is yours, and I hope you know that."

"Exactly how much do you have in there if you already paid almost thirty thousand and now are willing to pay ten more?"

"Enough."

"What's enough, Travis?" she asked, needing to trust him, and needing him to trust her enough to tell her.

"I wasn't going to tell you. I know you didn't marry me for my money, but I have over half a million in the bank."

"Half a million?"

"Yeah. Lots of expensive horses and some good investments, and I've done pretty well." A rueful smile spread across his lips

"I'd say so," she whispered, awed at the amount he had, but not willing to let it come between them. "But, I don't want you using your hard earned money to bail out John's mistakes."

"You aren't John's mistake. You are my wife, and I love you. The ranch is ours, not yours and his anymore. Ours."

"Do you have any idea how much I love you?"

His lips lifted in a smile. "I know how much I love you, and if it's even half that much, I'm one lucky man."

\* \* \* \*

The time for the first race stared them in the face, and Travis had to decide if the stallion could run or not. He actually thought it rather funny, because when the horse didn't know he or Ann Marie was there, he walked fine. No limp, no favoring of his front hoof – nothing, but when the animal got wind of them, he started limping again.

"Let me take him into his stall. We need to have a chat, just me and him," he told Ann Marie and Jacque.

"Are you sure?"

"Yeah, darlin'. You and Jacque go stand where he can't see you."

"All right. I hope you know what you're doing."

When they were out of sight, he pulled the latch on the stall and walked inside. The stallion lifted his front hoof.

"Knock it off, Black. You and me are gonna talk."

The stallion dropped his head.

"I know damned well there is nothing wrong with your hoof. Why you've decided to try to fool us, I don't know." Travis stepped to the side and looked straight into the stallion's eye. "You need to knock this shit off. Ann Marie needs you to run your heart out for her." He wasn't sure, but the animal actually looked apologetic. "Are you gonna straighten up and run right?"

The stallion bobbed his head and nudged Travis in the shoulder.

"Okay then, buddy. Let's do this and do it right."

Travis patted the side of Black's neck, pulled out a sugar cube from his pocket and fed it to him.

"All set," he said after he found Ann Marie and the jockey again.

"Yeah?"

"He'll behave now."

"What did you do?" she asked, her eyes wide and searching.

"We had us a pep talk, and he understands."

"A pep talk? You had a powwow with a horse?"

"Every good cowboy knows how to talk to a horse, and being a trainer, it's one of my special abilities."

"Okay. Whatever," she said, obviously not believing him.

"You'll see, darlin'. He's ready to run."

Jacque walked out seconds later, leading Black by his lead rope. The stallion no longer limped.

"What the hell?" Ann Marie asked with shock written all over her face.

"I told you—"

One hand came up to stop his words. "I don't want to know. It's between you and Black."

Travis grinned and kissed her on the lips. "Let's go find a good seat."

Kelly and Tyler joined them in the stands several minutes later, as Ann Marie watched with binoculars.

"I can see Black and Jacque. They are walking around behind the stables."

"Jacque knows what he's doin'. He's one of the best jockeys around."

She pulled the binoculars from in front of her eyes and said, "I know. I trust your judgment."

"Have I been wrong yet?"

"No, and don't go getting too smug there mister."

"I married you, didn't I?" he asked with a laugh. "I'd say I have pretty good taste and a wonderful eye for beautiful flesh."

One eyebrow cocked, and a smirk lifted the corner of her mouth.

The announcer came over the intercom and announced the first set of horses that would be racing. Black wasn't due to run until the third heat. For the next hour, they watched the other horses run, talked about which ones looked good and might be competition for Black in the final heat, should he qualify well.

When his turn came, they stood at the rail and held their breaths. All the horses lined up in the starting gate, and he could see Black fidgeting under the saddle.

"Easy boy," Travis whispered. "You'll get your chance in a minute."

As the gun fired and the gates dropped, Black shot out of his space like his tail was on fire. Rounding the first bend, he was in the lead by at least a head, but there were two others gaining on him fast. They rounded the final corner and ran for the home stretch with all three of the leaders running neck and neck.

The field came within sight of where they all stood, and Ann Marie shouted, "Come on, Black Jack. You can do it, boy! Run!"

Travis wasn't sure if the stallion heard her, but with a burst of energy, he stretched out his legs and pulled out in front of the others, beating them all by at least half a length.

"He won! He won!" she screamed, jumping up and down.

Travis grabbed her around the waist when she launched herself into his arms and kissed him soundly on the mouth.

"Easy, honey. He still has to run the final heat."

"Did you see that?"

"I saw it. We all knew he was fast." He grabbed her hand and said, "Let's go down by the barn. It'll be a while before he runs again, so he'll have time to rest."

When they reached the barn, they strode to where Jacque walked Black, cooling him down. Ann Marie rushed up the stallion and threw her arms around his neck.

"I knew you could do it, Black. I knew you could." With a kiss to the animals jaw, she stepped back. "One more time, buddy. You think you can do that for me?"

Black Jack bobbed his head, and they all laughed.

"We should go back up to the stands, darlin'."

"Okay. Take care of him, Jacque."

"Will do," the jockey answered, leading the stallion back to his stall.

"How long do we have, Travis?" she asked.

He looked at his watch. "About two hours. They have to run five more heats and then they'll let the horses rest for about an hour before they run the final."

"Shall we get something to eat and come back?"

"Probably a good idea. There was a restaurant not far from the hotel."

"Let's go then, so we can get back."

They walked into the local diner and were shocked to see so many people.

"Wow. I think everyone from the track, is here," Kelly said, brushing the hair from her face.

"Its race day and this place is fairly cheap. The food at the racetrack is expensive," Ann Marie replied. "I imagine lots of people hit places like this and McDonald's to save on money."

"How many?" the hostess asked, as she grabbed menus from the rack.

"Four," Travis answered.

"Right this way."

They found a large booth in the back and were looking over the food selections when a man approached the table.

"Well, hello there," he said.

"Mr. Armstrong. What are you doing here?" Ann Marie asked, glancing at Travis, then back to the other man.

"I came for the races, especially since I heard you had entered your stallion."

"Yes we have."

"Heard he's in the final heat, too."

"Right again."

"I look forward to seeing him race."

"You do realize, if he wins, the price of him being a sire for you just went up."

Mr. Armstrong's face turned purple, and he sputtered. "We had an agreement."

"Our agreement was strictly verbal, and since you never made the trip to the ranch to check him out after our lunch, I assumed you weren't interested."

Travis had to fight the urge to laugh at Ann Marie's statement. Her tactics had him in awe. On the other hand, he didn't think Landon Armstrong cared for them.

"Little bitch. I'll teach you a lesson or two," he said, stepping closer, until Travis stood and blocked his advancement.

"I would appreciate it, Mr. Armstrong, if you wouldn't call my wife a bitch."

"Your wife?"

"Yes," he answered. "Not that it's any of your business, but we were married not long ago."

"Shacked up with the trainer, did you?" Landon sneered.

"One more word and you'll be pickin' yourself up off the floor," he growled. "I suggest you move along, and don't bother wantin' anythin' from our place, including the stallion. To you, he's not for sale, and you aren't welcome."

"This isn't over," Mr. Armstrong grumbled before he turned and left their table.

"Is unpleasant too mild a word?" Ann Marie asked.

"Don't worry about him, darlin'."

"I hope he doesn't try to pull something." Her bottom lip disappeared between her teeth. "I thought he was so pleasant and helpful before."

"Obviously, he changes his stripes when he doesn't get what he wants," Travis replied.

"I guess so, but let's not allow him to ruin our meal."

The waitress returned, and they placed their order. Tyler and Kelly kept up the conversation while he contemplated the last development with Landon Armstrong.

*I think I'll call Mark and have him check the man out. Somethin' smells bad.*

Once they finished their meal, they drove back to the track.

"I want to check on Black and Jacque," Ann Marie said when they pulled through the gates. "I have a bad feeling."

"Sure, honey. I'll drive over there, and we can walk by his stall. Jacque may already have him out warmin' up."

The stall they'd chosen for Black sat back behind the barn in the corner. Ann Marie wanted the stallion to have a quiet place away from many of the other animals, but still be able to knicker to them if he wanted to, since he could be high-strung at times. They drove around the back and he pulled the truck into an empty spot next to their horse trailer.

"Who's that?" Kelly asked, pointing toward Black's stall where the stallion hung his head over the door.

"Who?"

"The guy standing next to the stall door."

"I don't know," Ann Marie answered. "Have you seen him before, Travis? Maybe he's a worker here at the racetrack."

"Not sure, but I think we need to find out," he replied as he stopped the truck and shut the engine off. The man looked around and then slipped inside the stall. "I don't like the looks of this. Let's go see what he's up to."

They climbed from the truck and approached the stall. The man hadn't appeared again, but Travis kept a keen eye on the door. Black nickered when they got close.

"Hey, buddy," Travis said while he stroked the animal's nose. He looked inside and saw the man crouched in the corner, trying to look small and not be noticed. "Somethin' I can do you for you, mister?"

The man shook his head.

"Get out here," Travis growled, and the man's eyes widened in fear and he shook his head again. "You ain't gonna like it if I have to come in there after you."

The man rose and slowly walked back toward the door, but Travis saw something drop in the hay in the corner.

"Kel, I saw a security guard around the other side of the barn. Go get him, please."

With a quick nod, she disappeared.

"I did nothing wrong," the man said in a thick, apparently Mexican accent.

"What were you doin' in this horse stall?"

"I check on him."

"I don't think so. This animal belongs to me and my wife. We did not ask you to check on him, and I'm sure his jockey didn't either, but we'll ask."

The wiry little man tried to bolt out the door, but Travis grabbed him, yanked his arm behind his back and shoved him against the side of the enclosure.

"Who sent you?"

"No one."

"Wrong answer." He pulled harder and the man yelled out in pain. "What's your name, and who sent you? If you don't give me the correct answer, I'll break your arm."

"Carlos."

"Good start," Travis said, pulling a little harder. "Now, the other name. Who are you working for?"

"I cannot say. He will kill me."

"Let me have him, Mr. Brooks," the security guard said when he arrived with Kelly. "I'll take him to the race office."

After Travis gave the man over to the guard's custody, he replied, "Wait one minute." He walked to the corner where he saw the guy drop something and picked up a syringe. "Take this with you. I want it tested. He obviously meant to harm the horse."

The Mexican struggled against the guard's hold, but he got him handcuffed and shoved outside before he walked the suspicious man toward the race office.

"Any idea on who is behind this, Travis?" Ann Marie asked.

"No clue, honey, but I'm glad we stopped that guy. We need to keep a closer eye on Black. I guess whoever wants him out of the races, will stop at nothing. I imagine once they test whatever the syringe contained, they'll find something that could have taken Black out permanently."

"Really? Why would anyone want to hurt him?"

"Because he's fast, and he could make a few people lose money on their own animals if he keeps winning."

"True, I guess. I don't understand how anyone can hurt an animal though."

He wrapped his arms around her waist and pulled her in tight. "You are a softy."

"For you, I am."

"And for the stallion."

"True." With her hands buried in the hair at the nape of his neck, she whispered against his lips, "But I'm desperately in love with you."

"I'm glad. I'd hate to be in this all by myself," he replied. He took her mouth with his and swept his tongue inside.

"Ewww!" Tyler groaned.

They pulled apart, and she smiled at Tyler. "You'll have someone someday, son, and you'll understand."

Jacque came around the corner and said, "Are we ready to run?"

"Yep. Need help getting him saddled?" Travis asked.

"No. The groomer will be here in a moment. I want to exercise Black a little before the race, but start time is in about thirty minutes."

"All right then. We'll go up into the stands to take our seats so we can root you on."

"See you in the winner's circle," Jacque replied with a saucy salute.

Ann Marie laughed, and Travis wrapped his arm around her waist to escort her and the rest of his family to their seats. Once they were all seated, she fidgeted.

"Sit still, darlin'. You'll wear a hole in the seat."

"I can't help it. I'm excited."

A couple of other owners stopped by and congratulated them on qualifying for the final heat. The murmurs of the crowd grew louder when the horses came trotting out, prancing for the starting gates.

"There he is," Ann Marie said, standing at the railing in front of them. "He's in slot number two."

"He's got a good starting position then," Travis answered, coming to stand beside her.

The announcer read off the horse's name, jockey's name and owner's name of each animal. The starting gate locked in place behind them, and Ann Marie grabbed Travis' hand in a fierce grip.

"And they're off," she whispered as the horses shot out of the gate.

Around each corner, they flew. Black hung onto second place. They rounded the outside turn and he nosed forward, running neck and neck with the leader.

When the field got close, Ann Marie yelled, "Run, Black! Run!"

Jacque flicked the riding crop over the stallions flank, and he shot ahead of the pack right before the finish line to win by a nose.

"He did it!" she yelled, jumping up and down as Travis wrapped his arms around her waist. "He won!"

# Chapter Seventeen

The stallion was loaded in the trailer and they checked out of the hotel while they got ready to make the long trek for home. Ann Marie had several phone numbers of people wanting Black to sire for them, and she couldn't be happier. The dream she and John had for him to be their crowning glory had finally come true.

"Excuse me?"

"Yes," she said eyeing the official from the racetrack, who stood in front of her and Travis.

"I wanted to get back to you on the investigation of the man you found in your horse's stall.

"Oh?" Travis asked, sliding an arm around her waist.

"Carlos confessed and told us the name of the man he'd been contacted by to harm your animal was Landon Armstrong."

Ann Marie gasped. "I shouldn't be surprised, I guess, after our run-in at the restaurant this morning, but I didn't expect him to work so fast."

"We've contacted the racing commission and the authorities. He will be prosecuted to the fullest extent of the law."

"Thank you, Mr. Jefferies. We appreciate your prompt action on this. Any idea about the contents of the syringe?"

"Yes, Sodium Pentobarbital."

"He planned on killing, Black?" she asked in a tortured whisper. "All because he couldn't get the stallion's sperm? God, Travis, he had every intention of killing him."

Travis pulled her against him and stroked her back. "It's okay, darlin'. The authorities will have something to say to him. Unfortunately, he'll probably get nothin' more than a hefty fine, but I hope the racing association bans him for life."

"But he would have killed him."

"I know," he murmured against her hair. "Come on, honey. Let's go home."

The ride back to the ranch seemed to take forever, but by early evening they pulled into the front yard.

"I'm glad to be home," she said.

"Me, too," Kelly replied, with another affirmation from Tyler.

"Let's get Black unloaded and settled. Why don't you go on up, darlin' and I'll meet you upstairs in a bit. I want to check in with Mark."

After a quick kiss on the lips, she agreed and disappeared inside.

* * * *

"Mark?" Travis called as he led the stallion into the barn.

"Yo," Mark replied, stepping out of the office. "You're back sooner than I thought you'd be. How'd it go?"

"He won."

"Really? That's great news."

"Yeah."

"Then why the frown?" Mark asked.

"A breeder tried to have him euthanized."

"You're serious?"

"Deadly serious. I'm angry, upset, pissed off — you name it, I'm probably feeling it."

"What did you do?"

"The race commission is dealing with him. The guy involved with the actual threat, squealed on his boss. They plan on prosecuting."

"Good."

"Any ideas on who is behind the shit going on here?"

"Yep."

"Who?"

"You know a kid named Sam?"

Travis had to think a minute, but when he realized who Mark mentioned, it was like a light bulb went on. "Isn't he like a stable boy? I've seen him around a bit, but not a lot. Maybe once or twice since I've been here. He kind of hung out near the bunkhouse."

"Yeah. That's him. After I did some checking on all the hands on your place, I got a bit suspicious when he tried buddying up to me. He wanted to hang out and got a bit nosy on why I came here. Then I found out his connection. His uncle owns the Bar X."

"Mitchell Payne?"

"You got it. I confronted him this morning, and after he admitted gathering information on the operation, supplying his uncle with numbers of head and so on, he high-tailed it out of here and haven't seen him since. My guess is since the Bar X borders this property, the old man wanted to buy Ann Marie out once her husband died, and expand his holdings. You showed up to train the stallion ,and he figured his chances were getting slimmer."

"The son of a bitch," Travis growled.

"Then when you two hooked up, he got desperate. The kid admitted to trying to tranquilize the stallion."

"I had to pay him off, too. When I found the notes about John borrowing against the ranch on the computer, Mitchell Payne held one of the larger ones. I'm sure he figured if she couldn't pay it, he'd get the ranch for half of nothin'."

"Probably."

"I'm sure he wasn't happy with his payoff, and then when Ann Marie and I got married, it put an even bigger crunch in his plans, because now she had the financial backing to keep things runnin'."

"My guess is something close," Mark replied. "I guess I'll be drivin' back to Amarillo come morning. You've got what you need here."

Travis slapped him on the back with a laugh. "Yeah, I do. My wife, my adopted son and a life I couldn't be happier with. I never thought I'd find a place to settle down, but this ranch has called to me from the first day. When I got here, I thought it was the challenge of taming the stallion, but the more time I've spent here, the more I realize it's the land and the lady."

"I'll be back at Christmas you check on you," Mark said with a laugh.

"You do that. You're always welcome here."

The two men shook hands, and Travis raced back to the house, taking the steps up to their room two at a time.

Ann Marie sat propped up against the headboard of the bed, reading a book.

"It's about time. I thought maybe you'd forgotten about me."

"No way, darlin'. You are my life, and I couldn't live without you if I tried."

"Then come here, cowboy. Your wife wants some lovin'."

"Yes ma'am."

# Epilogue

*Christmas*

"Any time, Travis. Good grief. You'd think you were painting a masterpiece up there."

"You hush, woman. The walls of this nursery have to be perfect for my son."

"You're so sure this little one is a boy?" she asked with a laugh, running her hand down the small bump beneath her shirt.

"You bet. I put in my request early," he replied with a grin.

"Well, you know, it's the man who decides the sex."

"Yep, and I made sure we had sex at night with the quarter moon, drank coffee beforehand, and had lots and lots of sex."

A roar of laughter floated from her lips. "Like those things work, but I know you enjoyed trying."

"We'll see, won't we?"

"In about six months, yes."

He climbed down from the ladder and wrapped his arms around her waist as a frown pulled down the corners of his mouth.

"What's wrong?"

"I hope you don't think that I won't love it, whether it's a boy or a girl."

"Of course not, Travis. You are fantastic with Tyler, and I know even if this one is a girl, you'll love her and spoil her rotten. Besides, it would give you more reason to try harder."

His face lit up like the Christmas tree downstairs. "True. Havin' a little girl might be fun. All the cute little dresses and teachin' her how to ride."

Ann Marie rolled her eyes. "And the shotgun you'll be carrying when all the boyfriends come to call."

"Boyfriends?"

"Yes, Daddy, little girl's turn into young women and they do get boyfriends."

"Nope. No boyfriends," he said with a stern expression.

"Until she wraps you around her little finger and smiles her first smile. You won't be able to tell her no if your life depends on it."

"Like her mother."

"Who, me?"

"You wrapped me around your finger the minute I stepped out of my truck in front of the house. You smiled at me, and it was over. Then, when you put your hands on your hips and gave me the what for, well I couldn't help but fall in love with you."

"What can I say? Gotta Love A Cowboy."

# *The End*

# About The Author

Sandy Sullivan is a romance author, who, when not writing, spends her time with her husband Shaun on their farm in middle Tennessee. She loves to ride her horses, play with their dogs and relax on the porch, enjoying the rolling hills of her home south of Nashville. Country music is a passion of hers and she loves to listen to it while she writes, although when she writes sex scenes, it has to be completely quiet.

She is an avid reader of romance novels and enjoys reading Nora Roberts, Jude Deveraux and Susan Wiggs. Finding new authors and delving into something different helps feed the need for literature. A registered nurse by education, she loves to help people and spread the enjoyment of romance to those around her with her novels. She loves cowboys so you'll find many of her novels have sexy men in tight jeans and cowboy boots.

www.romancestorytime.com

Other Books by Sandy Sullivan

Love Me Once, Love Me Twice (Montana Cowboys 1)

# Secret Cravings Publishing

# www.secretcravingspublishing.com

www.ingramcontent.com/pod-product-compliance
Lightning Source LLC
Chambersburg PA
CBHW050323200626
46810CB00022B/1159